For dad. Though he never read fiction, much less fantasy, I think he'd be proud anyway.

Acknowledgements

A special "thank you" goes to my family and friends, who have been very supportive and have put up with my yammering.

Also, my thanks to those who have purchased my first novel and hopefully want more.

Finally, to the Coffee Bean and Tea Leaf that adopted me after my original hangout closed down. Someone once described writers thusly: "a peculiar organism capable of transforming caffeine into books." So true...

THE CINDRA CORRINA CHRONICLES
BOOK 2

THE GALLANT RIDERS

MARK RUDE

All persons, gods and monsters appearing in this work are fictitious. Any resemblance to real individuals, living, dead or immortal is purely coincidental.

Conversely, if any of the gods or monsters described herein turns out to be real after all, the author takes no responsibility.

ISBN 978-0-9848275-2-7

Printed in the United States of America.

Contents

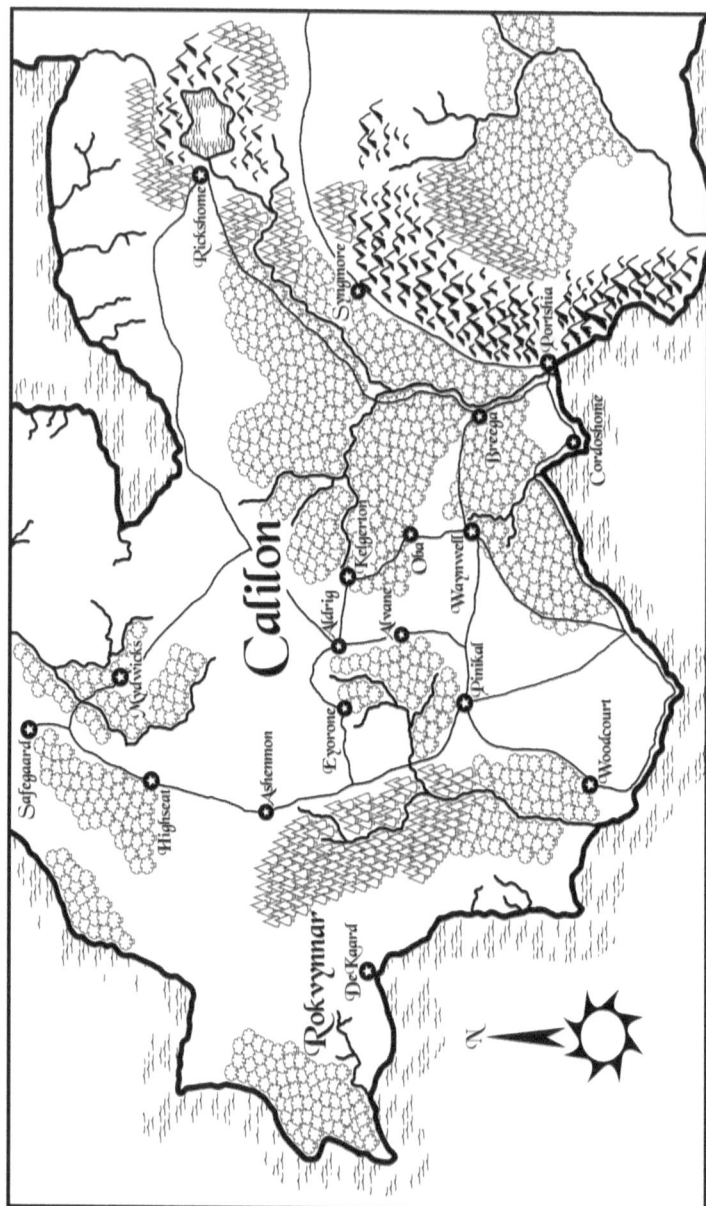

Chapter One

The Blood Jewel

The gale blew cold over the deck, the ocean spray flecked her face as she ran pushing through the thick air and making no progress; an invisible wind held her back and swept her nightclothes towards the maw of death. A voice from behind broke over the howl of the storm screaming, "Get away, Cindra!" Mineth was trying to warn her, trying to make her flee, but the thick air was pushing her back. She turned in panic to save her friend, but Mineth was far away and out of reach, the blade of the beast-man protruding from her chest. A scream of pain and anguish erupted, and Cindra recognized her own voice.

She awoke in the back of the Galindri caravan with Haani leaning over her, a concerned expression on her lovely, dark face. Cindra had dozed off on the small cot at the front of the caravan, which was separated from the driver's bench by a heavy curtain. The dappled sunlight played across Haani's face as the wagon passed under the

1

trees, and Navo, who was driving the horse team, turned to look in over Haani's shoulder.

"Were you dreaming, Cindra?" asked Haani gently. She was often there when Cindra awoke and the answer was always the same. Navo turned back to the road.

Cindra nodded and sat up in the cot. It was the third day since the Galindri had found her shivering on the side of the road, covered in dirt and flecks of blood. The dreams had come every night though they were worse the longer she slept. She had tried napping in the day to avoid these elongated night terrors, but she only experienced the dreams more frequently, though not as intense. It was frustrating and exhausting.

She turned her head to examine the caravan that had become her refuge. Drying herbs were hanging from the curved ceiling, which was made of overlapping slats of wood braced by curved wooden ribs, like an inverted ship. There was a window cut into each side, large enough to stick one's head through but not much else, and secured with folding shutters.

There were a few shelves built into the sides of the caravan walls and all had raised railings to secure their contents. These included pottery jars, tin cups, wooden bowls, knives, and cooking pots with ladles that were likely purchased or traded in the towns they visited. Thin, wide baskets secured to the walls helped make the most of the interior space.

Of all the things she could see in the wagon, the Galindri-crafted items had the most character. Each had flowing organic or geometric patterns carved or painted upon them, unlike the utility items that were acquired in more 'civilized' places. Cindra was used to fancy decorations on everyday objects, at least among the finer things in her house, and the attention to beauty and detail was a welcomed sight.

Majii, the old patriarch, was sitting on a large pillow in the back corner of the caravan with his back propped against the side wall. The wooden doors were opened and secured allowing for a breeze to pass through, making the space less stuffy. Majii smiled and nodded at Cindra as her eyes fell upon him, and she smiled in return. It was the man's sharp memory that she had to thank for her present acceptance, for he had remembered her from a brief meeting in the cold Portshia night as she walked past their camp months before.

He was convinced that their second meeting was more than chance, and Cindra was in no position to argue. She was alone and had only the vaguest idea of where she was. The Galindri had no maps and spoke of days of travel rather than miles or leagues, and she was unfamiliar with the names of the last few villages they had passed. She was lost in her own country. Well, it *was* a very big country to be sure.

Luka and Teya were likely walking outside the wagon, Luka near the door so she might tend to Majii if he called, and also to watch the goat as it walked along beside the wheels. Teya usually walked a distance ahead and kept an eye out for danger, but whatever shape it might take along the road, Cindra had no clue. She was not inclined to ask either, as Teya was frosty to her at best. Maybe there were fallen branches and large stones in the road, or fierce brigands and strange beasts that lurked in the woods preying on travelers. The more dangerous prospects might have made for a good read, but sounded less exciting since she was now among the travelers. She had already had her fill of violence on her journey. Mineth's face came to her mind unbidden and she pushed the thoughts away.

Haani drew the curtain aside and climbed through the opening to sit on the cot next to Cindra. She had taken her tasks seriously and was doing her best to teach the outlander girl about their language and ways, finding joy in the exchange of cultures. She arranged her skirts and hair and turned to Cindra saying, *"Yime, l'nók-da!"* This Cindra knew to mean roughly, 'Now is the time to speak.' She looked forward to her lessons, for they gave her a chance to focus her mind on other things.

The previous day they had been walking outside during the lesson and Haani had tried to teach her plants and animals. Cindra knew the goat was a *neko* and the horses were *jo'áman*, but whether that was one horse or both she was unsure. 'Tree' was *falón*, but Haani was either uncertain of or unwilling to share the words for the types of trees they passed. *They must have different names for oak, birch, shadowood and pine,* thought Cindra. Maybe they were harder to learn and would be saved for later.

It seemed today was for learning the contents of the caravan. Haani took up objects Cindra might use in a daily routine, a bowl, a cup, a pot, a knife and spoon. She coached her in the language's numerous subtleties, such as how long to hold a sound before blending it into another, and when to accent or arrest a sound suddenly. Many words were pronounced as much in back of the throat as at the tip of the tongue, giving it a strange cadence not unlike their music, which was springy and full of stops and starts.

Cindra loved their music. Navo played the flute nightly after they made camp, and Haani tried to teach Cindra basic dance steps. The results were not pretty, but proved amusing at least.

After exhausting the more common items and having Cindra repeat them as she pointed them out, Haani gestured to Majii. "*Ló-poh. Ló-poh teh.* My father," she said touching her chin with her fingertips. Cindra mouthed the word. Haani looked at her and asked, "*Ló-poh beh?* Your father?" It was a question about her past, her home. They were a kind but suspicious people and were always trying to get Cindra to give out little bits of information. Cindra took no offense, for she would be cautious as well if their places were reversed. Still, it was more than she was willing to share at this point; there were still too many unknowns. Would their treatment of her change if they knew she was nobility and worth a large ransom? Would they abandon her at the nearest village, wary of the trouble she might bring if someone recognized her name or face? She didn't want to think what the forbidding Teya might wish to do. Cindra was of the ruling class but she was also a girl alone in the wilderness, a little baby eagle at the mercy of kindly wolves.

Cindra played for time by pronouncing the words, her mind racing for a safe answer. Finally she pretended to understand the question and lied, "*Ló-poh teh*, my father is... Fedrick." It was a common enough name in Casselvane province, but it was also the name of her beloved Jaron's father. She wondered if she had picked the senior Dunlorden's name out of a desire to be close to his son. If they were wed, Fedrick would become her father by marriage. She blushed a bit at the idea and pushed it away. Marriage was impossible of course, but she could dream of another life, could she not? Things had already gone very wrong, so why not wish for better?

Haani mistook Cindra's color for discomfort and said, "It is alright if you do not wish to speak of home. Not all memories are happy and well. You were sailing away after all..."

Cindra noticed the attempt to draw her out further, so she decided to reward Haani with some further little half-truths. "It's not that I was unhappy, but..." she tried to think of a way to be vague and honest, "Father put me on a ship to work in another land. Mineth and I were to live with a lady in Rokvynnar and serve in her household." Upon reflection, Cindra decided that this version was as honest and true as any she had heard before, and she felt no guilt for leaving out the pertinent details.

Haani and Majii exchanged a curious look, unfamiliar with this custom among the Outlander people. Sending one's child far from home to work for another family seemed to defeat the purpose of raising children. Their guest didn't seem to care for it either, so they looked on her with pity.

Haani said, "I-I did not know that Outlanders gave up their children so. Is this done?" She wondered if Cindra had made an offense against her parents, or if this was something else.

Cindra nodded, "Yes, it is done, and often. Many children are made to live with those that would train them, be they noble or common. Some are sent to learn a new trade or craft, others to strengthen ties between families. Only the poorest of families raise their own children it seems." As soon as she said the words, Cindra hoped in her bitterness that she had not just insulted her hosts.

Majii spoke, "Are they so poor? What could children learn better than to love family, to respect father and mother?" He breathed and looked at the ceiling for a moment, considering, "*Gatéth-sho'a* believe that children are joy, that there is no greater than family. Yet we know that all ways are not our ways. The Mother has made it so."

Cindra had heard him speak of the Mother before, and she seemed to be someone of great importance. Was she a goddess? "Who is the Mother?" Cindra asked as Haani's eyes grew wide.

Majii smiled at her, "The people of the cities forget the Mother? The people of the lands know her, for they can see nothing else. She is *Ozh-shó-lapah* to us, but the Outlanders know her as Jayda, World Mother. All are her children, and all are joy to her, but all are not the same."

Cindra brightened, "I know Jayda! She made the world from the elements that Arathus and Llomaak brought her. One of the great spires of the cathedral is devoted to her." She felt a bit of pride for not seeming totally ignorant.

Haani was astounded, "*Wá-shad!* You speak the names so freely!" She crossed her hands before her chest, palms out, and brushed her fingers apart twice. *Was that a warding gesture?* Cindra wondered. *What have I said now?*

"All are her children," repeated Majii, "but all are not the same. The Mother understands this, but it is harder for us. Men will fight like mad dogs because they know a god by different names. We make war because it is easier than making peace." He lowered his head, resting his chin on his chest, and seemed to sleep. He spoke no more, so Haani nodded to him in deference and turned to Cindra, who seemed puzzled.

Cindra asked, "What were the words he used? Gatéth-sha?" She knew she had mangled it, but she was learning after all.

Haani corrected her, "*Gatéth-sho'a*, People of the Land. It is what we call ourselves. Your people came from across the sea and named this land... Gartetha, is it? It is from the word we use that is *Gáteth'a*, This Land."

Cindra smiled at the revelation, "This land is This Land," She giggled at the notion.

Haani continued, "And we are *Gatéth-sho'a*, People of the Land. We have been here since the early times when the Forest King led our people from the old wars. We have lived on the plains and hills, in the valleys and mountains, from cold white lands to the dry rocks and cracked earth."

Cindra mused, "But people call you the Galindri..." She had never before considered why; it wasn't a word in any language she knew.

Haani said, "It is easier to make their own names than to learn our words. Further south across the waters they call us Garéndiis. In the north we are Galendred, and in the time of Kraal's reign he called us Gallant Riders. Great King Kraal favored us and stopped the wars upon our people."

Cindra paused before asking her next question, unsure where it might lead. "Why do you call us Outlanders? We have been here for over a thousand years now."

Haani blinked at her and considered, answering with a question of her own. "Do you not know the history of your people, the story of how they came to live here?"

Cindra was well-educated and knew much of her family's history, dating back to the old empire, but she imagined Haani only wanted the short version of the tale, so she offered what she knew of the Norsican Exodus and the discovery of the lands across the sea. "I know that my people came across the Emerald Sea along the chain of islands east of Norsica, fleeing the grip of the Celvestrian Empire. They finally found this land, Gartetha," she smiled at the name again, "and settled here. They built a kingdom called Calilaar and ruled for almost three hundred years before the old empire came for them.

"During that time there were many wars, and eventually the king surrendered. Later in exile, he married a Celvestrian noblewoman and had a son named Orthicus, who would one day retake the throne. But that didn't turn out so well..."

Haani nodded solemnly, "Orthicus was an evil king, and all suffered beneath him, but the suffering of the *Gatéth-sho'a* began long before. They who built Calilaar did so upon the lands we hunted, they cut down the forests and broke the rocks and made houses and castles and walls. Our people moved far, but there were always new walls and new people. Enemy tribes were forced to share the same hunting grounds, and war broke out between them, and between *Gatéth-sho'a* tribes and the Calilaar warlords.

"There was much blood spilled in those times. My people took to the forests and mountains, fleeing the soldiers. We had lived on the land for countless seasons but those who came from beyond the seas, the Outlanders, claimed all the land as their own, killing anyone who challenged them. They hunted our horses to feed their war beasts, raided our stores for the winter. Many prayed to the Mother to deliver us, to drive the Outlanders back into the sea, but things only got worse. The Oldest War had come to our land, and we could only hope to survive while all was changed." She folded her hands in her lap and sighed, "We call your people

8

Outlanders because... we never understood how you came from the Mother but treated her so differently."

Cindra thought on this with a touch of confusion and guilt, for she had been raised to respect the king, the law of the land, and the teachings of the gods. She had never thought of the spreading of civilization to the wilderness to be a bad thing, indeed it was a commandment passed down from the heavens. The Galindri were a subject people and that was a painful thing indeed, but then all people were either conquerors or the conquered. Of course there was injustice and brutality in the earlier times, and that could not be excused, but were not her ancestors only doing the will of Arathus? After all, those were the days before the gods fell silent. Arathus was the god of kings and conquerors, so the domination of the native people was inevitable, even mandated from On High. A frown furrowed her brow as she considered this thought.

She knew the 'oldest war' Haani spoke of was the war between Order and Chaos, between Arathus and Llomaak. Civilization had come to Gartetha and brought the oldest war with it, into lands where the people only knew the World Mother. Some four hundred years after the 'Outlanders' had arrived in Gartetha, all was thrown into turmoil the likes of which had never been seen in recorded history; the Time of Chaos had shaken the entire world but had its roots in the old kingdom of Calilaar. It was like a horrid violation of the land, its people, and the heavens themselves. Maybe the gods had been wrong? It was a terrifying thought.

Haani decided to continue the lesson to raise their spirits; "*Gateshón'a* is the word for Outlander, but you will likely hear many more from Teya that are not so pleasant." Haani waved her hand before her as if warding off a bad smell. "The best and kindest of her names for Outlanders is *ma-shi'íni*. It is a pale pink flower that grows in the south lands. They cover the hills and plains in spring with a blanket of color." Haani smiled and sprinkled her fingers over the imagined fields of flowers, until Teya's voice came from the window.

"They choke the plants and grasses around them," Teya said over the turn of the wheels, "They steal the water and sun, and poison lives in their roots." Haani frowned at the window and turned to Cindra looking embarrassed, her eyes apologetic.

Majii lifted his chin from his chest and spoke loud enough to be heard outside the caravan, "Yet they are also part of the Mother, and they have their place."

It was after midday when the caravan stopped at the next campsite, for while there were many more hours of daylight to travel, this was the day for hunting and the extra time was needed because Cindra would be coming along. Teya was sure it would take too many hours before the Outlander girl was able to approach an animal without spooking it, and hours more to stalk a kill. Cindra had asked once if *Gatéth-sho'a* ever used traps, but Teya only looked at her in disgust. The others set up the camp while Teya gathered her bow and checked each arrow, making sure the fletching was straight and the shafts were not warped by the recent damp weather. She was far too careful with her weapons to allow this, but she checked anyway as a kind of personal ritual.

Cindra was pleased to surprise her hosts when she told them she could shoot a bow. She did not mention that it was one of the few sporting pass-times allowed a noble girl living within castle walls; she proved herself by burying an arrow into a nearby tree with Teya's bow. The bow was about Cindra's height and made of heavy dark Shadowood; its limbs were polished nearly black and the handle was wrapped in leather strips. It was much harder to pull than the bow Cindra had practiced on, but she was able to draw it and hold her aim on the third attempt.

While handing the bow back to its owner, Cindra noticed the strong arms and shoulders of the huntress, now bare save for her wrist wraps, and imagined Teya had been shooting all her life. It felt good to shoot a bow again, for it had been two years since Cindra last practiced her archery, having grown bored of it. Now it was practical and might save her life, so she was ready to embrace it again and longed for a beautiful dark bow of her own.

The strong black wood grew throughout the Shadowood Forest bordering western Casselvane province and was prized for its strength and resilience as much as its dark beauty. Many of the ornamental moldings and fixtures in Cindra's home were carved from Shadowood, as well as the grand stair in the entrance hall. It was costly to obtain for two reasons, the first being that the wood was so dense that it couldn't float, making the transport of lumber downriver impractical. The second reason was mostly due to local superstitions, for the Shadowood Forest was said to be haunted or possessed of a dark power that protected the trees. It certainly protected the profits of the wood dealers, whatever the case.

Teya was dressed in soft leather pants, tall laced boots, and a knee-length, embroidered wool skirt that was split for riding or running. About her torso she wore a length of coral linen that wound about her waist and neck, crossing her breasts and baring her arms. Her braided hair was bound further back than usual and tied to the left, keeping it clear of the quiver strapped to her back. She was rubbing a handful of leafy pulp over her arms and legs, leaving a yellow-green stain on her dark skin and clothing.

"It is to hide our scent, and it keeps away the blood flies," Teya explained as she prepared another handful of mashed herbs and leaves and helped Cindra apply it. Cindra wore some of Haani's old clothes including blue and green skirts that stopped at the knee, soft leather shoes with ankle laces, and a long-sleeved, dark green blouse cut to be bound in the front, leaving her midriff bare. She also wore a wrap about her chest like Teya's, which seemed to be a kind of traditional undergarment for men and women, although Navo and Majii wore them in a different fashion. Haani explained that it was called the *l'lash* and that it served many needs, including storing small items or medicines within the folds.

Now that Cindra was smeared with the herbal mixture and smelled like a bush, Teya decided they were ready for the hunt. She stalked off into the woods south of the road where the land sloped downward toward the distant sea. The Red Coast Road had moved farther from the shore where the terrain became less even and the woodlands hugged cliffs that sheltered hidden coves. Teya spoke softly and rarely, most often answering Cindra's questions with a hissing 'shush'. She pointed out signs on the ground that the girl didn't see and would stop and sniff the air for who knows what, for all Cindra could smell was the bug repellent masking 'her scent.'

It was obvious that Teya didn't like her and was only doing this to appease her father, and Cindra hated being led around like a child. Her huffing and sighs did not go unnoticed by the huntress, who glanced back at her with warning stares. It was only when Teya stopped and pointed to a deer nestled in a distant bush that Cindra made an effort to be silent and pay attention.

The huntress motioned for Cindra to stay where she was as she readied an arrow and began to stalk closer for a shot. Her steps were measured and carefully placed, sometimes pausing for several minutes before moving again. The wind was blowing towards them from somewhere inland, keeping them downwind of their quarry; the silent footfalls of the huntress were carried away from the resting creature and Cindra slowly moved behind a tree to watch the spectacle. The deer was perhaps a young male by its velvet-covered antlers, which almost blended in with the branches of the bush. It had light russet hide and dark markings down its mane to the middle of its back; its nose was tucked away from the danger but its ears flickered slightly, making Cindra hold her breath.

Teya was drawing her bow now, the black wood creaking ever-so-slightly like the bough of a tree in the breeze. The wind shifted, moving now from the seaward side and rustling the leaves overhead. The deer pricked its ears and lifted its head suddenly, looking into the distance. It caught sight of Teya out of the corner of its vision and leapt to its hooves, but the huntress had released her arrow and the shot struck true. The deer staggered for a few fleeting steps before tumbling to the ground in the bushes.

Cindra felt a thrill at the final moment, when it seemed their meal might get away, but as the animal collapsed into a heap she felt a pang of remorse for the beautiful beast, taken in a moment of panic and flight. Still, she had no illusions about where her meals came from and this death was better than meeting the slavering jaws of the wolf-beast that had nearly eaten her shortly after she washed ashore.

Teya ran to the kill and drew her horn-handled knife, being careful of the animal's hooves and horns as she bent in and opened its throat, making sure it had a clean death. She pulled the arrow from the beast and cleaned it on a rag at her side, a troubled expression on her face as she looked about into the seaward forest.

Cindra came up to the scene, her eyes bright with excitement, "That was amazing!" She had only heard of noble women hunting small game with falcons, but never of a woman tracking game through the forest to make a kill such as this. The huntress glanced at the girl, wondering what she found so worthy of praise, and returned her attention to the southwest. "What's wrong?" asked Cindra, noticing Teya's distraction.

Teya stood up from the kill and sniffed the air. "Do you smell it? That which spooked the *t'ora*?" Cindra shook her head, assuming *t'ora* was the deer. "Smoke," said Teya, "smoke from a campfire." Teya sheathed her blade, notched another arrow and moved towards the scent of burning wood.

Cindra wondered if it was the trappers who set the snare that saved her from the wolf-beast. She might thank them if they were pleasant enough, but she would let Teya be the judge of that. Cindra had told the Galindri of the spike trap and snare, but they knew of no local people who set such devices. Galindri saw traps as cruel and unnatural, and the only other people about were peasant farmers; any hunting rights belonged to the local lord.

Galindri were an exception by ancient order of Kraal, who had favored these native people enough to grant them special privileges. They could hunt small game as needed when passing through, and were allowed to follow the migrating herds of furdeer, the meat of which outlanders could not stomach. *I am an Outlander*, Cindra silently reminded herself. It was so easy to leave that life behind her.

The sun was sinking into late afternoon as the pair walked many cautious steps through the forest. It was several paces until Cindra smelled the faint hint of smoke on the breeze. It was coming from a downward incline where the land ended in sea cliffs beyond the thick foliage and trees. The sounds of the ocean could be heard as waves crashed upon the rocks and seabirds squawked, circling the shore. Teya motioned once again for Cindra to stay behind as she scouted ahead; the girl crossed her arms defiantly but remained to lean against a tree and pout. The huntress crept farther into the brush and was soon out of sight.

Many minutes passed. Cindra could still see the spot where the deer had fallen and the thought occurred to her that one of those horrid wolf-creatures might be drawn to the scent of blood and pay the deer a visit. She had no weapon this time and was unsure how far away the huntress had gone. Weighing the possibility of losing their meal to hungry creatures against being scolded by Teya for following, Cindra decided it might be better to

14

brave the temper of the Galindri woman. She quietly advanced down the path, keeping low and trying to replicate the stealthy pace of the huntress as she moved through the undergrowth.

Teya could hear voices from beyond the thick bushes as the campfire smoke drifted overhead. There was a clearing just past the trees and the land gave way to a steep decline, possibly a path leading to a sheltered cove. Standing in the clearing were four figures about the fire pit, conversing in unguarded voices. Teya stifled a gasp and froze as she saw that three of them were large Minozhian bull-men; the fourth was a man in a dark cloak and a deep hood, his hands resting on the pommel of a sword, blade drawn and point down in the dirt at the ready.

The huntress had never before seen a beast-man, and the Minozhians were fiercer-looking than she had imagined. Their great shaggy heads were topped with curving horns, carved and painted with unknown symbols and capped with metal tips. They had broad ears beneath the horns that were pierced with rings of gold and hung with delicate chains, perhaps plundered or bartered from more skilled craftsmen. Their snouts were short and broad; dark noses rimmed with hair that fell about their mouths like beards or whiskers, and manes of longer hair hung behind their horns in braids, or was bound in metal rings.

They were all broad-shouldered and tall, perhaps a forearm's length taller than the man before them. Their muscled arms and chests were bound in leather and red fabric tunics, while layered strips of boiled leather served for scant armor. They had no tails or hooves, as some accounts told, but trousers of dark linen covered their legs and leather sandals encased their thick, somewhat stubby feet. The fur length and coloring varied between them. The nearest to Teya was brownish-red with shorter hair, while the other two were shaggier about the head

15

and arms, the middle one with light tan hide and the farthest with dark brown. All of them were armed with broad wicked *Kos* knives, and all had bestial black eyes that were set deep under a formidable brow.

The man on the other side of the fire was standing calmly at ease, but the placing of his feet told Teya he was ready to fight. He wore black and dark green clothing, a vest and traveling trousers with tall leather boots. He had black velvet gloves with red trim and tassels, and a sword belt hung at his waist. His voice was muffled beneath the hood, but his words were clear enough.

"You bring no proof of the deed then, Vaenmar Traaken?" he asked in a sharp voice, making the bull-men bristle and shift their weight, "Not a head or finger, or a scrap of clothing?"

The tan-hide Minozhian spoke in a deep, gruff voice, the sound making Teya tense even more. "We do not make trophies of women or children," Traaken said as he leaned forward, "Besides, one of them fell in the water and was pierced by a spear. The other was burned with the ship."

The man inclined his head beneath the hood. "I imagine you took the girl's treasure from the hold first? Do you not have something of hers to show for it?"

The tan bull man nodded to the dark one beside him, who was wearing a kind of short robe of red and black, and the dark Minozhian reached into a leather pouch at his waist, withdrawing a silver object that he presented to the man in the hood. The man took it and held it up in the waning daylight. "Very well," he said as he handed it back to the robed one. "Wait here and I will retrieve your payment." He moved off into the trees opposite the huntress and returned moments later with a bundle in soft fabric.

Teya's instincts told her to move away and flee, but as she turned back she saw the distant shape of a girl moving among the trees. The wretched Outlander child had followed her! Teya tried to motion to the girl to stay, but she was still too far away to see such a guarded gesture.

"As I promised," said the man as the dark Minozhian unfolded the bundle carefully, the other two looking intently at it. The creature's thick fingers held a jewel that caught the sun's fading light, radiating a glow of rich, deep purple from its uncut surface. The dark one inspected it with a practiced eye, while the other two gawked with treasure-lust and rumbled approving noises in their throats.

Finally the dark Minozhian wrapped the gemstone in its protective fabric and tucked it away into his robe, saying to the vaenmar, "The largest I have seen! It will do well for us!"

The vaenmar nodded and made something like a smile or a snarl as he regarded the hooded man. "Our business is finished Ghethas, but I am puzzled. What was the blood of this noble girl that you buy it with such a treasure, this jewel and the fortune she carried with her?"

The man was about to answer when Teya's bow caught upon a branch and rustled it slightly. The large ears of the bull-men pricked up and they spun towards the noise, seeing the Galindri woman watching from the underbrush. Teya's eyes widened in panic and she started to run, when the man threw something at the ground before her. It burst in a flash of blinding white light, making her head spin as if she had been struck. She stumbled a few steps before feeling an iron grip upon her arm, and hearing muttered curses in a deep, bestial voice. She was yanked off her feet, her shoulder nearly pulled out of joint by the force of it; she had lost her grip on her bow and heard the arrows scatter from the quiver. Before she could fight back, she was being forced to her knees by a pair of large, powerful hands. Her arms were immobile and she could not reach either of her knives. Her vision swam with blue spots and her ears rang with a din like the high-pitched screams of battling squirrels.

"Cursed wizardry!" Traaken shouted, rubbing his eyes,

17

"You might have warned us first!"

The man chuckled, "It was meant for you and your fellows if things went awry. Besides, it is not wizardry, but Divine Alchemy. The Countless Lord has given his faithful many such devices."

"Curse your alchemy then," Traaken snorted, "All I see is big blue spots. Who was spying on us?" He squinted at Teya as she squirmed in the other Minozhian's grasp.

"We caught a bush cat, vaenmar!" The reddish-brown bull man snarled near Teya's ear, his hot breath snorting moisture on her shoulder, "A woman of the horse people, brown skin and green eyes." He took her wrists behind her back and held them fast with one hand, using the other to pull back her head so the others might see her face.

The man leaned close to Teya, his hood filled her vision but his face was hidden by her momentary blindness. She blinked to clear her eyes as he spoke, "You seem to have stumbled into the wrong camp, my sweet. Whatever are you doing here?"

"Hunting," Teya gasped as the Minozhian squeezed her wrists.

This brought a chortling laugh from Traaken, who said, "I doubt there will be much here. We have been trapping all week along the coast while awaiting our true prey."

The hooded man spoke, "She has heard much she was not meant to hear, not that it matters. Still, we should take precautions..." As he loomed closer, Teya's vision allowed her to glimpse his face. She shrank at the sight, for his eyes were those of a man, but below them was the grimacing mouth of a beast, fangs of white and yellow and a snout like a wolf. When he spoke, the horrid jaws did not move and Teya cursed herself for being fooled by a mask. "Perhaps we'll take your head for safekeeping, hmm?" He caressed her chin and straightened, nodding to the Minozhian restraining her.

Cindra saw the flash ahead and feared for Teya's life. She could see shapes down by the edge of the woods and perhaps a clearing for the campsite, but little else. She resisted the urge to call out and thought perhaps to run for help, but it would surely arrive too late. Whatever had happened, Teya was either dead or in mortal danger. She needed to learn her fate at least, though she might not be able to help. Drawing her skirts close to avoid making more noise, she hurried down the meager trail.

The voices she heard as she approached made her hair stand on end. Through the haze and smoke of burning chemicals and firewood she heard the gruff, throaty voices that haunted her dreams, beast-men from the sea that burst through the door and murdered her closest friend over and over again each time she slept. There was another voice as well, like a man trying to fit in among monsters, arrogant and boastful. She froze for a moment but moved closer when she heard Teya's cry of pain. *She is alive!*

The forest was growing dark but the light was enough so that Cindra could see the huntress's fallen bow and several arrows lying scattered about a nearby bush. There was also a smoldering spot in the grass where the flash bomb had likely struck. She reached for the bow and took up as many arrows as she could without exposing her presence. As she looked through the branches she beheld three large Minozhian butchers, one holding Teya by the arms and the other two standing nearby, rubbing their eyes. There was a hooded man in a hideous mask kneeling before her, probably questioning her. Cindra moved back into the woods to hide behind a tree and get a better view of the clearing.

Her heart was racing now and her pulse pounded in her ears like war drums, the fear she held quickly became hatred as she set an arrow on the bowstring without thinking. Her arms were trembling and her insides quivered with the urge to act, fighting the desire to run away and not look back. Teya was helpless and would soon be dead, just like Mineth, impaled on a Minozhian blade. The only difference was that Cindra was out of sight and armed; no longer helpless, no longer trapped. She felt the courage within her well up again, like it had so many months ago in the dark streets of Portshia. She had saved a life that night, and by all the silent gods, she would do it again or die trying.

The masked man had stood up and stepped back, sheathing his sword. The Minozhian who held Teya pulled out a long, wicked knife with his free hand, raising it slowly as if to behead her. Cindra raised the bow and drew with all her might, grunting with the effort, and held her breath as she aimed at the exposed ribs under the bull man's arm. Her eyes watered with the exertion, or perhaps something more, and before her tears could blind her she released the arrow. It flew between the trees and struck the murderous creature under the arm, piercing his heart. His knees buckled and he fell towards his fellows, pulling Teya down with him. His knife fell from his grip and stuck point-first into the earth.

The other Minozhians blinked and looked into the dark woods, anger and panic in their faces. "Ambush!" shouted Traaken as he drew his blade, "Cursed alchemy! I see nothing!"

The dark-robed Minozhian tried to free his knife from its sheath but only succeeded in tangling his hand in the leather pouch at his waist, spilling some of the contents. Something silver tumbled to the grass as he turned and fled, clutching the prized jewel to his chest and heading down the trail beyond the clearing, roaring an order into the cove below. There was a bestial answer from somewhere down the path.

Cindra had moved from the spot after watching the bull man fall, her mind racing too fast to take in what she had just done. She circled around the clearing, keeping her head low, until she had another clear shot at the remaining villains. The hooded man must have seen her shadow through the trees and threw another flash bomb into the brush, flooding the woods with white brilliance. Cindra managed to clench her eyes shut and dodge behind a tree, opening them moments later as she heard the Minozhian captain, or 'vaenmar', cursing and roaring with rage. The hooded man was gone, having fled into the woods, so she drew an arrow on the remaining bull-man. He was ignoring Teya, blinking as he tried to find his assailant. Cindra took advantage of his confusion and shot, this one being poorly aimed and not fully drawn. It whistled past the monster and struck a branch overhead, raining leaves down on his shoulders. The bull man flinched, blindly turning and stumbling towards the safety of the descending trail.

Cindra raced into the clearing, leaping over the dead bull-man to reach the huntress. Teya was looking about, searching for enemies before raising herself from the ground. Her legs were unsteady as she rose, her vision returning slowly. Teya stared in amazement at the dead Minozhian lying beside her, one of her arrows protruding from his ribs. Cindra pulled the woman to her feet, returned her bow and ran to the edge of the cliff trail, looking after the retreating monsters. Gazing into the cove, she saw a familiar battle-damaged longship with red sails pulled onto the narrow shore; a small bonfire surrounded by large figures was burning before the horned ram of the vessel. The commander and the robed one were calling for reinforcements from the trail, and many were drawing weapons in answer.

Cindra backed away from the edge, wondering how long they would be pursued, when she saw a glint of silver at her feet. She stooped to pick up a familiar hairbrush marked with the Corrina family crest. Anger burned in her heart as she watched the approaching soldiers, wishing to avenge every soul that had perished on the *Indisputable*, and especially that of her dear Mineth. The sensation lasted but a moment before the reality of her situation struck her; she had to escape with Teya before they were both killed like sheep. She spun and found Teya picking up the dead Minozhian's large knife, tucking it into her belt before retrieving her quiver. There were only two arrows left inside and she had no time to collect the ones scattered about. Taking the lead, she darted into the brush and up the slope, heading towards the northwest away from the carcass of the deer. Cindra realized they could not make it back to the caravan with the meat, and she felt a silly regret that the hours of hunting had been wasted.

As they made their way through the woods, twisting and turning through the brush to confuse the trail, Cindra looked about for signs of the hooded man. He likely had a horse tethered nearby and was far away by now, and she wondered at his part in this conspiracy, meeting with those murdering pirates. Her hand clenched around the smooth handle of her brush, taken from her luggage in the very cabin where Mineth died. They had plundered her personal belongings and probably her dowry as well. She heard shouts in a rough language behind them, but there were no footfalls or the sounds of crashing through foliage, so it seemed they were making good their escape so far. She wanted to sneak back and reclaim her things but the idea seemed beyond foolish, just like avenging the crew of the *Indisputable*. Well, at least she had killed one for Mineth.

They had made it to the road about a half-mile west of the caravan and Teya led them through the woods on the opposite side of the road, making their way back in a serpentine trail. Minozhians were reputed to be vengeful, and Cindra wondered what they would do to repay the death of their companion. Would they really risk a long chase through unfriendly woods? She felt like the ghost of the bull-man had followed her and was pointing her out to his fellows, demanding revenge. She told herself this was untrue and that he had deserved his fate, but she still felt stained or marked somehow; she felt exhaustion creeping up on her so she had little energy to linger on this ill feeling. The noise of horses told her they were close to the caravan now and Teya let out a twittering bird-call.

As they entered the campsite by the road, they saw Navo, Haani and Luka frantically packing the wagon as Majii doused the fire. None were speaking but they all moved with a practiced efficiency as the horses were harnessed and the goat was led into the back of the caravan. Teya sought out extra arrows and reloaded her quiver, jumping onto the driver's bench as Navo took up the reigns. Majii was helped into the back and the women, Cindra included, loaded the last of the cookware and settled in, making fast the door. They were soon moving west down the road at a fair pace, making the contents of the wagon rattle and shake about. No one spoke, but Haani and Luka sat at the windows on either side, keeping watch as Cindra held on to the nervous goat.

It was about an hour later before they stopped, this time driving the wagon off the road a bit further than usual and unpacking only the essentials lest they need to move quickly again. Teya spoke to her family rapidly in their language, explaining the events of the last few hours; many glances were cast at Cindra, their eyes wide in amazement. Then Teya began speaking of something else, drawing cautious questions and mysterious looks at the Outlander girl. Cindra understood nothing of the conversation and was in no mood to talk. Instead she took out the hairbrush she had stowed in the folds of her clothing, staring at her family crest. The silver shone brightly in the firelight, sending orange flickers into the darkness. The Galindri watched her turn the treasure in her hands, watched the sadness play across her face.

Teya spoke again, this time for Cindra's benefit, "The masked man served one called the Countless Lord, and he gave the Minozhians a large jewel as payment... for the blood of a noble girl traveling by sea."

Cindra's hands fumbled the brush, nearly dropping it as she looked at her new friends, searching for a sign of

23

possible betrayal. They returned her stare with wary eyes.

Teya continued, "The man wanted proof of the deed, and they showed him that silver brush," she pointed to the object in Cindra's hands. "It was taken from the lady's treasure. They said one girl fell into the sea and was pierced by a spear... the other..."

"The other was Mineth, and she was impaled on a Minozhian blade," Cindra said quietly. "She bought my escape with her life. The spear only scratched me." Cindra stared into the heart of the fire, watching a chip of wood being devoured by the heat, turning black, cracking and withering as its vitality was drawn out and turned into flame, smoke and ash.

Haani said, "Then... then you are noble born? You are a lady of Portshia?"

Cindra nodded, still looking into the fire, "I am Lady Cindra Corrina, daughter of Count Casselvane. I was to be wed to a boy duke in Rokvynnar on the 28th of Balmoth, this month."

The Galindri exchanged worried glances, unsure of what to say. It was Luka who murmured something in their language that finally stirred them. "*T'emeko'a Tol'ózh...*" she said to her husband and Navo barked a nervous laugh.

Majii asked, "The girl who we saw in the market that night; that *was* you? How can this be?" He knew enough about Outlanders to find it strange that a noble girl had been in the streets alone.

Cindra looked at him, trying to be reassuring. "That was me, I was in the market. It was my birthday and the night I learned that the duke I was to marry was a boy of twelve. I was upset and I escaped the castle for a while. There were some... tricky situations that night."

Majii nodded, glad he had not been deceived about their first meeting. All was not as it seemed, but at least all was a kind of truth. He felt the hands of the gods in this. "It seems we were meant to save you, and you were meant to save my daughter. For this, I will always be grateful." He nodded again and waved his hand downward, and he was silent. The others could say what they would, but his mind was known.

Haani sat near to Cindra but not as near as usual. "What should we call you, milady?" She was awed again as she had been when Cindra first stumbled into their camp, but now it was mixed with fear.

Cindra shook her head and said, "No! No, Haani. I don't want to be held at a distance. We are not in the city, and I am no more than you found me."

Luka said, "Besides, it would be dangerous to call her such things. She was being hunted, and they think her dead."

Navo nodded, "Luka is right. This Outlander who met with the Minozhians... what if he knows Cindra's face? What if we meet him on the road?"

Teya scowled, "I would end his life if we meet again, but... I did not see his face. He wore a mask over his mouth; I do not think he will be wearing it on the road or in the villages."

The discussion went on for a while; Navo and Luka urging caution, Teya wanting to track the man and hunt him down, and Haani's opinion teetering back and forth while Majii stared into the fire. Cindra had ceased to listen but she did notice that no one was considering abandoning her at the nearest village. It seems that it was no longer an option, and for that she was grateful.

As she looked into the heart of the fire her mind kept going back to the moment she let an arrow fly and ended a life. In all her time she had only killed insects that bit her in the night, slapping at a twinge and thinking nothing of it. She used to fantasize about war and battle; driving enemies from her father's castle, but the death of imaginary armies were nothing to her, just child's play.

She had begun to cry and the Galindri stopped their discussion and turned to her. Haani scooted closer and placed an arm around her shoulder, much like Mineth had done to comfort her when she was beset by the now minor troubles of her castle life. Luka was the first to offer words, but she had mistaken the cause of the girl's pain.

"Do not fear Cindra, we will not let harm come to you," Luka held Navo's hand for support, "We will keep you hidden, though we move from one end of the road to the other."

Cindra sniffed, wiping her eyes, "Thank you Luka, but... I was just thinking of earlier... I've never killed..." She broke down in fresh sobs as Teya moved to her side. "I know he was evil, they attacked us, killed everyone to get to me! But still... He'll never go home to his family again, never eat or drink again, never have a chance to..."

"To murder again," said Teya firmly, "Some people live good lives, but others live on the cliff's edge. They do things..." her gaze grew distant, "...things that lead to death for those they meet. It is not your place to look after every soul. The bull-men came here for murder and payment, nothing more. Every murderer inherits vengeance."

Cindra was silent but understood. She knew then as now that Teya would be dead if she had not acted. Still, it didn't make the stain on her soul go away. It was so confusing and troubling; was she sorry for what she did? She recalled watching the Minozhian fall as if he were a great tree crashing to the forest floor, remembering the look in his dead black eyes, tongue lolling out on the grass, seeing an ear twitch as he lay there motionless. Could she ever make up for that? Or was it justice, vengeance, divine retribution that led him to meet his end at the hands of the very girl they had been sent to kill? Valdak the Just and the other gods were silent on the matter as usual, and she had to struggle with these questions herself.

Teya drew the Minozhian knife from her belt and presented it to Cindra, who took a few moments to bring herself to look at it. Why had Teya taken it, just to give it to the person who never wanted to see one again?

Teya explained, "It is your *Lok-shíneh*. Every *Gatéth-sho'a* warrior has a war-token of their first kill in battle, but I know of none who carry a Minozhian *Kos* knife." She waited for Cindra to take the blade. It was a big wicked thing, curved along the spine like a crescent moon, the sharp edge of the blade was thicker and shaped like a long leaf but for the curved spurs near the handle. There was a ringed finger-guard on the hilt to protect a rather thick forefinger; the handle was made of horn or bone, carved and engraved with quasi-Norsican symbols that were the bastardized script of Minozhia. The base of the handle was a sharpened iron tip that made it just as deadly on one end as the other. Cindra trembled as she accepted it, putting it in her lap as if it were a dead fish beginning to stink. Her grip on the silver hairbrush tightened.

"I'm not a warrior Teya," she said, "I was terrified and wanted to run. If I had thought about it, I would have. I feel sick..."

Teya smiled, which was something Cindra had never seen her do before. "Yet you did not think; you acted and I am alive. It does not matter that you were afraid and wanted to flee. All warriors are afraid once in a while. I was afraid among the bull men, and I was not ready to die."

Cindra looked at the murderous weapon in her lap and asked, "What do I do with my war-token? Do I have to keep it?"

Teya said solemnly, "It honors the lessons that one killed to learn, that one died to teach. If you value this, then value the *Lok-shíneh*."

Cindra thought on this for a moment and ran her finger along the handle of the knife, wondering how it would help. It would always make her remember, but what could it teach her? A thought occurred to her and she asked Teya, "Do you have one, a war-token?"

Teya rose and patted the second knife at her hip, the one with the brass pommel and wire-wound handle, saying nothing more as she went into the caravan.

Majii decided that Cindra should sleep in the wagon for the night just in case someone was to happen upon their camp and notice the fair-skinned girl. Word of her presence among them must not travel to the wrong ears and there was still much to discuss. The bed was made for Cindra and she lay there staring at the hanging herbs, trying to listen to the conversation by the fire. The strain of the night's ordeal soon overtook her and she drifted into a fretful sleep, dreaming once again of traveling by sea with her dear friend and looking forward to a new life. Then the pirates attacked. The wind blew cold over the deck, the ocean spray flecked her face as she ran pushing through the thick air and making no progress, invisible wind held her back and swept her nightclothes towards the maw of death. Mineth gave up her life as always, but this time things ended differently. Bow in hand and endless arrows at the ready, Cindra piled the doorway high with Minozhian corpses as they tried to reach her, climbing over their fallen comrades and meeting the same fate. Soon Mineth was buried beneath them and Cindra tried desperately to move the heavy bodies to reach her friend. When she had pushed and pulled as many of them out of the way as possible, she was distressed to find that Mineth was gone, her blood mingled with that of the mountain of Minozhian pirates filling the small cabin. She stood up finally and went to the window, instructing Gavagul the messenger bird to tell her parents that everything would be alright before jumping into the sea, the golden bracelet on her wrist calling to the sea god's favorite minions to bring her ashore.

She awoke early the next morning in peace, breathing deeply of the forest air and seeing all things in the pale blue of morning.

Chapter Two

A Year of Mourning

The weeks had been kind, and so had Stable Master Gorin. Nixy had hardly felt the man's meaty hand smacking the back of his head anymore, and didn't know what to think of it. Was it because the boy was being schooled each day to learn his letters? Was it out of respect of Cindra's wishes, or had Nixy himself become more behaved, not giving the sour little man an excuse? Whatever it was, Nixy was grateful for the change.

He finished raking out the stalls after the morning feeding and went about helping the older boys prepare a horse for its rider. One of the castle folk needed to go into town, so his horse was done up in tack and harness. It had been Nixy's job to give the saddle a good polishing, as if the rider's rump would notice the difference. Nixy never complained, for he loved his work; he loved the chance to be free of the cares of his old life. He had three meals per day, he had a bed of his own, and was given one silver calimark per month, which he saved as best he could. As an added bonus, no one was trying to kill him.

The thought gave him a shudder as he remembered the night he met Black Will in the old church courtyard, and Lady Cindra had saved him. It had been the most frightening night of his life, he was sure, although he had been having some powerfully disturbing dreams of late. Black wolves, shadowy figures, and the beating of great leathery wings haunted his sleep. What did it mean? And why did he feel a knot in the pit of his stomach when a mouse or cat scampered across the roof of the stable lodgings? He couldn't figure it out, so instead he lost himself in his work and went to bed satisfied, too tired to care about what was lurking in the night.

After polishing the saddle and cleaning up, he headed to the rectory in the bailey for his lesson. Suddenly a streak of fire passed overhead and resolved itself into a brilliant bird, which circled and landed on the castle roof. Nixy had heard of firebirds before, but hadn't seen one before today. He meant to ask his teacher about it, but the man arrived late to the lesson. His teacher, a minor priest of Eyorona, was one of the castle scribes; he had agreed to take an hour or two from his duties to instruct Nixy in reading and writing. Brother Dane was a nice fellow, who had seemingly endless patience, but today he was shaken and distracted, and the lesson was a short one.

On this day the castle was strangely silent. Everyone went about their duties as usual, but with a little less pep than they might, and with eyes gloomy and downcast. Something was wrong, that was for sure, and he heard many a servant asking another what the matter was about, but they were only met with uncertain looks and shaking heads.

The man he had readied the horse for was late in coming, and when he finally arrived, he mounted up and

30

rode away like a shot. Later in the day, a great many people arrived at the castle, but few were leaving. Most were obviously rich and important, and there was much work to do finding stable space for the newcomers. Priests and priestesses came too, and judging by their cloth, they represented all the temples of the city, and many said prayers before the gates before entering.

"Something's happened," said one of the older boys who handled the horses, "Something bad, I'll warrant. All these priests, it reeks of death, it does."

"There's been a battle, I'll bet!" squeaked a younger lad, "A war's started 'tween the king and the rebel houses. Maybe a castle's been taken, or..."

"You don't know nothing," the older stable hand said, "If there were a war, they'd not have all these priests. There'd be knights and men-at-arms marching about, and that firebird would've been sent out somewheres else. No, it's some grim news that just concerns the lord and lady." He stopped speaking when he noticed that Nixy was growing pale and nervous. They all continued working in silence.

By nightfall Nixy had little appetite. The other boys were quiet and broody, having seen the day's activities as a bad omen. Some of the more vocal ones were spinning wild tales of war and foreign intrigue, and others were talking of the death of the king or a plague in the neighboring province. Nixy heard enough to realize that no one had any real idea what had happened, not that he took comfort in it.

At mealtime they sat on the edges of their cots as Gorin and Minerva came up the stairs to serve them their supper. Gorin passed out the wooden bowls and spoons, and when he came to Nixy, it seemed he held on to the bowl a moment too long, as if he wanted to speak. Nixy looked up uncertainly, but Gorin averted his eyes. Minerva came by with a pot of stew and ladled it out to the lads, giving Nixy a few extra potatoes. He looked up and smiled, but the woman's face was grave.

He ate the stew in silence, the warmth of it doing little to ease his fears. Gorin gave them a bit longer to finish, or so it seemed, and collected the bowls and spoons without comment. Nixy waited with a growing dread, sensing that the pair had very bad news to share. Gorin put aside the bowls in a pile by the door and made as if to speak, but his voice failed him. He looked at Minerva for support and she stepped forward, all eyes on her.

"There has been a terrible tragedy, lads..." she fiddled with her apron, "The messenger bird arrived today, straight from the ship bearing our lord's daughter to her new home..." She choked up a bit and looked at Nixy, whose eyes grew wide in understanding. "The word is that the ship was attacked and... and the lady..." she sniffed and tears began to fall as her strength failed her.

Gorin stepped forward saying, "It were the Minozhian bull men that did it. That much is known." He took the kitchen mistress's hand and patted it. "The lord and lady says... that there's to be a year of mourning for th-the Lady Cindra, just as there was for her baby brother a few years back." He glanced at Nixy and found the boy staring at a spot on the far wall, his face drained of color. Gorin tried to sound like his old brutish self, but his voice cracked. "S-so, fer the next month there's bound to be a lot of comings and goings at the castle, and we best be prepared for it." He squeezed Minerva's hand and turned to retrieve the bowls and leave. She remained for a moment to run her fingers through Nixy's hair, seeing if he needed any support. He only sat there, unblinking, looking at nothing at all.

"Cindra had a brother?" he asked quietly, to no one in particular.

The other lads knew all about Nixy's friendship with the young noble lady, even if few believed she had saved him from a monster. They all watched him silently and looked at each other, waiting for someone to make the first move. Then one of the older boys came forward and placed a hand on Nixy's shoulder.

32

"I'm sorry, Nix." He gave him a pat and turned away. Several other boys followed suit, offering their condolences as best as they were able. They were used to being obnoxious to one another in their daily exchanges, and had little practice at sympathy.

Minerva picked up the empty soup pot and gave Nixy a pat on the head saying, "If you need anything, little one, just come and see me, right?" She sniffled and departed; there would be many guests to feed over the next few weeks, and she would need all her rest.

The boys went to bed early with little talk, and all gave Nixy a respectful distance. For his part, Nixy just lay in his cot, staring at the ceiling with the blood pounding in his ears. He felt empty, as if all his joy and sorrow had poured out of him onto the floor and seeped away through the cracks. Cindra had gone; he had dealt with her absence and the sadness that followed, but at least he knew she was safe and well in another land. Now was he supposed to accept that she had died at sea at the hands of monsters? That the girl who had befriended him, though he didn't deserve it, was lying at the bottom of the ocean? That wasn't fair, it wasn't right. What had she done to deserve that? He waited for an answer, hoping the gods would break their silence to explain it to him, to help him understand what it was all for. But there were no voices from on high, no light shining through the window bearing divine guidance, only the setting sun and the ocean breeze.

He wondered, as gloaming turned to dark night, when he would feel like crying. His eyes stung from looking at the rafters for so long, but there were no tears. He almost wanted to have the void within him filled by something, sorrow, anger, anything. The emptiness was so much more difficult to face; it absorbed any misery or comfort, and left him cold and lifeless. He wanted to cry for her, for himself, he owed her that at least.

From somewhere deep inside his head came a keening wail, like a cry on the wind, until it wound itself around his heart and squeezed, pulling his insides down through the floor. A dark ache spread all the way through his shoulders to his fingertips, and his breath escaped in a soft moan of suffering. It was as if his bones were throbbing with every heartbeat, trying to turn to jelly and melt away. Breathing hurt. Seeing hurt. He curled in a ball and trembled.

That-that's better, he thought as tears streamed down his cheeks. The dogs howled in their kennels, the air grew chill, and from the rafters came the soft scratching of claws upon the roof tiles.

The Guadim could wait; it had all the time in the world. The boy would be driven from the safety of the castle walls and into the open. The death of the noble girl, his savior, was the perfect catalyst for the song of despair the Guadim was pouring into the boy's mind. It folded its long, powerful limbs and sat like a gargoyle, retracting its leathery wings against its back and settling in for the night. The guards on the wall would ignore it if it didn't move; they would walk their patrols along the battlements and feel a strange chill that had nothing to do with the night air. The horses might stamp and the hounds might bay, but nothing on two legs would perceive it. Human eyes would see only a shadow among shadows, an owl, a cat, something expected and familiar, anything but the ancient evil that sat within the bailey of Casselvane Keep. Night after night it would return until the boy could bear it no longer.

Then it would have his blood.

Chapter Three

The Divine Court

It might have been an instant or an eternity since the little creatures had been given their task and carried it out, guiding the attention of the priestess to the two young lovers. The day had been cold and clear in the world of Jayde; a festival was being readied for the Mistress, but one of her mortal servants had her eyes turned inward instead of towards the blossoming romance before her. The Mistress had sent the butterflies to intercede. Now they were flying back to her with tidings of success.

Shedding their material forms in a flash of fire, the spirit butterflies soared on the winds that swept between the worlds. They enjoyed the times they were allowed to enter the world of elements, and quickly volunteered for the brief but important mission. Such excursions were rare since the portals were shut, and only the least of Powers could pass through. When the King decided to sever the Realm of Jayde from the Realms Outside, the Mistress was outraged, for she loved her influence over the people of the world, mortal and immortal alike. Nevertheless, it was not a matter of choice, and the Age of the Gods came to a close. Now, mortals called their time the Age of Omens, for signs and portents, true or imagined, were the only things that linked them to the divine. The poor creatures would now have to make their own destinies.

Rivers of ether flowed through the Void, signposts and landmarks in the vast emptiness. The realms of the Powers drifted and bobbed within them, like corks in a stream. The butterfly spirits dove for the borders of one such realm, a swirling ball of light transforming into a flat oval plane of silver glass, reflecting the splendor before it. The butterflies headed straight for its surface and passed within, sending tiny ripples across the glass, like pebbles in a vast, still lake.

The goddess of love and desire, of beauty and fulfillment, this was the Mistress of the realm. In olden days, when she had chosen to walk the world of elements, she often took the form of a beautiful maiden; she was one whose grace and loveliness defied the skill of poets and the art of sculptors and painters. Unique to each person's vision, her form and essence was born in the eye of the beholder, and was therefore perfect to all.

The Mistress was not hard to find, for she was always in the center of her garden, and the center was wherever she chose to be. She walked upon a labyrinthine path lined by rosebushes, her toes barely touching the stones, as her hair and garments blew in the breeze only she could feel. She was tall and shapely, elegant of form and curve, and her hair was gold, or copper, or streaked with both, as she desired. She wore a wrap of coral silk, finer and softer than any material of any craft, and it clung tightly to her breasts and hips, crossing and caressing, and flowing behind her like wings. In her wake was a bouquet of bright butterflies that fluttered after her adoringly. The air was rich with the scent of roses and earth, heady and intoxicating.

Selvina extended her finger for her two arriving servants to land on. The butterflies danced upon its tip as she favored them with a smile saying, "Welcome back, little ones. You have done well. Now join your family." Her voice was sensuous and rich, and her praise made the two butterflies glow brightly with pleasure as they joined their fellows.

The goddess walked in her garden, tending the roses with a touch or caress. Every bloom was a love held for another, a longing either fulfilled or unrequited, a reason to live or die. The roses were varied in size and health, as were the loves they held. Some were budding, others were in full bloom, and others still were withering and faded, dropping petals and leaves before wilting away. Eventually she would prune these roses, taking them in hand and making them dust to feed the garden anew.

But for now, it was new love she was seeking, the budding flowers of chance and fate. She had her hand in its making of course, but it needed encouragement that was now, sadly, beyond her power. Subtlety was never one of her strengths, but she was learning; sending her two little servants to catch her priestess's attention was one of her more clever and simple ploys. She reached out for the two young buds, already beginning to open. She loved this time of potential most of all, when anything could happen and often did. It was so rare when two buds grew and blossomed into fullness together, remaining sweet and fragrant until they were cut. When that happened, she would adorn her gazebo with such beauties; they were triumphs of her will and gifts.

A voice cut through her musings and gave her a start. "And they call *me* a meddler!" A high nasal giggle drifted up from the rosebushes.

Selvina hunted for the offender and found him hiding

amongst the flowers; a rose with a mischievous face surrounded by petals was leering up at her, high-arched eyebrows waggling. The flower face took a bow, bending its stem and flourishing its leaf-arms as it dipped low.

"You!" shrieked the goddess.

"Me!" sang the flower, growing and stepping out of the bushes. As it uprooted itself and trod upon the path, it was suddenly a man, or perhaps a boy of indeterminate age. He had a mane of pale blond hair, a heart-shaped face, and large pointed ears that swept as high as the top of his head. His grin was wide for such a pointed chin, and his emerald eyes were bright. His form was light and muscled, like a dancer's, and over it he wore a loose green silk jacket bound at the waist with a red sash. Beneath was motley of yellow and black, and he danced about in pointy green shoes. Tavenji was his name, and he was the messenger of the gods, among other things.

Selvina folded her arms before her and said sternly, "Defile my garden again, Tavenji, and I shall fertilize it with your carcass! How did you get in here?"

Ignoring the threat, Tavenji said, "Come now, Selvina. Unexpected entrances are my specialty, and it's not as if your gate key is that hard to figure out. A mirror can only hold so many things, after all." He loved to taunt his siblings' attempts at maintaining their privacy, so long as he was vague in doing so. No sense in letting them get too wise.

"I am on official business, so perhaps we could adjourn to someplace more suitable?" Tavenji looked hopefully at her, for he took pride in his one official function and had his standards to maintain.

At once they were in the gazebo, a large white edifice many stories high with great pillars supporting a circular roof overhead. It was the only structure in the whole landscape of rosebushes, and was currently the center of the realm, for Selvina stood within, her hands on her hips, awaiting her so-called sibling's message. Apparently she was not in the mood for chit-chat.

Happy to be accommodated, Tavenji stuck an oratory pose and began, "Our father and lord, the High King Arathus, summons his most beauteous and loving daughter to attend him at the Divine Court!" He smiled as he finished, perhaps awaiting applause.

None was forthcoming. Selvina was terse with her response, her brow creased in worry, "Again? So soon? Why?"

Tavenji had no answer to give. "Er... daddy misses his kids?" He offered helpfully.

Selvina was relieved, then confused. "All of us? He is summoning all of us then?"

Delighted that his sister caught on so fast, he grinned and bowed, congratulating her. "He has sent me to say so," Tavenji said, "I am but one of two messengers, actually. He dispatched his eagle to tell the others, while I am to fetch you, the Mother of Mercy, and the big, bloody, *unpleasant* one." He shuddered a bit, which brought a knowing smile to the goddess's face.

"Lelonetha will indeed be pleased to see you," she began, "but *Balkon*, oh my, I recall he promised to do *horrible* things to you if you ever set foot in his realm again." *Surely deserved,* she added to herself.

Tavenji waved her off, "If the big lump would only develop a sense of humor..." He bent to examine an ornate flower vase on the central marble table. The vase was adorned with funny little figures chasing about and fornicating in the way humans do. The roses within were highly prized, no doubt.

Selvina watched him closely around her vase. "He *has* a sense of humor, just not about himself."

"Pity," Tavenji said wandering about the table, "so much wasted potential." He began to sniff the flowers decorating the gazebo. "So, sister," he asked nonchalantly, "what was the reason... no, that's not right." He didn't like to use the word 'reason' with her, for Selvina's actions so rarely deserved it. "What was the eh, *purpose* behind that tiny little, um, *divine intervention*?"

39

He spun at her with the words. "You know," he said, "with the butter-flappies?" He hooked his thumbs together and flapped his hands like wings.

Selvina did not like to be baited, for she took to it too easily. "It was *inspiration*, half-brother dear, not intervention!" She gave him a scornful look and said, "That gloomy little priestess of mine needed to pay attention to her duties. Surely I can still inspire my own priesthood at my own festival! Or am I to be stripped of that power as well?"

Tavenji looked her up and down, leering. "No," he said, "I think you've been stripped quite enough." He began examining his fingernails, a habit he'd picked up from his time in the world of mortals. "However, you never know how father might react. After all, he wasn't too pleased with your last little stunt."

Selvina leaned over the table in a seductive manner, even though her mood was dark, for it was simply in her nature. "Don't play the innocent with me!" she snarled, "You all thought he deserved it, closing the portals to Jayde, but only *after* he had his little tryst with that mortal woman."

Tavenji shrugged, "He probably thought they'd be better off without our constant meddling in their affairs."

"You don't understand... I am Love, yet I am cut off from those who love me... You couldn't know what that is like. You never had much of a priesthood, never had so many devout worshipers..." Her lovely face grew dejected as her pain became palpable and manifested, darkening the sky. The delicate prized roses in the vase wilted under the weight of her sorrow, dying in moments. All but one remained unscathed, and she gasped in horror at what she had done.

Tavenji smirked at the wilted roses, wondering whose loves they had been. "So you took it upon yourself to make him feel the loss more personally. Oh yes, sister, *very* clever of you."

He felt the change in the air as her rage peaked. The

goddess whipped around, hair and garments blowing in a sudden blast of fury. She raised her arm, causing her anger to take form in her open hand. Butterflies made of radiance and power struck the smirking god square in the chest.

"Get out!" she screamed, and forced his body through the fabric of her realm and out into the Void. Tavenji's ears flared out and his eyes lit up with the shock of the attack; he let out a cry that faded and died as Selvina's realm closed upon the rift of his passage.

Alone again, she took a few moments to calm down as she turned to assess the damage her anger had caused. The wilted flowers in the vase were dead or dying, and there was little she could do to help them. Her power had its limits after all, and love once lost was not so easily repaired, even for a goddess.

Only a single rose remained in her prized collection, the same rose that had been in bloom since ages past. *Would it ever die*, she wondered? All things had to end; even love was meant to fade over time, and time enough had passed for this one.

She knew all the details of course, and understood this rose's tragic circumstance, but she was powerless to alter its destiny. *How far we've fallen*, she thought sadly, *when even the gods cannot correct their own mistakes.*

Tavenji drifted in the winds between realities, shaking off the effects of Selvina's outburst. "Was it something I said? Hn-hn-hn-hn-hn!" He giggled nasally and set off through the blackness to his next destination.

The youngest of the gods didn't mind being misunderstood, for he felt it added to his mystique. He was known as the Trickster, the Laughing God, the Storyteller, the Fool, Master of Secrets, Lord of Thieves, and the Lord of Lies. To many of his siblings, he was known as half-brother, for they were not entirely convinced that he was a creation of the God of Order. Llomaak, the God of Chaos, seemed a more likely sire, and the others mistrusted him. No matter, Tavenji knew his place in the scheme of things, as did his father Arathus, king of the gods and lawgiver, Order incarnate.

Lelonetha accepted him too, and for that he was eternally grateful. The Mother of Mercy was like a mother to him, at least he imagined so, since he had never really had one. She lived in a realm called Haven, where all was peace and beauty and bliss. He would have visited more often were it not for the goddess's barriers of pain. He approached Haven and sighed, for as much as he loved Lelonetha, he hated her idea of fairness.

A burning sphere of fire drifted before him now, immense and imposing, like a sun. He knew that the souls of those who journeyed to Haven were judged as they passed through the barriers; those who led easy lives had to suffer much, while those who suffered in life found it easy to reach their goal. That left few choices for gods, who didn't suffer any more than they wanted to. Lelonetha compensated for that.

He took a deep breath and plunged into the fire. The first layer was almost more than he could bear; blazing waves of solid heat almost blackened his fingertips and the points of his ears. He squinted against the brightness until he broke through the wall of flame, and his eyes were still dazzled when he entered a layer of blackness. No light, no wind, no way to get one's bearings, just the horrid howling of the dark as cold hands reached out to touch him.

He sought for a way out and found it, a tiny tear in the fabric of the trap, a shortcut through the suffering that only he could have found. He spilled out of the shroud amid a wall of tumbling boulders, drifting and floating in space, bumping into one another and changing direction.

Tavenji took a moment to find the pattern and dove in, ducking and weaving through the rocks like a living breeze. *This might not be so bad after all*, he thought as he navigated the falling rocks, leapfrogging over one and bouncing off another. Suddenly, as if responding to his confidence, sharp spikes rose out of the stones like morning stars. One snagged his sash and jerked him to a halt, and he missed his next timed dodge. Rebounding and trying to free himself, he narrowly missed being crushed by a 'smaller' stone as large as his torso. He began to panic, making matters worse. Freeing his sash, he scrambled over a boulder that spun against his advance, voiding his effort. More stone spikes emerged and pierced his hands and legs, pinning him to the spinning rock. The great stones closed in and began to crush him slowly, so that he feared he might actually die from the pain. That wasn't possible, was it? With his last gasp, he cried out, "Mercy!"

Haven surrounded him. The marble halls were warmed by braziers and draped with lush fabrics. The columns were hung with ivy and stood beside luxurious couches. Peach trees stood in elegant planters, and the sounds of water falling in a fountain could be heard, making music to accompany the aroma of sweet blossoms. The spirits of mortal men and women drifted aimlessly through the halls, awash in the bliss of divine mercy. Tavenji gulped the air and checked his body, making sure nothing was broken or shattered. To his relief, he was whole and complete, without a scratch to commemorate his passage through the barriers. Only the scars on his mind remained.

Lelonetha was there to greet him with arms outspread. "Welcome, brother dear! It has been too long since your last visit." Her smile was warm and genuine, and her pale skin reflected the warmth of the fires. Her eyes were blue-gray and happy, and her golden hair was pulled back and bound with a simple ring. She wore a yellow dress made of a single sheet of fabric, bound at the waist and gathered about the neck. Golden bracelets adorned her wrists.

Tavenji was mildly surprised. "You don't wonder at my absence, do you? Your barriers get harder to pass every time!"

She sat on the wide edge of the fountain, patting it for him to sit beside her. "Only for you, dear one; you used to simply ignore them."

He pouted and replied, "I just never understood your sense of hospitality." He sat on the marble surface and hugged his knees to his chest.

Lelonetha said, "Haven must have a meaning for everyone, *especially* the gods. Now, to what do I owe the pleasure of your company?" She grew concerned, "I hope you're not hiding out from Balkon again."

Tavenji shook his head, saying, "Actually I have to see him next."

Lelonetha nodded "So you have a message then."

Tavenji stood dramatically and proclaimed, "Arathus, his most high majesty, has summoned the benevolent and most magnanimous Mother of Mercy to attend him at the Divine Court."

Lelonetha curled her legs up on the bench and smiled at his recitation, saying, "Oh my! Balkon too?"

Tavenji plopped down on the seat again, looking thoughtful, "All of us. I just came from Selvina's garden, and father's eagle is fetching the others."

Lelonetha frowned. "Well! You'd think he would send Aminus to fetch Balkon instead of you, poor thing. Balkon has a fondness for birds of prey."

Tavenji nodded slowly and looked up at his sister with big, soulful eyes. "It's why I came to see you first. I have a big favor to ask, and I know it's irregular but... will you go with me to Balkon's realm?"

Lelonetha sat back and regarded her brother with concern and doubt. "I don't know... I do hate that place; all those poor souls constantly at war, all the blood and gore..."

Tavenji sank his face into his knees and sobbed, "But last time I was there, he made me fight my way out! He raised up the Bythian Royal Guard and set them on me... I barely got away." He snuffled and wiped his moist eyes. Gods could cry if they chose to.

Leonetha was outraged and exclaimed, "Oooh, that rascal! Very well, I shall accompany you just this once."

Tavenji brightened immediately, perking up and willing the water from his eyes. "Oh, thank you sister, thank you!" He pointed hopefully towards one of her prized peach trees; each bite of its fruit was full of the Nectar of Bliss. "Can I have a peach?"

She nodded and looked at the tree thoughtfully as Tavenji helped himself with glee.

The Fog of War surrounded the vast plains of Strife, obscuring its borders and hinterlands. Cold and gray, it caressed the skin of the newcomers as they found themselves drifting in a small boat on the water. Leonetha wrapped her traveling cloak more tightly about her shoulders, and Tavenji sat upright and alert, eyes darting to and fro in a vain attempt to pierce the fog. The smell of decaying weeds swept over the waters, suggesting a nearby riverbank or shore, and the call of scavenger birds echoed in the distance. There was no breeze to disperse the gray mist, and the boat's passage caused the only stirring of the veil.

Tavenji's voice was hushed. "Boat. Don't like it."

"Perhaps our brother has spared us from walking across a bloody battlefield. Perhaps he is becoming more accommodating," suggested Leonetha, who always liked to hope for the best.

"Not likely," said the nervous messenger. "He's not going to let me just walk in without a fight. He has it in for me, especially after..." His voice trailed off as his ears perked at a new sound. There was something moving through the water, something close. He darted his head about to find the source, and his movements rocked the little boat. Leonetha placed a calming hand on his knee, but it only made him jump.

"What is it, brother?" she asked, steadying the boat.

"Can you hear...? It's almost..." His voice caught in his throat as he turned back to his right, for the tall bow of a longship was passing the little boat; its ornate prow was carved in the likeness of a screaming eagle's head, with twisted knot designs down the length of the neck as it joined the hull. Tavenji remembered these ships in the mortal world, for they were manned by bold traders and explorers whose names were both respected and feared. The Norsicans, as they were called, were also bloody pillagers and pirates at times. Not the best of neighbors and not someone whom Tavenji wished to meet in this realm of eternal war.

As the rest of the ship came into view, even Lelonetha was taken aback. The sail was faded and tattered, as if exposed to centuries of wear; its red eagle symbol almost vanished on the pale sheet. The crew, numbering a dozen, looked centuries old as well. They were all but skeletons dressed in ring mail, yet still standing in grim purpose, with dim points of cold light burning in their empty eye sockets. They were brandishing spears and swords, and one or two were drawing back ancient rotted short bows, which were probably deadlier than they looked. One of the frightful specters was even hefting a flail with a spiked ball, upon which was impaled the cracked skull of a vanquished adversary. The dangling skull grinned menacingly, as if eager to be dashed against another head. The crew let out a ghastly battle cry, each sounding like a dying cow echoing in the depths of a well. They shook their weapons aloft, rattling the tarnished armor and jewelry about their bones.

"Norsican Raiders!" Tavenji exclaimed as he clung to his sister in fright. "And he didn't even bother to put skin on them!" He really disliked his brother's sense of humor.

"Oh, how perfectly horrid!" Lelonetha said, more disgusted than afraid.

Tavenji searched the bottom of the boat for an oar, and finding one, used it as a shield against spear thrusts and flying arrows, moving with the speed of a desperate god. He could not keep this up forever; he hoped Balkon would tire before then.

46

A great roar of triumph and mirthless laughter pealed like thunder across the sky, and the Fog of War parted to reveal the battle-scarred landscape of Strife. Dominating one full quarter of the heavens above was the frightful visage of Balkon, the god of war and conquest. Broad and powerfully built, even at normal size, the god was armored in silver mail and plate, which was stained with dried blood and viscera and brightly reflected the sun. He stood with his hands on his girded hips, or so it seemed, for his waist was hidden below the horizon. From under his raised visor sprang a thick and bushy beard, the brown hair stained red and matted with gore. His mouth was wide and cavernous as he laughed, and his teeth looked like snowcapped mountain peaks. His cheeks and nose were rosy from too much wine, and the forests of his eyebrows shaded his cruel eyes.

"Ho ho! Now here's a contest! A cockroach of a god and a merciful healer, pitted against the most feared pirates of all time! This could be amusing for a good long while, and there's plenty more where they came from." He parted the sparse clouds with a motion of his gauntlet, indicating the ranks of desiccated soldiers lining the banks of the dark river. "I'll let you heal him once per hour, if you wish, dear sister. These soldiers are the Dishonored, so I'm afraid you cannot offer them Haven as a means of thinning their ranks. They are mine." He smiled wickedly.

Strife was one of the places a warrior might go after death, in order to fight the perfect battle, to win the perfect victory. Unable to truly die, these elite warriors fought until they won, or littered the battlefield until the day began anew, fighting until they had nothing more to fight for. Those who cleansed and perfected their spirits through combat moved on. The Dishonored, however, had fought for blood-lust and the joy of slaughter in life, and so were doomed to the role of eternal enemy; their fate was to test the mettle of the never-ending armies of the brave and proud.

Lelonetha was having none of it. "Stop this foolishness at once, brother! There will be no fighting. We are here with legitimate purpose and we demand, *I* demand, that you treat us as the honored guests that we are!"

Balkon barked with laughter, the shock wave stunning birds in flight and sending them tumbling. "HA! Honored guests, what do *you* know of honoring guests? You make them pass through your accursed barriers of pain and suffering before they reach Haven, be they mortal or god! What kind of welcome is that? I don't need lessons from you on honoring guests!" He loomed over the landscape and scowled, blocking the sun.

Lelonetha stood in the boat, using her power to steady its violent rocking. Tavenji had taken up a fighting stance on the bench seat and was swatting at the animated corpses with his oar, parrying every hack and blow with panicked grace. He managed to knock the skull from a pirate's bony neck, and its teeth gnashed at him as it plopped into the river. The headless body continued to swing its sword.

Lelonetha looked at her massive brother, incredulity on her face. "When mortals or gods pass my barriers, they receive the rewards of Haven, brother. But when we finish muddling through this nonsense, there will only be you and your cold, unwelcoming hall."

Balkon stiffened and sputtered, unused to being insulted to his face. "Rrrrgh, very well, a deal then! You may come up and visit, but the cockroach stays and fights! I insist!"

"Where I go, Tavenji goes with me." Lelonetha was resolute.

"Then you may both go to the Abyss!" the god roared, spittle flying like wet artillery through the cold air.

Lelonetha folded her arms and glared at her giant brother. Tavenji's oar was getting whittled down considerably. "Is there nothing I can say or do to change your mind, brother dear?" she asked, showing her endless patience.

Balkon bellowed "Nothing!" and folded his arms with the horrendous din of mile-wide armor plates rubbing together.

"But," she withdrew a hand from beneath her traveling robe, "I brought you my peaches." She held up a perfect specimen, ripe and fuzzy and begging to be bitten.

The very next moment, the two visitors were standing in the War Room in the heart of the Fortress of Strife. "Well, why didn't you say so?" Balkon exclaimed. He was standing before them, now only towering over them by a head-height, arms wide in greeting. His sister embraced him, careful to avoid the spiked bits of his armor.

The hall was small and almost cozy by godly standards, with torches illuminating tapestries depicting historic battles, the images slowly moving to make the scenes more dramatic. Several passageways met in this room, and winged women known as the Kyraine could be seen coming and going on unknown business; their short skirts and scant armor reflected the torch flames, and their talons clicked on the stone floor.

In the center of the War Room was a large circular table fashioned of dark marble, streaked with veins of red. It was supported by the twelve carved figures of men, and things like men, who strained against the immense weight. They were the imprisoned spirits of the worst of the Dishonored, fated to be slowly crushed by the weight of their crimes.

Upon the surface of the table was Balkon's Field, the landscape of Strife that most who were not gods were familiar with. Vast armies clashed upon its surface and sieges were waged against crumbling castles, with catapults hurling minuscule artillery at the walls. Ships traded volleys across lakes and oceans, hills were defended and taken, and cavalry trampled men under hundreds of hooves. Tavenji leaned over the table and found a familiar looking river and a tiny Norsican ship floating next to an itty-bitty rowboat.

He grinned wickedly, "Not so tough now, are you?" He

dunked the carved eagle prow of the ship with a finger, tipping it on-end and tossing the crew, who scrabbled for a foothold as they poked the mighty digit with useless weapons.

"Don't touch that!" bellowed the war god, who had been distracted from his table by the prospect of Peaches of Bliss. He was now climbing the dais to mount his throne, a massive seat made of iron and bone. "Ziowyn," he bellowed, "Bring fresh gore! We have guests!" One of the winged women, with a face as perfect and impassive as that of a porcelain doll, bowed and departed. Balkon regarded his brother with the warmth most mortals reserved for toenail fungus. "Well, you have a message then? Out with it, and the sooner I can be rid of you!" He took a bite of the peach in his steel gauntlet, and a look of utter pleasure crossed his face.

Tavenji just stood and blinked at him, mystified. "Aren't you going to remove your helmet when I speak the words of the Divine King?"

The pleasure left Balkon's eyes and his brow creased into a deep frown. "It's fine where it is, now out with it," he growled.

The messenger folded his arms across his chest and heaved a great sigh. "Father wants to see you. Now." He examined the ceiling as he spoke, noting the multitude of daggers stuck in the rafters.

The war god rose from his throne, nearly crushing his peach in a clenched fist. "DO IT PROPER, DAMN YOU!" Balkon had a passion for protocol, when it suited him. He settled back as Ziowyn returned and smeared a wet coat of blood over his breastplate and pauldrons, making him more presentable.

Tavenji bore an unhappy glance from his sister as he straightened himself, clearing his throat. He straightened his jacket, adjusted his sash, and made as if to deliver a solemn oration; he then fell upon one knee and spread his arms wide, eyes crossing with the strain of his most theatrical voice. "LO! The King God Arathus, Highest of

High, Father of Order and Giver of Law, has hereby called and summoned to his Divine Presence, his utterly sanguineous and most contentious son..." His voice petered out and he took a deep breath, "Balkon, giver of abrasions, master of fractures both large *AND* small, creator of well-disciplined discord and Lord of Strife... " he pretended to search his thoughts for a second, "...er, who must at once leave for the Divine Court in the City of Dormos." He rose to his feet, and then fell to a knee again to conclude, "Presently. Now. At once." He stood, made a quick curtsy, and wandered away.

The war god glared at him as he chewed another bite, not quite sure if he had just been mocked. "That's better," he said around a mouthful of peach.

Lelonetha stepped up and intervened, lest the bliss wear off and Balkon become properly insulted. "Thank you for being so kind and understanding, brother. Father would have sent Aminus, but knew only Tavenji could deliver his message so... eloquently." She offered a weak smile.

Balkon finished his peach, licking the juice from his stained gauntlet. "Well, you did bring me a peach. You know how I love them..."

Lelonetha withdrew another from her robes and said, "And I know how you can't eat just one."

Balkon was indeed pleased, and a warm smile stretched across his broad face. "Ha! Now you spoil me, sister!" He gratefully took the peach.

Tavenji, now forgotten, wandered by the table and peered through the fog. An idea overtook him, and glancing over his shoulder to make sure he was unnoticed, waggled his fingers over the tiny skeletal hordes upon the shores of the river, working mischief.

"Well!" Tavenji said, spinning to face his siblings. "We must be off. Lovely place you have here, brother. Come, sister, let us depart." He took her hand and waved, and the duo vanished from Strife.

Balkon took his time finishing his peach before he

51

called for his chariot to be readied. He stood and walked to the table, wiping the peach juice from his mouth with his beard. Leaning over the table, he said to the assembled throng of Dishonored, "We gave the little runt a good scare, did we not? He would have soiled himself if he were able! Now, let's see what we can..." His words trailed off as he leaned closer, examining his skeletal forces. A rage boiled up inside his chest and his blood hammered in his ears. "Stop that! Stop it!" He shouted at the troops, holding a mailed fist over them to exert his will. It was not having the desired effect. "That little.... BASTARD! I'll kill him for this! I'll KILL him!"

Ranks of fearsome warriors, the worst of humanity's savage killers, were arrayed in rows and dancing with perfect choreography, joining bony hands and kicking high from side to side. Spear-men twirled their weapons, swords and shields were used for rhythmic percussion, and some of the doomed soldiers had even acquired little handkerchiefs, which they flourished daintily as they danced.

Balkon had to crush them into dust before they stopped, and there was peace on the fields of Strife, at least for a little while.

The Ether Dragon carried the traveling gods on an ornate divan upon its back, its long serpentine body undulating as it beat its feathered wings against the spirit currents. *Lelonetha likes to travel in style*, thought Tavenji, as he relaxed and heaved a sigh of relief. "That went better than I expected," he said happily, "Bribery. I never thought of that."

Lelonetha put her arm over the back of the divan and adjusted her traveling cloak. "You must have something he wants more than blood," she explained.

Tavenji considered, "More than *my* blood? Hmm. Never mind."

Lelonetha turned to face him. "So brother, 'Especially after' what?"

The prankster just stared at her, baffled.

She said, "You told me that Balkon would not let you walk into his realm without a fight, that he had it in for you, especially after... what exactly?"

Tavenji recalled their earlier conversation, before skeletal marauders so rudely interrupted them. "Oh! Well, a while ago I went ah, *shopping* in Obamir's Market and I found a vial of dragon bile; real stuff from the ancient ones, older than most of the gods!"

"Oh my," said Lelonetha, her eyes widening. Dragon bile was extremely potent, and not just in the mortal world. She gave him a wary glance. "What did you do?"

Tavenji had a look of pure glee as he hugged his knees to his chest and grinned from ear to ear, giggling. "Hn-hn-hn, on my last visit, I poured it into his helmet!"

"Tavenji! What... what will that do to him?" She was really worried now.

"No idea," said the Laughing God, "but he didn't want to remove it, did he?"

The divine city of Dormos sat in the center of the Plains of Dromoth, at the very utmost top of creation. It was a vast and unlovely city, bereft of the architectural flair of the mortal world of Jayde. If there was beauty to be seen, it was in its pattern and symmetry, its perfect organization and exquisite alignment, its Orderliness; it was a city best enjoyed from a distance. Massive granite structures stretched for miles in every direction, if such measurements had meaning here. In the center of the city was a high ziggurat, a step pyramid with a flat pinnacle, upon which stood a fortress of stark majesty. A winding path crawled up the face of the structure leading to a tall gate at the base of the fortress; hundreds of tiny figures lined the path waiting for their turn to enter, their arms clutching supplications written on stone tablets or scrolls.

The visitors arriving in Dormos this day did not need to use the path or the gate, for they were beyond such things. The Divine Court was, after all, the meeting hall of the Gods of Order and Civilization, and they were allowed to pass through portals designated for them alone. Eight pillars lined the main hall of the court, and upon these pillars were formed the likenesses of deities, five male and three female.

A lone figure paced the hall, pausing before each pillar and gazing at the faces of the effigies. His appearance was that of a tall man of older years; a golden crown with three points adorned his head, and a rich purple robe, with gold thread-work and jeweled embroidery, hung to the polished, mirror-like floor. Upon his shoulders was a mantle of exquisite silver fur taken in elder days from the Father of Wolves. A red sash bound his waist, and golden sandals could be glimpsed under the hem of his robe as he walked. Beneath his feet, just visible under the polished floor, was an impossible arrangement of gears of all sizes, which turned and meshed endlessly, giving the hall the faintest smell of oil and metal.

The head of Arathus wore no mane of hair to contend with his crown, but his jaw bore a silver beard, perfectly trimmed. His face was aged, but held a power and majesty beyond any mortal king. His golden skin creased about his eyes and brow; his irises were like platters of gold, dark pupils bearing three points like the crown upon his head. He viewed the universe with the eyes of perfection, seeing the imperfection in all things.

His mood had been dour since the news had reached him that the cursed Dark Heart was missing from what was to be its final resting place. There were few others in all creation who knew where the Dark Heart had been hidden; there were in fact seven others, all his godly children. The eighth god was no longer of any consequence.

The king god paused before the last pillar in its row, bearing the faded effigy of a tall elderly man with a great beard and robe, holding a carved staff. Arathus had not desired to harm his child, but the world had grown beyond the need of him, and the king god had stripped

54

him of his power and purpose. Now he was lost, wandering the fringes of creation, seeking his own destiny rather than keeping the destiny of others. Arathus felt a twinge of guilt and regret, but no more than that. He had given up his base emotions and instilled them into his children, his Divine Courtiers. They now governed the passions and desires that led to orderly civilization, for they had been his gift to the First Children, and later to humanity; they were by his will begotten or undone.

At one end of the main hall was a raised dais bearing a large throne carved from a single diamond, its facets throwing off shards of light. At the other end of the hall was a balcony with an enormous archway opening to the stark golden sky. The beating of mighty wings heralded the return of Aminus, the king god's confidant, spy, and messenger. The great eagle swept onto the balcony, bowed its towering bronze-feathered head to its king, and then folded its wings to enter the hall and loom behind the throne. The clacking of its massive talons on the floor was like the ticking of a mighty clock, sharp and metallic in the empty hall. The king of gods climbed the dais and sat, awaiting the presence of his children and wondering which had betrayed his edict.

First to step from her carved pillar and leave it bare was Eyorona, goddess of wisdom and learning. Her skin was tan and rosy, her hair like polished copper, swept up behind to cascade down her back. Delicate pointed ears gave her the look of her favored people, the Ilvayiin, the People of Light. She smelled of oaken woods. The goddess wore a coral gown that left her shoulders bare, and she spread its long sleeves to curtsy to her king before joining him at the foot of the dais. She did not speak, for there was no need. Questions would be pointless until all were assembled. She made herself content to wait.

Valdak and Obamir came next, stepping from their imaged pillars and striding across the floor. The gods of justice and prosperity respectively, the two could not look more dissimilar. Valdak was tall and dark, with concealing robes of charcoal gray, and a flowing scarlet sash that draped over one shoulder. Beneath his hood he had umber skin and a short black beard, which greatly emphasized his pale, blind eyes. The staff he carried was long and gnarled and topped with a curved blade, perhaps just large enough to encircle a head and neck.

Obamir was short and portly, dressed in extravagant attire from his ample velvet cap to his platinum-laced shoes. He had a ruddy complexion and a curly red beard about his jowls, and his pug-nosed, full face always seemed ready to laugh. He rubbed the tips of his many-ringed fingers together as he walked; he smelled of exotic spices.

The gods stopped before the dais and bowed, Obamir taking his hat in hand, and then both stood to the side before the throne. Arathus wondered if Valdak had the ability to find guilt in a god, to see into the depths of their hearts and minds as he did with mortals. He had not been created to judge the divine, but perhaps his perceptions could be of use. That is, if he himself was blameless. Obamir, however, was a giver and taker, bounty and avarice, and Arathus held him in his golden gaze a bit longer.

Selvina came next, her pillar bursting with butterflies of light that faded as her own radiance gathered about her. The sweet scent of roses and feminine skin filled the air, announcing her presence as much as the dazzling lights had. Her clinging strips of silk changed their hue from coral to violet, and her hair turned from copper and gold to rich brunette, so she was distinct from her sister in more than just the brazen display of attributes. She smiled and walked to the dais, hips swaying hypnotically, eyes like a tigress. She gave a graceful curtsy to her king and endeavored to look as innocent as she was able.

Lelonetha and Tavenji arrived together, each taking the image on their pillar with them as they stepped onto the polished floor. Lelonetha threw off her traveling cloak and it became nothing, yet the scent of peaches wafted across the hall. Tavenji skipped along behind her, twirling and capering about like the jester he was. They gave their father their respects before the throne.

Lastly was Balkon, armor polished to a high shine and rich red cloak flowing behind him. Tavenji noted his larger brother was still wearing his helmet as the war god clanked across the floor towards the throne. Stopping and bowing stiffly, Balkon took his place in the semi-circle of his siblings at the base of the dais. The coppery scent of blood surrounded him.

Arathus looked at each of his children in turn and began, his voice vibrating with command and authority, "We imagine that..." He stopped abruptly as soon as he noticed Balkon, and gave him an impatient stare. Balkon shrank under the gaze and looked about at his siblings nervously. Giving his king an apologetic and tortured look, he reluctantly removed his helmet.

Tavenji was then filled with such mirth that his toes rose above the floor and his knees buckled as he struggled to contain his laughter.

The war god's head of bushy, brown hair was now bare to the scalp upon his crown, with the longer, fuller sides brushed up in an attempt to cover the loss. Blotchy red spots colored the bald patch, and several scratch marks attested to their itchiness.

The gods and goddesses reacted in mild shock, unsure if this wild appearance was intentional. Balkon cleared his throat and shook his head to unfurl the futile grasp at vanity, making the bushy mane flare about his ears. "It helps the helmet fit better," he explained, as if it was perfectly obvious.

Tavenji shook with repressed giggles and felt as though he were about to spring a leak.

The king god was neither amused nor distracted from his purpose. He began again in a louder voice, as if it were needed. "We imagine that you are wondering why you have been summoned here..."

Tavenji perked up, converting his glee into nervous babbling. "I have a theory about that; as I'm sure Your Majesty is aware, Selvina recently sent her butterflies to the mortal world-" The love goddess stiffened and shot him a killing look.

Eyorona spoke to the little god as if to an unruly child, "Be silent, Lord of Fools. Now is not the time for your jests." Tavenji pouted and Lelonetha placed a restraining yet gentle hand on his shoulder.

Arathus continued with grave import, "Divine power moves among mortals once again, power capable of throwing off the balance we have forged with our own blood. Someone is intervening in the course of human events. We will know if it is one of you."

The words hung in the air like a hammer waiting to strike. The gods looked at one another in puzzlement and fear, wondering which one had raised the king's ire in such a scandalous and foolhardy way.

Divine intervention? It was not only forbidden but near impossible, as the portals were shut so tightly that not even the Kyraine, winged servants and heralds, could pass through.

"I have a question, Your Majesty," said Tavenji, suddenly at Selvina's elbow, "I was just wondering, what is the difference between intervention and inspiration? Selvina and I were discussing it earlier, and *she* seems to think..." His prattling was brought short by Selvina's elbow impacting his chest.

Eyorona stepped forward saying, "The law of Arathus is clear. We may offer signs and omens to our faithful priesthood, letting them make of them what they will. The least of our powers we have granted for their alchemy, which they may use as they will. Our influence must be as a scent on the breeze, no longer as a storm on the horizon. Their free will must not be subverted."

Balkon looked about in worry, "And one of us has managed to do so?" he asked, "One of us has taken the right to choose from a mortal? But how?"

Tavenji shrugged and offered, "Maybe someone has fallen madly in love?"

Selvina had endured enough of his innuendo, and she rounded on him. "Or maybe someone has been tricked! Mortals are easily tricked, aren't they, Trickster?" She spat the words.

Tavenji pranced away from her and around Balkon, saying with a smile, "Not just mortals."

Obamir ran a finger through his curly red beard, calculating. "This sounds like something far more serious than the changing of one mortal life," he said in a high, aristocratic voice, "There must be more at work than a trifle like that."

Valdak spoke slowly, with a deep and resonant voice, drawing everyone's eyes to meet his pale gaze. "A law has been broken, and an action is known by its effects. A small tumbling stone can start a great avalanche."

Selvina tossed her hair and waved dismissively, "A wonderfully dramatic analogy, brother. But I don't see why it has to be one of us. The portals are shut. We are weakened and bound by law. More to the point, we are not the only gods! There are those who answer to the Mother, bound to the nature of the mortal world; there are the denizens of the Abyss, great and small; there is Your Majesty's brother..."

This made the golden eyes of Arathus narrow; the name of Chaos was not to be uttered here.

Lelonetha stood by her sister's side in agreement, and she entreated the king with her hands spread, saying, "Surely, father, there are others more likely to defy your will than we are. Why suspect one of us?"

Arathus rose to stand over his children; his form was smaller than the giant eagle beside the throne, but suddenly became far more imposing. He spoke in a measured voice, lest his rage be unleashed, threatening the integrity of the hall. "A great power has entered the Ninth Realm: the abandoned wastes of the Sands of the Ages. That power has walked the sands and found what was hidden there, and taken it back to the mortal world of Jayde. If it finds its way into the hands of a certain mortal scion... it has the potential to shake the world to its foundations, possibly bringing all creation to ruin."

Tavenji no longer felt like laughing.

Chapter Four

Breaker Test

Nixy DuQuayne had endured it for as long as he was able and he had reached his wit's end. Ever since the night he learned of Cindra's tragic death, he was unable to find any comfort in his new life. The faces of everyone he met were either drawn in sorrows of their own, or looking on him with pity, like he was a sad dog that lost his master. Gorin's ranting had lost its edge, which was good, but every time the squat little man spoke to Nixy, he mentioned 'the Lady' and how she would have wanted him to work hard and earn his keep, as if he needed to be reminded.

But the worst of it came at night, where lying in his bed, he felt the grief pressing upon his chest, the sorrow that couldn't be lessened by crying, but grew stronger with every tear he shed. The nightly sounds haunted him;

61

wolves howled in the distance, and the scratching of claws upon the rooftop of the stables reminded him of his strange dream. He wanted to get away from this place and go back into the city, with its constant life and noise.

Spring was returning and the days were getting warmer, so there would be much more traffic in the Market Square and shops. There'd be plenty of opportunity for someone of quick hand and sharp wit. Was he still that someone? The ten-year-old boy flexed his fingers experimentally, then wiped his upturned nose.

He began to think back to his time with the Circle of Gold, the brotherhood of thieves that had taken him in and trained him. They were a scary bunch if you were on their bad side, but they were also a family, at least as much of a family as he had ever known. Dexer was waiting for him, and had made it clear that they were still on good terms. Nixy was on borrowed time in the castle anyway, as he was expected to return to the streets and his mentor's care.

He wondered if he would be welcomed back by everyone, or if his old enemies would still bear him a grudge. Daymi and Cricket had been Dexer's favorite students until Nixy showed up, and they never let him forget it. Still, even in the Circle, where you always watched your back, it would be better than here. The castle was like a tomb for his happy memories and they died anew each night. He ran his fingers through his unruly blond hair, attempting to shake out the feelings of sorrow like bits of debris.

Escaping was easy since he wasn't a prisoner and the guards ignored him. To avoid Stable Master Gorin and his temper, Nixy hid under a blanket in one of the hay wagons that delivered feed to the castle stables, riding out in the back until they crossed the drawbridge from the Highcourt into the Copper District. Nixy slipped off the cart and disappeared into the crowd before the driver could notice.

Once he was on his own, he regretted not saying

proper goodbyes to a few of his fellow stable-hands, but the less they knew, the better. Someone would try and stop him for his own safety, but whether the monster man, Black Will, was waiting for him or not, he couldn't bear the thought of another night within those bleak and suffocating walls of stone.

Nixy had his most prized possession, his magic knife *Cutter*, hidden in a sheath under his tunic. It was a comfort and he kept it close at hand, for if there were any monster-men still out to get him, he knew the knife was his best protection; Cindra had used it to drive off Black Will before taking Nixy to the castle. He was sorely tempted to use it on some of the fat purses he saw crossing his path; he needed the practice after all. He resisted however, because he knew that would be poaching. This part of the city had its own district boss and brothers, and even though they were in the same gang, it was considered very bad manners to thieve outside of your group's territory. Bad manners in the Circle often meant losing life or limb. It was better to avoid the notice of other Circle of Gold members until he was well within the Silver District, lest they think he was up to no good.

As he walked past the shops and houses, he was distressed to see the black ribbons tied around the door handles and streaming from the signposts. There had been a huge black banner draped above the main gate of the keep to mark the year of mourning for Lady Cindra, and that had been bad enough. Now everywhere he looked there were little reminders in dark fluttering fabric. It had been over a month since the news of her death had arrived by firebird messenger, and already some of the ribbons were looking faded or a bit tattered.

He wondered briefly where these people got the cloth of the right color for times like this. Were they handed out by someone or sold door-to-door? Did everyone just keep lengths of colored ribbon in a box at home, waiting to be told what to hang up? He figured if he lived long enough, he might learn the answer. It seemed like a wrong thing to just ask.

He trekked across the bridges to the Harbor and Silver Districts, finally finding himself in the Market Square at the height of activity, with the sun creeping toward noon and the air thick with the smell of food, bodies, strange perfumes and animals. He was a monkey and this was his jungle, he was a little fish in a pond of plenty, snatching what the big fish wouldn't miss. He felt more awake and alive than he had in the past month as he measured up every person within reach, his hands itching for the handle of his knife and his feet ready to fly over the flagstones, dancing through the crowds with a newly won treasure. He felt safe in the crowd, invisible and invincible; Black Will wasn't going to grab him and carry him off here, and the things that troubled his dreams were driven away by the light and noise, driven out of his thoughts and worries. He tried to whistle a happy tune as he made for the Warren, failing not so much because of his mood, but because he had never managed to whistle properly.

He walked a route he had not taken in some time; in fact it was the very route he had used to follow Cindra on that fateful night when they met. He passed the corner where he had cut her purse, remembering how she had shouted and actually chased him. He had never told her how stupid that had been; after saving his life, it seemed lucky she had been so careless.

He passed the jousting field on his right and the courtyard on his left where the attack had taken place. The Temple of Lieutrella stood beyond the archway as a mute witness to the events of that winter night and he shivered despite the warming air.

Further on down the street was the candle shop where Dexer had warned him against trying to leave the gang; the owners knew the gaunt man well because many shops in the area paid protection to the Circle, and Dexer was the debt collector.

Further up the way was the Temple of Valdak, located between the corner of the nearby building and the cemetery. Valdak was a scary god, if his pictures and statues were accurate; he wore a black robe and red sash and had dark skin like the Galindri, but he had blind white eyes that saw all of a person's sins and allowed him to judge their soul. He carried a staff topped with a wicked-looking metal hook, which Nixy didn't want to know the details about. It was enough to know that Valdak was the first god you met when you died, and he decided where you ended up. That's why his temple was conveniently close to the cemetery.

It was then rather cheeky and irreverent that the Circle had used this spot for the Warren. Not the temple itself, but the building kitty-corner to it, and the passages and catacombs that ran under the streets throughout the neighborhood. Nixy passed the church, avoiding the stony gaze of the all-seeing god's effigy, and entered the gate into the quad building's courtyard.

From there he passed the doorways of the small orphanage that served as both cover and recruiting pool for the Warren. He scratched his chest with his thumb to let the watchers know he was alone and family, before going to the far door where he knocked thrice, waited for a thump from the other side, then knocked two more times. The door was unbarred and the latch opened, admitting him into Nanny's room.

'Nanny' sat at the workbench in the back room of the orphanage, mending and sewing garments for the urchins who lived there. She was also the doorkeeper of the Warren and knew all the boys by face and name, keeping a set of special needles at hand for those intruders who didn't belong.

Nanny met him at the door and blinked in surprise saying, "Bless me, if it isn't little Nixy! I didn't think to see you again lad!" She tousled his hair and beamed at him.

Nixy liked her well enough, for she was always friendly and charming to him, but he knew she was as hard as

Dexer when she needed to be.

After bolting the door, Nanny led him to the mural at the back of the room and inserted a long needle into a discreet little hole until a *click* was heard and a portal revealed itself, the edges cunningly hidden in the pastoral scene of frolicking children and swaying trees. Nixy smiled and waved to her, ducking into the doorway and heading down the stairs; happy to know he was still on good terms. If he were marked, Nanny would have stuck him in the back of the neck with her special needle.

"Dexer is in the parlor, dear!" Nanny said as the door swung closed.

Nixy felt his way down the dark stairs, his hands on the walls as his eyes struggled to adapt. There was no one to meet him coming up, for this was the way into the Warren and there were many ways out. At last he reached the bottom of the steps and the faint light of a single lamp could be seen, guiding the way to an iron-shod door with no handle. A large knotted rope was hanging next to the frame like a bell cord, but Nixy knew it was anything but. An unwelcome visitor might think it was such an obvious way to open the door that they would pull it, expecting the maid to answer or something. In fact it was an alarm that alerted the Warren to intruders. Younger boys would scarper, and the older ones would set traps in their wake to snare whoever had made it that far into the Circle's little hideout. Nixy ran his fingers along the outer door frame, found the hidden latch, and opened the heavy door.

The Warren was a twisting maze of cellars and tunnels joining the older catacombs of the nearby temple and graveyard, making for a perfect blend of safety and spooky. Nixy never felt quite at home here, but it was like a fortress if you knew your way around. There were many modifications to the walls and alcoves after the gang took it over, so the place was loaded with secret doors, bolt holes, traps, false walls and pitfalls. Many of the bolt holes were just big enough for a boy or very thin man, so it was wise to make sure an escape route hadn't been outgrown. There were exit routes that led into the sewers, the cemetery (Nixy avoided those), several different cellars in nearby buildings, and even the church.

The Valdakian acolytes that worked in the catacombs were in league with the Circle, though the priests they served were none-the-wiser. It was an arrangement that might not have worked so well before the Age of Omens began, when the gods would speak to their faithful. Or maybe the servants of the Blind God turned a blind eye because the pay was too good.

He passed dozens of boys of differing ages on his way through the tunnels; all were engaged in some kind of activity, for it was too cold down here to just sit and do nothing. Some were wrestling, some were being taught blade work, and others were chasing each other through the maze of corridors. All of it was good practice for life on the streets, and he fondly remembered some of his early days exploring the Warren with the other lads.

Nixy made his way to the parlor, which was actually an old wine cellar beneath the orphanage, back in the days when it was a famous tavern that served the workers in the silver mines. Once the mine dried up, so did the tavern, and the business moved further into the city. Some of the large wine casks remained, since they weren't that valuable at the time. Now that a few hundred years had passed however, Nixy understood that they were quite a treasure. It seems that wine got better with age, unlike say... milk.

The parlor had an arched ceiling and cracked plaster finish. Nice rugs covered the cold stone floor and there was a constant dripping that echoed off the walls. Dexer had a nice desk and a few comfortable chairs around it, although he rarely invited anyone to sit. There was also a newer stone fireplace off to the side of the desk that had been added after the Circle took up residency; the smoke was piped into the orphanage kitchen's chimney so not to arouse suspicion. The place was lit with candelabras (possibly stolen from the church) and splattered mounds of wax surrounded their bases.

Dexer was seated at his desk, his hat removed, his hood exposing only the long oval of his face, while covering the rest of his head. The firelight made him look more ghoulish than usual as he glanced up from his papers and focused his intense gaze on Nixy. The boy bobbed his head in a kind of bow and shuffled forward, waiting for some sign of what was going to happen. He had assumed that since he had made it this far, that everything was going to be fine, but you never knew; Dexer may have just wanted him to feel safe so he could get him in close and make an example of him. Maybe Nixy had walked into a trap after all? He tried to push the thought from his mind because it was making him stumble on the rug.

"Nixy. Good to see you boy," Dexer croaked from the end of the room. It seems he had a bit of a cold and it made his voice even more frightening. Nixy wondered if the man caught colds on purpose just to scare people. "Have a seat." He motioned to one of the nice chairs across the desk. Nixy gulped and forced a smile, sitting down but not getting too comfortable.

"I hear your little lady friend... met with a terrible end at sea," his face showed something like sympathy, as if a snake tried to look sorry for a mouse. "Minozhian pirates, they say. Ships have set sail to hunt them down, but you probably know about that."

Nixy shook his head.

"No?" said Dexer, "The count launched a fleet to scour the coastal waters looking for revenge, justice, whatever you wanna call it. They might even attack Minozhia itself, or so they say."

The news gave Nixy little comfort.

"The latest word arrived at the castle by firebird. Seems the Rok escort ship pulled a boy from the water, a cabin boy or something... he hid in the water near the rudder during the attack... clever kid. He saw the girl,

68

Lady Cindra, fall into the water and... a spear took her. She never came up... I'm sorry."

Nixy sat there stunned, like he was hearing of her death for the first time. Why had Dexer told him this? He obviously had eyes and ears in the castle if he had the latest news. Nixy had only seen a firebird arrive in the sky two days ago. Was Dexer just trying to show him that he was always being watched, that nowhere was safe? Nixy squirmed in the chair and looked at his toes.

Dexer waited a few moments before speaking again, studying the boy's mood. "I want you to know that there's no hard feelings. She saved your life I hear; took you to a nice safe place. Better food, good honest work, a chance to start over..." He paused until Nixy looked up into his eyes, "But there is no starting over for us. The Circle of Gold is a family; the life is in our blood. You," he pointed a gloved finger at Nixy, "you were the best I had ever seen, quick with a blade and quicker on yer feet. Slipping in and out o' the shadows like you owned them. You belong here boy, more than anyone that's passed through the Warren in years. That's why..." He stood and Nixy sank back into his chair, "...I'm gonna give you another shot at the test."

The test. The chance to be made a Brother, with elevated status and respect. He had failed his test last winter when Cindra ran him down, and he expected to have to work his way up again because of it. Those who failed the test weren't given a pass. Ever. Was Dexer really that forgiving? He had never spoken to Nixy like that before in all his time among the den of thieves, indeed he had never heard Dexer shower anyone with the kind of praise he had just been given. It made him feel proud but no less wary.

"Well? What do you say, boy?" Dexer leaned on the desk, looming over him. "You want another shot?" It was a silly question; to refuse would be incredibly stupid. Nixy nodded.

"Good, good. Same as before, you get two watchers,"

Nixy knew that meant Daymi and Cricket, senior brothers who didn't like him one bit. "This time the test will be different, I can't let the lads think I'm too lenient with you..."

Here it comes, thought Nixy. *The catch.*

"This time," Dexer said with a cold gleam in his eye, "it's a breaker test. The watchers choose the break. You choose the hour. House rules apply." His raspy voice echoed like it came from the Abyss itself.

Nixy felt his throat go dry. A breaker test was for burglars, not pickpockets. He would have to break into a house and steal something to prove his skills, and house rules meant no weapons, only tools. If a burglar was caught with a blade, it meant they had lethal intent, which usually led to a hanging at least. He'd have to leave *Cutter* behind, and if that weren't bad enough, the watchers would be picking the target house. Nixy had no doubt that they would find him a real challenge. What was it Cindra would say at a time like this? *Oh, splendid.*

Nixy spent the next week in the Warren, building up his skills for the test. He didn't own a set of breaking tools, but Dexer gave him some on loan, setting him up with locks to pick and one of the older instructors to teach him. There were also places in the Warren that served well for climbing practice; the deep drops and shafts with irregular handholds, combined with a safety rope, gave trainees a good challenge. There were few boys training now since housebreaking was a dying art. Magic had made life difficult for burglars, lighting the streets brighter than before and providing protective spells to those who could afford them. There were a handful of lads sponsored by the Circle that trained at the Mystic College in town just to learn ways to counter such defenses. There would come a day when the best thieves would be wizards, some said.

Nixy had avoided Daymi and Cricket while training, knowing they would only try and discourage him. It was enough that they were picking the house for him; he didn't need anything further to sink his spirits. The night of the new moon was past and the moon was getting brighter, making things more difficult, but there was a bit of hope to be had. Spring showers were due in Portshia and the sky might soon be cloaked with clouds and maybe rain. Rain was no good for housebreaking since the burglar left a wet trail everywhere, but nothing about this would be ideal. He would have to make do.

He had no clothes suitable for the job, so again Dexer came through, finding dark trousers and a tunic in his size, complete with a hooded cloak. It was unnerving how generous the man had become. This was a big test after all, and if Dexer meant half of what he said about Nixy's place in the family, then he was going to want the boy to succeed. What might be in store for him if he did succeed was not even in Nixy's thoughts yet, he was just focused on surviving the ordeal.

The skies grew dark over the next few days and Nixy decided that things were as good as they would get, so he informed Dexer, who in turn informed Daymi and Cricket. The boys had spent a good deal of time talking behind Nixy's back, throwing sly glances at him as they determined his fate and imagined how he might fail spectacularly. They were now in full form as they ushered him out of the Warren through one of the cellar exits and brought him into the cool night air. Lightning lit the sky over the mountains and the thunder followed moments later; the storm not yet upon them.

Daymi snorted, "Looks like you get a bath tonight, DuQuayne. Hope a little rat like you don't drown; that'd be sad, it would."

Cricket cackled dutifully.

They moved through the streets, dodging carriages and crowds of street people looking for a dry place to stand once the rain started. Most decent folk were indoors at this hour and the city watch was making the rounds, dressed in heavy cloaks to ward off the coming showers. The boys led Nixy through lesser-used streets until they were in the Market Square itself, and Nixy's mind went back to last winter, when his nerves were up and his stomach queasy before his test. The boys were more loathsome to him on that night than they were on this one and for some reason that made Nixy really troubled.

They stopped in the shadows and he waited for them to tell him which house he would be violating tonight. Daymi raised his arm to point across the square towards the buildings between the canal and the Temple Walk. He said the words and Nixy's blood froze, "Clavemont Manor."

There were many who paid protection money to the Circle to keep burglars away, and there were those that trusted in the magical protections they had purchased, but only Lord Clavemont had publicly issued a challenge to the city's underworld to do their worst. He had magic wards and the best locks money could buy, but he was also opening his home to parties and social gatherings throughout the year. Many had tried to make off with his finery both night and day, party or no, but none succeeded. Either the alarms ran them off, or they made it past the alarms, never to be seen again. Some said he had trained dogs that roamed the halls; some claimed the paintings watched you. There were enough tales about the dangers of Clavemont Manor to fill two nights worth of storytelling to wide-eyed boys in the depths of the Warren.

"We'll be watching you get in, but then we're off," Daymi said gravely, as if just watching someone try to steal from the manor was dangerous. "We want something of his lordship's, something personal, a seal, a ring maybe."

Cricket started across the way to his spot near the temples where he could act like a beggar while watching Nixy's progress.

Daymi put a hand on Nixy's shoulder and said with a

smile, "See you back in the Warren, breaker-boy." Then he gave Nixy a little push and waited for the show to begin.

Nixy's feet were numb as he moved across the wide street towards the quad building and its high walls. There were windows on the top floor, but the ground level was solid stone that was plastered smooth with no handholds or embellishments to use for purchase. The windows all had glass and showed no means of opening, and heavy drapes covered most of them. The top floor had light streaming out from a row of windows that overlooked the temples and cathedral. The arch of the main gateway faced the street as well, with statues of wyverns perched on either side of the entry, and heavy wrought iron gates baring the way into the courtyard. The Clavemont coat of arms hung above the arch and on the iron bars of each gate, a welcomed sight to invited guests, but a warning to the likes of him.

Nixy walked in a wide circle around the manor house, searching for a way inside. The most promising angle was on the western side where a street separated it from a larger quad complex next door. The only advantage here was that someone either had to look down this street or look out a window to see anything. The other three sides were wide open and offered no cover.

"Trickster's wick," Nixy cursed under his breath. He was no housebreaker. Daymi and Cricket picked this place because they wanted him to disappear. He wondered if he might someday get revenge on the rotten lads, but he was even worse at revenge than he was at housebreaking. It just wasn't his thing.

He took a mental inventory of his tools. He had a rolled-up pouch at his waist that held lock picks and small cutting tools, as well as a polished metal mirror on a rod for looking around corners. Around his waist was a leather belt with a folded harness, that when combined with the folding hook on the end, would allow him to suspend himself on a ledge and free up his hands for other things (not that he wanted to try it). Around his neck was his glowstone, should he need some light. Strapped to his back and concealed under his cloak was his most vital tool: a length of braided silken cord that was knotted every few feet to aid in climbing. It was worth more than the rest of his gear and Nixy was thinking that if things went horribly wrong, Dexer would mourn the loss of the rope at least as much as the loss of his best pupil. Maybe more.

The lightning flashed again and a light rain started, thunder following close behind. The storm was getting near and time was running out. If he was going to climb anything, it was best to do it dry. He walked out of the street between the two buildings and found himself looking over the canal on the southern face of the manor. There was no cover here either, just a railing along the river-walk and a stairway leading down to a floating pier. Barges or small boats could moor there and unload their goods, although by law, anything for sale needed to be unloaded on the Harbor District piers across the canal where they could be taxed. The usual smells assaulted his nose; rank sewage, slaughterhouse runoff, and slimy green growths on the walls of the canal gave this part of the city its distinctive aroma.

Water oxen were tethered across the canal, awaiting their keeper to hitch them to a barge and begin their swim up the Joshian. They clacked their curved horns together as they grunted and lowed, obviously having been fed already; they made quite a stink even from here.

A thought crossed Nixy's mind at that point, and he was immediately sorry because it was at once his best chance and most unpleasant option. Sewers emptied into the canal, and the river current carried the refuse out to sea (usually). That meant there might be a very close entrance to the manor that was unguarded and easy to get to. At the worst, it meant that he would drown in sewage instead of dying a horrid and mysterious death within the manor house. He started for the stairs leading down to the pier, thinking if Daymi and Cricket wanted to follow him this far, they were welcome to it.

Part way down the stairs, Nixy saw the sewer outlet partially submerged in the current of the canal. The outlet looked about as broad as he was tall, and had an iron grating over the opening that was wide enough to admit one desperate little thief. He continued down to the pier and took out his silk rope, tying one end to the dock post while building up the nerve to take the plunge.

This, he thought, *is really going to be nasty*. He lowered himself into the water, gasping at the cold and hanging on to the rope lest the current take him. Once he was up to his neck, he held his breath and let the water carry him to the sewer grate, using the rope to control his progress. *If it rains hard*, he thought, *the river might rise and this might all be underwater soon*. He wished he could recover the rope and use it later, but a knot was a knot, as the saying went. Gripping the slimy bars and wedging his way between them, Nixy entered the sewer pipe. There was enough room for him to walk while pushing against the curved top of the tunnel, keeping his head above water. *Eyes open, mouth closed*, he repeated in his head. It was a saying he lived by while in the gang, but it had a special significance here. The stench was choking.

The tunnel rose steeply, and to Nixy's relief, the water level receded to his knees. He guessed he was somewhere under the manor house now, for he had walked more than thirty steps from the grate. It was pitch black, and only the sound of running, dripping water filled his ears.

He took out the glowstone and held it tightly, whispering "*Ilda*" to make it glow softly. Tiny little eyes blinked at him from the dark and scampered away, balancing on the raised sides of the tunnel with long rat-tails. There was other movement as well, as if the walls had come alive. Bugs. Lots of them. *Eyes open, mouth closed, eyes open, mouth closed...*

Several holes lined the sides of the sewer pipe at

irregular intervals and a mighty stench surrounded him. Nixy figured it was safer to breathe through his mouth now and tried not to gag. The pipe branched off in different directions farther on, and it occurred to the boy that he might easily get lost with no way out. There were a few exits from the Warren through the sewers, but those tunnels were on higher ground, and anyway, he had never explored them. This was territory known only to the guild that serviced the sewers, and he was unlikely to find someone he could ask for directions. The sewer workers were known as 'rat men' because of the company they kept, at least, he hoped that was why.

He felt a breeze on his left cheek and turned the light in that direction, spying a small tunnel that led up a gentle slope. The edges of the opening were slick, but the light showed the inside to be dry and little used. He placed the glowstone back around his neck and hoisted himself up into the small tunnel, crawling on hands and knees, and scattering bugs while the light slowly faded. He was soon under a metal grating that felt dry and cold, and with a little difficulty, he was able to lift it, pushing against it with his back. Once the seal of filth and age was broken, Nixy slid the grating to the side and listened. No footsteps or alarms, no dogs; so far, so good.

He wiggled out of the drain and got to his feet in the dark room. Once again he used the glowstone to get his bearings, illuminating a cellar lined with casks and bottle racks. His mind went back to the parlor in the Warren and he smiled, imagining the look on Dexer's face if he added to the gaunt man's wine stock. Closer examination revealed the Clavemont coat of arms on the casks, and Nixy rejoiced silently that he was in the right house. His joy turned to cold fear as he remembered that *no one* wanted to be in this house unless they were invited. He had made it this far and there was no need to hurry to his doom. He could take his time and prepare for the main break.

The first thing he did was to search the room for some

kind of sink to wash his clothes. The wine cellar had a faucet against the far wall that drew from a cistern in the roof and emptied into a plugged basin, which could drain into a gutter and down into the sewer grate. Nixy loved indoor running water; it was like a kind of magic to him, and the sound was soothing. Most people still had to draw from a communal well and pay a guild wizard to purify it, but the rich had other means. He began to strip off his wet, filth-stained clothes and fill the basin, taking a chunk of lye soap from a shelf over the faucet. There was a mop nearby, and even a large sponge; Nixy squished the strange matter in his fingers while waiting for the basin to fill. Sponges were weird and fun.

He soaked and scrubbed his clothing with the soap, wringing them out over the gutter and sniffing to see how clean they had become. It would do him little good to sneak around in the dark if he reeked like a sewer, leaving a trail of stench in his wake. If there *were* dogs prowling the halls, they would be able to find him anywhere, even if they had a cold.

Once he was satisfied that he could no longer be smelled a mile away, he donned the damp clothing and belted on his tools, shivering in the dark cellar. The fact that he had still not been discovered was encouraging, and he began to wonder at the manor's reputation. Maybe the other thieves who disappeared just got too greedy and bold for their own good? He wasn't gonna let his guard down to find out though; he needed to find something valuable and personal and get out any way he could.

His leather shoes were squishing on the stone floor, so he decided to take them off and fasten the laces to his belt. He climbed the well-worn steps up to the cellar door and pressed his ear to the wood, listening for noise on the other side.

The sensation on his ear was warm and tingling, not unlike a dry summer breeze that tightened the skin. Placing his hands on the door he felt the same sensation in his fingertips, warm flowing waves like the heat of a fire. He sniffed for smoke. He felt the wood along the frame. There was no fire beyond the door as far as he could tell, but the warm flow persisted, moving along the length of the wood and back again like little rivers of feeling.

A spark of insight tickled his brain and he stepped back from the door. *Could this be a magical ward?* He had never come up against one before, and his brief training didn't cover such things. What was he supposed to do now? He touched the door with a fingertip, testing it again. The tingling warmth flowed over him like a thick fluid covering his skin, slowly moving up his arm. Was this what magic felt like? His knife or glowstone never felt like this, but maybe the spell on the door was a more strong and dangerous kind of magic.

He wished desperately that he had never come back, that he had only stayed to endure the sorrow in the castle and face his fears, that he was safe and warm in his cot instead of shivering in a cellar with death on the other side of the door. He said a silent prayer to Tavenji, Lord of Escapes, to get him out of this mess alive, promising to never be so foolish and reckless again. After all, Tavenji favored thieves, not idiots.

As he prayed, he felt the warmth of the door turn cool and pass over him like a gentle breeze. The experience left him feeling dizzy and out of breath, and he blinked at the colored spots that danced in his vision. The room was still dark, but had lost much of its gloom, for he could see from the top of the stairs to the central drain without any extra light. The grains of the wooden door were smoother under his touch and the warmth had faded, leaving behind only a hint of the funny tingling. Somehow the door had lost its menace. It seemed to be nothing more than a door between this room and the next, made of normal wood with iron hinges and a brass latch. There was a hint of light through a keyhole but he could make out nothing beyond. He reasoned that he couldn't stay in this room forever (at least he didn't want to) and the only way to go now was forward. Taking a deep breath, he put his hand on the latch and opened the cellar door.

A breeze blew past him into the cellar, bracing him as it hit his damp clothes. The air carried the lingering smell of baked goods and cooked meat from a meal prepared hours earlier. There was a high window on the far wall that admitted light from the cloudy sky, tinged with pink and orange from the city's wizard lamps. Lightning and thunder struck, illuminating the kitchen with a stark white light that flashed against the polished surfaces of knives and cooking pans hanging about on iron racks. The preparation tables were clean and orderly, and sadly, there were no leftovers available. He remembered the first night in the castle's kitchen and the feast of unfinished meals that beckoned him. His stomach grumbled and he thought, *keep your mind on the work, or your belly will wake the house.*

There were three doors from this room, one leading to the larder no doubt; he needed to find a way upstairs where the lord's chambers were located. The left door led to a darkened dining room and beyond was a flight of stairs spiraling upward, a wrought iron railing twisting with it like a black ribbon. *Good enough*, he thought. As he passed the long table, he glanced out the large glazed doors leading to the courtyard, noticing the rain had begun to fall. The courtyard had a winding stone walkway that encircled a patch of open grass, with two fountains standing in opposing corners, one in the shape of a woman reaching out for an embrace, the other of a man in similar pose. His eyes flicked about the courtyard to see if there was a good way to leave. Finding none, he moved to the spiral stairs.

Halfway up the staircase, he heard voices from below, so he took the steps two at a time and hid near the darkened landing to listen. A candle was lighting the way as two figures approached the base of the stairs. Two male voices could be heard, one deeper and subservient, the other light and melodious with a manner of speaking

79

that Nixy had only heard around Cindra and her parents. *Noble,* he thought.

"No, no, an excellent game Lian, you are improving. One day you will get the better of me!" said the light and cultured voice.

"Oh, never I fear, milord," said the deep voiced man who carried the candle, "You are beyond my meager skill." Nixy caught the word 'milord' and confirmed that the owner of the manor was right below him. He held his breath.

"I hope you are doing your best, Lian. I would not wish for you to let me win." There was a laughing reproach in his voice.

Nixy looked over the edge and saw the two men standing at the foot of the stairs. The man with the candle was wearing a long night coat of deep red or maroon, bound at the waist with a matching sash. The other man was shorter and slighter of build, with an elegant gray coat and dark hose that ended in thin shoes of the same color. The light of the candle set off his white hair and pallid skin. The pale man, who must be none other than Lord Clavemont, extended his hand to the man with the candle, saying "I know it helps you sleep, Lian."

The taller man took the offered hand and held it for several moments, his face unseen from the top of the stairs. Nixy couldn't tell if they were speaking quietly or just standing holding hands. It was odd to be sure. The candle flickered and the men broke their grip.

"Good night, Lian."

"Thank you, milord. Good night," Lian said with a drowsy tone.

The tall servant departed down the hall towards the kitchen, feet shuffling as the candle cast his shadow about the room. The pallid man in gray stood watching him for a minute until the light of the flame was almost gone, and then he turned his head slowly upwards to look at the top of the stairs. Nixy met the lord's pale blue eyes from the shadows and quickly withdrew from the railing. *He saw me! He must have!*

His heart began to race, his palms grew clammy and he was suddenly cold. There had been no expression on the man's face, no hint in his eyes that he had spotted an intruder, but somehow Nixy felt as if the ghostly man had looked into his very soul, as if he knew the boy was there the whole time and could now devote his attention entirely to him. Nixy backed against the wall, feeling like he wanted to melt away. He dared not look over the railing again, but he could not move from this spot without being seen from below. He wanted to wrap himself in darkness and slip away, to sink into a corner and run, like he had done so long ago when his father had come at him with a switch on his birthday. His feet started to inch towards the hallway when he saw a shock of pale blond hair rising up the stairwell, the white face turning in his direction as Clavemont ascended the spiral steps.

How? His mind staggered. Nixy had heard no footfalls, no creaks from the framework. Even his own climb hadn't been so quiet, light as he was and with bare feet. The lord turned to look about the landing, almost playfully, his eyes catching the glare from the distant windows as lightning flashed again and the thunder shook the house. Nixy froze in the sudden flare, sure he had been seen, but the man only stared at the landing with a bemused expression as if he had discovered a joke being played. He laughed, musical and light, and continued to the landing and into the next room. Nixy peeked around the corner to watch him go as the man passed by open curtains, the light and rain-shadows speckling his face and hair with dark rivulets. The boy took a deep breath as silently as he could. Clavemont passed out of sight.

The hall was unlit by candle or lamp, and the light from the windows was dim and scattered by rain, but Nixy could see well enough. The brass curtain rods and latches on the windows were clear to him, as well as the deep maroon of the curtains and carpeting. He looked the other way and saw a hall with doorways along its length, probably private rooms for guests or upstairs servants. There was no one to be seen that way, and Nixy did not want to follow the lord, so he ventured down the hall.

His steps were cool and muffled as he glided past the stairwell and into the dark hall with its drapes drawn against the light of the neighboring building. He listened at the various doors and heard only silence or snoring, for the upstairs servants had gone to bed hours ago. There was nothing he needed in these rooms, so he went on, hoping to find a study or library where the lord might keep personal things. He did not want to find the man's bedchamber for some reason. The thunder rumbled on, making Nixy jump, though he was happy for the extra noise to cover any sounds he might make exploring the manor. *It might even cover the thumping of my heart,* he thought.

He passed another corner and another stairwell and continued towards the adjoining room. The door was closed and the brass handle shone in the gray shadows, beckoning him. He reached for it carefully and felt the warm tingle of magic again, the dangerous currents moving through his fingers and up his arm. He knew opening the door would result in something nasty, so he said another prayer. *It seemed to work last time,* Nixy thought desperately. The warm feeling continued like an army of tiny ants crawling up his arm, threatening to bite. *Maybe I said a magic word before?* He tried to remember and realized he had said nothing. He thought about being safe and secure, being in bed under a blanket, being in the castle behind large walls. He went through every thought or feeling he had experienced in the cellar, until finally the feeling of the door handle changed and the tingling waves drained away as they had downstairs. The dizziness hit him again but left just as fast. *Funny,* he thought, *it's not a magic word that makes the magic go away; it's wanting to be safe.* He slowly picked the lock, pressed the latch, and the door swung open silently. *Gotta remember that.*

The room was definitely a study or library, much like the one in which he and Cindra had met the wizard and the dweedragon. The curtains were open and the rain struck the window, admitting light from the street lamps below. There were shelves full of books and scrolls, swords and knives of different styles, a nice desk with a comfy chair, portraits in nice frames, even a funny spinning ball on a stand. The ball was painted with little areas of green amid big patches of blue; words were written all over it, though Nixy had no time to spell them out.

He looked at the portraits next, feeling eyes on him. They were all Clavemont lords by the look of them; men with light blond hair and very pale skin, some with blue eyes and some with pink. Some had facial hair in much older styles and wore funny clothes and hats. Nixy guessed that the pale skin ran in the family, along with the shape of the nose, chin, eyes and mouth. He thought back to the encounter on the stairs and wondered if they had trouble with their eyesight too. What would it take to make a Clavemont look normal-colored? Maybe if he took a Galindri wife? That wasn't likely to happen.

He went behind the desk with his back to the window, looking for something small, valuable and personal. The lightning crashed beyond the cathedral and lit the room in white light, giving him a brief view of everything in sharp detail. A book was open in the middle with a long ribbon marking the place, a crystal goblet with a lead or pewter stand was empty nearby, a quill and ink set was arranged within easy reach, a roll of sealing wax sat near an unlit candle. His eyes settled on a dagger bearing the wyvern seal of Clavemont. It was poised on a wooden stand, point-down, with some kind of engraving marking the blade. The brass handle and small cross-guard held little jewels. He grabbed for it quickly, holding it up to the light from the street lamps to get a better look. *Perfect!*

He thought, as he tucked it in his belt.

The light was suddenly blocked by a shadow, not his own. He turned, an icy terror gripping his chest. The windows flew open, letting in the rain and cold wind. A dark form was huddled on the sill, clutching the frame with claw-like hands, a snarl of pain escaping its clenched teeth. Nixy spun in panic and bumped into the desk as a bolt of lightning cracked, setting the entire study aglow in a harsh, white luminance. The house shook with deafening thunder.

It seemed one of the portraits had come to life and stood before him, face and hair of radiant white and eyes of lightest blue, gray coat and dark tights, standing just on the other side of the desk. It couldn't be the man himself, there was no time, no sound, and no way could he have gotten so close without warning. The little thief pushed away from the desk with a shout of surprise, only to be grabbed from behind by unforgiving claws and snatched out into the sodden darkness.

The pale man in gray moved to the opening, his brow furrowed in dismay. After a moment, he closed the window and drew the drapes.

Nixy was crushed close to the body of his captor, the rain doing little to wash away the stench of Black Will. The creature had jumped to the cobblestones after snatching him, and was now running through the deserted streets as cold spring rain came down in gray curtains. Nixy's arms were pinned to his sides, but he managed to get the stolen dagger from his belt. The wild darting and leaping of the monster made it hard to act; Nixy's legs dangled uselessly and he strained to keep his head still. He jabbed as best he could with the dagger, but it had little effect.

The monster-man only rumbled in his strange, doubled voice, "*Hrrrrr, spelled glass, nasty spell too,*" he said into Nixy's ear, "*Still worth the pain to get to you!*" He laughed in a horrid chortle that echoed itself, "*Waiting for a long time to bleed you, boy...*"

Nixy kept stabbing with the dagger, waiting for the man to howl and let him go, waiting for the thing inside him to show its black bones and cry in pain. But the dagger wasn't his *Cutter*. His precious magic blade was hidden in the Warren, safe and sound. *Stupid house rules,* Nixy thought.

He had little sense of where they were headed, but they were soon leaping in the shadow of a large building. Black Will began climbing with his unnatural claws, finding purchase on the wet stone with toes and fingers, leaping from height to height. They seemed to climb a long time, and Nixy dared to look as lightning flashed across the sky. To his horror, he was gazing down at the street from a long way up, higher than he had ever been before. There were white stone pillars and buttresses on either side as the rain fell past him, vanishing into the distance long before hitting the glossy flagstones below. He managed to find the time to feel sick amid the panic and fear, and his vision spun wildly. He convulsed and vomited into the air, his last meal fading into the sudden darkness as it fell. Black Will pulled himself and Nixy over a ledge and began clambering up a steeply inclined roof coated with overlapping sheets of lead. The jostling made Nixy drop the dagger and it bounced and slid to the edge, passing between stone moldings and falling silently to the street.

Finally, they reached the top of the structure and Nixy got a better sense of where he had been taken; he was deposited on the three-foot wide crest of a roof, with a long steep drop to either side. There were six tall, pointed spires lining each side of the roof, the tallest of which were at the far end. Perched on the points of the spires were the stone figures of gods, their backs to the hapless boy as they looked dispassionately over the cityscape. Along the crest were statues of kings, their sandstone faces worn by weather and time. He was on the roof of the cathedral, where no one could find him and no one could help.

Black Will squatted down near his feet, leering at him with wicked, glowing eyes and rotten teeth; his pale, tallow skin defied the rain to cleanse it as he sat under the soaking torrent. His shaggy mess of dark hair and bedraggled beard were plastered against his face, giving him a thinner, more corpse-like appearance.

The monster-man looked up past Nixy and the boy heard the beating of leathery wings; dread gripped him, like it had once in his strange dreams, as something settled on the rooftop behind him, claws scratching metal and a foul wind buffeting the boy's soaked hair and clothes. Nixy was too frightened to move as the meager years of his life passed before his eyes, summing up an existence so brief it hardly seemed to matter as it neared its violent end.

The rain beat down on his face and body, stinging his eyes and chilling his skin. There was a hiss from behind his head, and looking up, he saw a pair of wings loom over him; the sickly green skin and veins were stretched between long, spindly fingers, briefly illuminated by the angry sky. The wings covered him like a tent, blocking out the rain with a cacophony of tiny drumming sounds. As he looked further back, a hideous face came into view, like a nightmare come alive; horns and spines twisted from its head and a long pointed nose met a prominent chin, with a set of sharp yellowy teeth between them as it pulled back its black lips in a grimace. *The dream was real!*

He screamed, or tried to, but his voice was swallowed by some dark magic. Putrid odors filled his mouth and nose; icy fingers of fear crept down his scalp and threatened to lock his jaw in a permanent cry of terror, his chest felt a great pressure as if he could hardly breathe, and he wet himself. The creature looming over him coughed a revolting laugh and produced an earthen jar in one of its clawed hands, removing the lid with the other.

"I've been waiting many years for this, child; ever since

I learned of your birth." The horned horror ran a sharp claw along the boy's jaw, teasingly. "There is no help for you here, no black wolves, no magic blades," it licked its lips with a dark purple tongue, "and the gods will not save you either, even as we take your blood on the roof of their holy place. They are impotent and blind, caring nothing for their once-beloved children."

Nixy managed a sound, moving his lips and whimpering, "Why?"

The creature smiled, baring its needle teeth and narrowing its snake-like eyes, "Because we do not want the Elder Ones to return. It was their meddling that cost us the First War and many since." The creature snarled at the memory, "It took ages to topple the old dynasties. Most of my kind was killed in the First War. Since then, the Elder Ones have slowly departed for their precious Alhanna, leaving humanity ripe for the spoiling. Now the gods have left you too." The creature smiled and a string of drool fell from its mouth to mark the boy's cheek. Nixy flinched as the spittle itched and burned like a rash. Black Will took Nixy's feet and made ready to lift him like a deer to be bled and gutted.

"He entered my house and stole from me. He is mine." The voice was light but strong, carrying over the wind and pitter-patter of rain.

Black Will dropped the boy's feet and spun, a bestial growl issuing from his throat. Standing before a stone effigy of a forgotten king was Lord Clavemont in his gray coat and dark hose, a gray cloak billowing from his shoulders. The lightning from beyond the mountains flashed in his hair and face, his eyes were ablaze with blue fire, and his posture was regal and still, like the many statues that lined the roof. The wind whipped at his clothing, but the rain seemed to fall around him, as if the drops dared not stain his attire. Nixy could not understand what was happening to him. *How did Clavemont manage to get up here? Is he a wizard?*

Black Will lunged at the elegant intruder, ready to tear

him to shreds with his filthy claws and powerful bony fingers, but the pallid nobleman cocked his arm and struck Black Will with the back of his fist in a movement only visible by the trail it left as it parted the rain and air. There was a popping sound and the shaggy, bearded head of the monster-man went spinning through the air, trailing water and blood-spray as it hurtled towards the distant canal.

Nixy gasped as the headless body wobbled on its legs, spurted from the neck once or twice, and tumbled down the side of the steep roof, leaving a trail of filth and dark blood that was soon washed away in the rain. All that remained in its place was a shadowy skeletal form with eyes like burning coals and a matching wound upon its cheek. It wheezed a curse in the gruesome speech of the Abyss and faded away, as if the rain had scoured its taint from the night sky.

"I have tolerated his predations long enough," said the nobleman, advancing a step towards the boy and the winged nightmare crouching over him. "I trust he will find another host before long, but not in *my* city." He spoke in a commanding tone that was impossible to ignore. "As for you..." His cold, blue eyes drilled into the vertical pupils of the troll creature.

The Guadim known as Paugh hissed and spat, "Why do you interfere? I have hunted this one for years, and now I have him. You have banished the pathetic demnox; so be it. Leave the boy to me."

"No, I think not. As I said, he is mine. He entered my home uninvited."

"We need him for the war!" Paugh croaked with rage.

"I care nothing for your war, in fact it is the last thing I desire. I am quite content here." He smiled charmingly as thunder rolled across the sky.

"Fool! You are of the Abyss, spawn of Krumn, a *Vemlok*!" The Guadim's wings snapped back, arching menacingly. The rain assaulted Nixy again as he blinked up at the pale visage before him. Vemloks were only stories... but then, he used to think that about trolls and Black Will.

"I control the thirsting spirit, it does not control me," said the lord as he took another step, "Now leave, before I stain this rooftop with your foul blood. Leave and do not return to my city." Clavemont was standing at Nixy's feet now, staring down at the Guadim.

Paugh stood slowly, rising to its full height and extending its wings. It glared at Clavemont for a moment, as if considering its options. Then, smiling or snarling, it took the earthen jar and leapt into the night sky, its wings beating against the torrent, its emaciated form fading in the rain.

Nixy watched it go until he felt Clavemont kneeling beside him, making him flinch and almost lose his balance. The man was leaning in closer, his piercing eyes brighter than they had been in the manor house and his skin and hair more eerie in the storm light. Clavemont lifted a hand to the boy's face, as if to caress his cheek. He wore no gloves and there was no trace of blood on his knuckles from knocking Black Will's head off moments earlier. Nixy tried to move away as the man's cool hand cupped his face, his fingertips brushing wet hair. There was a cold, tingling sensation on his skin where the pale man touched him, and Nixy suddenly felt lightheaded.

Clavemont was saying, "Now let us see what..." His blue eyes flashed in alarm and he withdrew his hand, the palm of which was now pink and warm. His lips parted and he revealed clenched teeth through which he inhaled in a long hiss. Standing up, he was suddenly several feet away, his back to the nearest statue. His hands were grasping, his fingers like talons; a wild fire burned in his eyes as he began moving slowly towards the boy once again, pain and conflicting emotions on his face.

Nixy's legs kicked for traction and he tried to get to his feet, but there was no place to go but down. He slipped and landed on his arm, crying in pain as he tumbled and slid towards the deadly drop. The curve of the roof made his descent faster and faster until his feet hit the border molding hard and his knees buckled; pieces of masonry broke and fell to the street below as he flailed for purchase. His left arm found a handhold and his right fumbled with the folding hook and harness at his belt, fastening it to the edge of the roof. His grip on the wet stone gave way and he fell for a split second, before the harness snapped tight and the hook held him dangling over the hundred-and-forty-foot drop.

He could see Lord Clavemont standing on the pinnacle of the roof, a statue among statues; unmoving save for the billowing cloak.

Looking beside him, he saw a white stone spire and flying buttress just out of reach, upon which the headless body of Black Will was draped like a wet towel. His stomach leapt into his throat as he looked down at the drop, wondering desperately if someone might happen by with a *really* long ladder. Lightning flashed again and illuminated the side of the cathedral, highlighting the relief work and the carved faces of gods and men. *There's some really nice stonework up here*, he thought, just before the masonry gave way.

Nixy screamed as he fell, the rain around him seeming to stand still as the world rushed up to meet him. He wanted to pass out from fright before hitting the ground, but he was still awake and almost there. *Things never go my way*, he whimpered in the back of his mind.

Suddenly hands were upon him, grasping his belt and shirt and slowing his fall. He heard Clavemont's voice in his ear, clear and commanding over the sound of the rain, "You are safe for now, so long as you never speak of this to anyone." They descended until Nixy's feet touched the ground, but the powerful hands held him still, "I will let you go back to your life, such as it is, but know that we will meet again. I have many questions."

The hands released him but he dared not run; something in the man's voice told him that would be a very bad idea. Instead, he turned around slowly and faced

Lord Clavemont, who stood between the raindrops in the light of a street lamp, his face contorted with restraint.

"When I am ready to speak with you again, I will send for you. Until that time..." He reached into his coat and withdrew the bejeweled dagger stamped with his house seal and held it out for Nixy to take. "...I hope this was worth the risk."

Nixy's hand trembled as he took it, unsure what this man, this Vemlok, wanted of him. He was happy to be alive, but something told him his life had gotten much more complicated and much more dangerous.

The albino Lord Clavemont, generous host and darling of polite society, shot into the stormy sky like an arrow and vanished over the spires of the cathedral.

Chapter Five

Valerian and Sand

The goddess reclined on the divan upon the back of the Ether Dragon, its scales rippling in the twilight gloom between creations. The audience with King Arathus had shaken the divine siblings, and all had felt the heat of his wrath. None would admit to any wrongdoing of course, for whoever had taken the Dark Heart from its eternal hiding place was playing a most dangerous game; the outcome might result in the very undoing of the world, for starters. Lelonetha did not know what to do, for it was not within her nature to suspect and pursue the guilty; for she was mercy itself and did not judge others for their crimes. Her realm was peace and rest for the weary and a path of meaningful service for those who were served in life.

Tavenji was uneasy in the divan chair, fidgeting more

than usual; his pale blond hair waved between his long, pointed ears, echoing his agitation. The little mischief god was deeply disturbed by the king's indictment and had been abnormally silent during the trip to the borders of Haven. Lelonetha wanted to talk to him, but the young god was pensive only once every few centuries, so she decided to leave him to his thoughts. If he wished to speak, she would listen.

She closed her eyes and felt the ripples of the Ether about her, stirred by the beating of the serpent dragon's feathery wings. Rivers of spirit power flowed between the outer realms, causing them to drift and bob in the currents of timeless space, eternal and moving, engaged in an endless dance. She let the currents of Ether blow through her golden hair and fill her with the semblance of breath as it rustled the yellow fabric of her traveling cloak.

Something was disturbing the peace of the flow. She opened her eyes and looked about, sensing a ripple approaching them like the wake of a passing ship upon the water. She was suddenly reminded of sitting in a little rowboat on a river, with a ship of the dead drawing close. Tavenji felt it too, and he became animated, spinning his head to and fro, searching for the source of the disturbance. The Ether Dragon turned its serpentine head to look upon its riders for direction, its forked tongue flickering to scent the danger.

Tavenji saw it first, for his eyes were sharper: a chariot of black iron, its wheels spinning in space and leaving a trail of smoke and flame. Upon the platform stood a huge bearded figure in bloodstained armor, a whip in one hand and a spear in the other; the war god Balkon, terrible in his wrath, bore down upon them. His eyes flashed like fire and he cracked his whip over the heads of three mighty, bronze geese that drew his chariot. It seemed to suddenly race at incredible speed, but it was actually growing larger, expanding to immense size along with the team and driver. The geese were soon large enough to snap the ether dragon up like an earthworm in their gleaming beaks; their great bronze feathers were as long as pine trees, and each was razor-sharp. The beating wings were as the rumbling of nearing thunder, but their noise was drowned out by the roar of the war god as he lifted his visor and called to his prey.

"You will not escape me this time, Trickster!" Balkon bellowed and the Ether trembled, "I don't care if sister is with you, I will make you pay for what you've done!"

Tavenji wished he had been there to watch Balkon smash his little armies into powder to make them stop dancing. It may have been a step too far, but it had been rather funny at the time.

Yet things were not so funny now. Lelonetha was worried, for they were in a neutral region, neither guest nor host. Vendettas were carried out in the Ether in the early days before the gods learned to get along with one another. Now it seemed that Balkon had been dealt all he could take and was looking to settle a score with Tavenji once again. Violence was Balkon's specialty, and his fury could take centuries to recover from, even for a god. She had never earned his ire before, but Tavenji made it a point of pride to do so, and now it seemed that she was in the path of his retribution. She sighed. It was going to be a long day.

The whip cracked overhead again, and the geese began squawking with the noise of a thousand trumpets, bearing down on the dragon's feathery tail. The iron wheels sent sparks flying like an erupting volcano. The visage of the war god loomed over the massive rail of the chariot, his spear charged with the destructive powers of the cosmos. Forked bolts of lightning leaped towards the ether dragon, which banked and beat its wings madly to escape; its feathers were singed and its passengers struggled to keep their seats.

Tavenji ran towards the head of the terrified dragon, balancing perfectly on its undulating back and stopping just behind the beast's feathered mane. He spoke to the creature and it dove, folding its wings and snapping its tail, flying like an arrow away from the pursuing giants. The spirit flow enveloped them like a fog and Tavenji balanced upon the dragon's nose, leaning into the currents and holding his hands before him, palms together. The ethereal wind buffeted his green jacket, and Lelonetha wondered what he was up to; she hoped that the trickster god had learned a trick or two since his last tangle with Balkon.

The war god shouted and drove his chariot into the flow, the screams of the bronze geese rising in crescendo as they dove into the obscuring mist. "You can't hide, Mavaram! I shall kill you thrice! I shall feed you your innards while I beat you with your own arms! Mavaram dog!"

Mavaram? It was one of Tavenji's first names, spoken in the language of the First People of Jayde. When Arathus created the gods of the Divine Court, Mavaram the Herald was the last and the strangest. The other gods saw the taint of Chaos in him and shunned him, believing he was somehow a tool of Llomaak. Only Lelonetha offered him unconditional love, as was her way. Now they were once again in the same boat, as it were. *I cannot let Balkon have him*, she thought resolutely. *His fate shall be mine, and I shall spare him all the pain I can take upon myself.* She stood on the divan and prepared herself for the approaching storm of godly wrath.

But Tavenji was unmoved by the war god's bellowing. He whispered into the flow and flung his hands wide, brushing reality aside and throwing it back like a gray curtain. The ether dragon folded its wings and passed through the rift, and before Lelonetha knew what was happening, the young god clapped his hands over his head, closing the rift behind them.

They were no longer in the Ether, but had entered a realm Lelonetha had never seen before. Balkon was no longer pursuing them, and Lelonetha wondered what kind of obscenities were spewing from his bearded mouth as his quarry vanished right in front of him. The thought gave her a touch of pleasure, and for a brief moment she shared in the perverse thrill Tavenji took in enraging the blusterous war god. She pushed the feeling aside, for it was unbecoming of Mother Mercy; she contented herself with the fact that she and her little brother had been spared a good deal of suffering, albeit deserved in some measure.

She looked about at the vista before her. A veil of stars hung overhead, supported by mighty pillars of ancient bone. The land below was a collection of strange mountains that rose about a valley; each was a different shade of earth tones, recalling the seasons of the world of elements: rust, brown, green, blue, and the orange and red of autumn. There were even bright smatterings of spring flowers scattered about in a perplexing heap of patterns. Indistinct structures were obscured in the distant horizon, and the sweet, pungent scent of Valerian blossoms permeated the sky.

Tavenji was skipping back along the dragon's spine now, a happy smile on his lips and a look of relief in his childlike eyes. He clapped twice and suddenly he and Lelonetha began to grow, or the landscape started to shrink, she could not tell which. The ether dragon flew out from under them, diminishing in size rapidly as they filled up the valley.

The details of the terrain became clearer to the goddess and began to make more sense; the veil of stars overhead was indeed a veil, for it was a fine woven fabric of dark velvet, embellished with points of silvery thread in the patterns of constellations. The whole of the 'sky' was supported by the ribs of ancient dragons, long gone. She found herself seated now on the patchy mountains of color; they were pillows of varying earth tones and patterns, making a small valley in the middle between her and Tavenji, who reclined on the pillows opposite. The walls that made up the horizon were quite close now, a collection of gray and blue fabric that bowed out where they rested on the dragon ribs, draping in between them like folds of old skin hanging on weary bones.

Secured to some of the ribs were shale slabs, flat pieces of driftwood, and other 'found' items that served as makeshift shelves. Upon the shelves were a strange assortment of knickknacks and trophies from uncounted years of 'collecting' from every plane of existence. There were acorns in a neat row, coins and jewels stacked in pretty little pyramids, and scraps of paper with arcane writings that seemed to gather dust unto themselves. There were little representations of creatures and people that capered and cavorted within the bounds of their shelf space. Rose petals, oak leaves, seashells, coppery eggs and snowballs could be found among the compilation. A vial held an amount of white sand, stopped with a wax seal; a fragment of sharp, bright metal glinted in a corner; and a pile of peach pits sat in a gauzy, translucent bag, cinched with a yellow ribbon. Lelonetha could account for every one of the pits, for she had given the fruit to Tavenji on each of his visits to her realm. Valerian flowers hung about the little tent and gave a calming scent that permeated the close air, manifesting as a misty cloud between their heads and the velvet cover of stars.

Tavenji looked very relaxed and at home here surrounded by his belongings, which by all accounts were once someone else's. He took in the calming mist and sighed happily, sweeping an arm before him and saying, "Welcome sister, to my realm." Lelonetha smiled at the word, for his 'realm' was low enough to make her stoop if she stood.

"Thank you brother, I had hoped I might visit one day under different circumstances." She sat back on the pillow-mountains, which were not as soothing as her own furnishings in Haven, but were still quite comfortable. The ether dragon could be seen flapping about like a moth, finally selecting a landing place next to a wyvern on a nearby shelf.

The walls of the tent shook slightly, causing the ribs

and fabric to sway; the items on the shelves rattled but stayed in place.

"He's really mad," said Tavenji, as he looked about the tiny fortress of blankets and bone. "He can't find this place, no one can, but he sure is trying." He hugged his knees to his chest as he did when anxious.

"We shall wait out the storm of Balkon's fury in here then," said the goddess as she looked at the stars above, appreciating their twinkling rhythm. "But I was wondering why you wished to travel back to Haven. If you could hide here, why come through the barriers of pain with me?" She could tell the little god had something weighing on him beyond the wrath of Balkon, which he had earned and nurtured over eons.

"I... I wanted to talk about what Father said. About the Dark Heart being stolen," he muttered to his knees.

He looked in her eyes and she looked back at him, resisting the urge to scan the shelves for the missing artifact. He had not admitted to taking it. Besides, Arathus had claimed it was in the mortal world now. She chided herself for the impulse and resolved to listen calmly. "Go on," she said carefully.

Tavenji flipped his feet nervously, rubbing his insteps together and reminding Lelonetha of a motley cricket. "I didn't think much of it at the time... it was a few mortal lifetimes ago when it happened, and no one said anything back then, so I kind of forgot about it and didn't tell anyone. I figured Father would be mad anyway, even though nothing bad happened, at least I didn't *think* anything bad had happened..." He was rambling now and Lelonetha put a hand on his knee to still him.

"Just take it slow and start from the beginning, little brother," she said.

Tavenji stopped flipping his feet and sat up straight. He nodded and asked, "Would you mind if I showed you? It's easier for me that way."

Lelonetha blinked and wondered what he meant, but then this *was* his realm, and its reality was defined by his wishes. He might have a power here that she had never seen. "Of course," she agreed, hoping it was not too unpleasant.

Tavenji closed his eyes and the little tent vanished, replaced by the endless expanse of the Void and the spirit-ether that flowed throughout, starless and dark. Lelonetha found herself floating alongside the little god as he flew through the darkness towards almost imperceptible points of light in the distance. At first he did not acknowledge her presence, but as they got closer to the luminous blur ahead, he turned and spoke to her.

"I was exploring the Ether, looking for the old gates. It had been a long mortal age since the Thinning, but I was hoping to find a place I could look through. I wouldn't create an avatar or anything, just, you know... look." They flew on towards the luminous blob and it resolved itself into a circle with many raised shapes about it, like fingers pushing though silk. It formed a soft, pulsating pattern of muted light that crept though the fabric of the universe to reflect in the little gods' eyes. "Then I saw it, heard it, *felt* it." He slowed and acted surprised, falling into the Now of his story, instead of acting as narrator of things past. Lelonetha followed his gaze and opened her senses, and she felt it too.

There was a *presence* in the old gate. Someone was waiting there, trying to be heard from the other side. It was not the dim, whispered echoes of the spirits of mortal worshipers, but something more potent, something that was empowered by the gate as it struggled to be noticed. It was old to be sure, for nothing in the world of elements was born in these times with such strength. But it was faltering and weakening as well, like a flame about to be extinguished, lest the breeze relent.

Tavenji switched between Now and Then as he told his story, letting things happen as they did, and acting as he had, but maintaining a commentary on events as they unfolded. "Hello? Who is there? I strained to hear, to see... Hello? Who calls beyond the gateway? Who summons the Gods?" He floated closer now, drifting amid the raised, glowing pillars and feeling about, like a man in the dark, for some sign. "There was a reply. It touched me through the gate! It actually made it possible to feel beyond, to the world of elements!" Lelonetha felt it too, and a shiver went down her spine; it was a feeling she had borrowed from mortals, so she might know the fear of imminent peril, or excitement. The voice and touch from beyond the gate was almost familiar, like an old creation long abandoned and forgotten.

It whispered through the dim luminosity of the gateway, *"Help me brother, it is so cold, so very cold."*

Lelonetha gasped at the words, though the voice was unknown to her. *Brother?*

Tavenji explained as he approached the presence in the circle, "I knew that only the least of powers could cross the boundaries between worlds on their own, but I thought perhaps... Take my hands! I shall pull you through," he said to the voice. "Perhaps if I helped it pass the barrier, if I lessened the strain... Come through! I can hold it..." his voice was quavering as he struggled to help the presence enter the Ether.

The goddess felt the stranger growing weaker and fainter, leaving behind more and more of its strength as Tavenji pulled, like a wet cloth being drawn through a wringer. Would he survive? What *could* survive such a transition, typically reserved for the spirits of the mortal dead?

The little god strained at the gateway, the force of his will allowing the stranger to pass. The presence became less and less potent, until the fabric of the Void no longer stopped him. Suddenly Tavenji held a body in his arms, the limp and emaciated form of an old man, with desiccated skin, wispy hair, and a tattered robe of gray linen, soiled by decades of travel through unknown realms.

The face of the man was unfamiliar to Lelonetha, but the feeling of him, the vibrations he left echoing in the

Ether, like a breath on the waters, were all too memorable; she knew him and she wept.

Tavenji did as well, lost in the Past of his tale as the ancient figure raised a weary limb to touch the young god's face. *"Brother,"* said the old one, and Lelonetha moved forward so that he might notice her and call to her as well, but it was all a memory, and her lost brother could not perceive.

Eldest of the Divine Court, he was called Thesram in the beginning, *Lord of Ages* in the first language. Later, he gained names such as Epoch, Destiny, Fate, the Keeper of Ages, the One Who Knows, and hundreds of others. He was once the god who charted the path of history; upon his staff was carved the life story of the world and all things in it, and he could know all there was to know about the past and future by tracing what was etched upon it. His cloak was white as snow then, his hair and beard were long and silver and they fluttered as the passage of time blew through them. That was before the Thinning, before Arathus fathered one last child upon a mortal woman, and the portals were forever shut.

The gods could no longer act in the world directly, and each being's destiny was its own. There was no more need for the god of fate, so Arathus took his power from him, sending him into exile. None of the other siblings understood the Father's intentions; never before had a god been rendered obsolete. Was banishment better than oblivion? Was Lord Epoch being punished for some unknown reason? It made no sense, but the word of Arathus was law, and none questioned it openly. There was sorrow and mourning, but no doubts were given voice.

Now he had returned to the Outer Realms with Tavenji's help. The trickster god held the frail old form in his arms and turned his tear-stained eyes to Lelonetha, bringing himself out of the memory to explain, "I know it was wrong to bring him back; Father had banished him, and pulling him through nearly destroyed him, but he was begging for help... Brother, can you hear me?" He turned back to the old man, cradling his head.

The fragile shell that was once a god croaked out a request, "Take me to my once-realm, brother. I need... I need what I left..." The old man fainted from the effort.

Now Tavenji was flying through the flow with the old man in his arms and Lelonetha beside him, his keen eyes searching the blackness for something only he could find. He explained as they flew, "I didn't know what he wanted, but I knew that the Void would kill him in his weakened state. I took him into the spirit flow to keep him strong, but it wouldn't last."

Stopping his flight suddenly, he launched out of the gray mists and headed for seemingly-empty space. Lelonetha watched as he scratched his fingers in the velvet darkness and drew forth grains of sand. He scratched again with more vigor and a rift appeared, spilling fine white sand upon the spirit wind and spreading it like vapor.

Was this one of Tavenji's secret paths? Does it truly lead to the Ninth Realm?

They flew into the rift and were engulfed in the raspy, abrasive flow as it moved down to seal the damage to its borders. Finally they broke through and found themselves standing upon an endless sea of white sand dunes under a brilliant blue sky. There was light but no sun, no stars. Lelonetha looked about the bleak realm searching for some structure; she remembered that Epoch had lived in a tower carved with past and future history, but she saw no sign of it here. Tavenji still held the withered man in his arms, but the figure had changed somewhat. He was no longer so weak and fragile, and his hair had regained a bit of its old luster, but the eyes were still ancient and weary with much pain. She wished she had been there to relieve his suffering, but she was only an observer now.

Tavenji gingerly set the old man on his feet, helping him straighten his soiled robe and find his footing on the shifting sands. The stooped former god was not much taller than the Trickster as he stood beside him, though in his power he had towered over the other siblings, his height matching his standing as first created of the gods of the Divine Court.

He looked about the landscape, as if getting his bearings, and Tavenji spoke, "I brought him here because he asked it of me, but I had an odd feeling. Something was not right. Brother had changed... Brother Epoch?" He spoke to the old man, who took a few moments to notice Tavenji was addressing him. "You said you needed something here. Something you left behind?" The old man chuckled and nodded, looking back towards the distant dunes. "He was always so serious and grim before, but now he was almost... delirious? I don't know, but it frightened me. I asked him again... Brother? Can I help?" The old man waved him off and began walking across the dunes. Tavenji and Lelonetha followed as best they could.

Dune after dune they crossed, walking with difficulty over the unfamiliar landscape, forced to abide by the rules of this reality. The old man who once ruled here was much more able, and his speed seemed to increase with each step. He was becoming strong again, though still only a pale shadow of his former glory. Soon he was out of sight over the crest of a dune and the siblings hurried to catch him. As Tavenji and Lelonetha reached the top and looked down, they saw the old man digging in the sand.

"What have you found?" Tavenji called as he ran down the slope.

The ancient figure giggled and drew a white cloak from the gleaming sands, dusting it off and shaking it clean. He smiled through his silver-gray beard and drew the cloak about his shoulders, taking great comfort in it. "It was cold," said the once-god, "So cold there, always too cold." He turned in another direction and walked off, forcing the gods to catch up. He was soon out of sight again, and this time his trail led in a twisting path that suggested he was lost. Once in a while the pair would see him ascending a dune or crossing its ridge line, only to vanish down the slope.

Lelonetha asked Tavenji, "Where is he going? What does he find next?"

Tavenji looked a bit sheepish and stopped in his tracks, remembering that he was the storyteller here, and his story was going overlong. He smiled apologetically at Lelonetha and said, "Sorry," before closing his eyes and getting to the point.

The landscape blurred and the siblings found themselves climbing towards the top of a dune where the old man was taking handfuls of sand, lifting them and pouring out the contents. He did this over and over until the sand began to coalesce into a thin pillar at his feet, growing taller with each pouring. Lelonetha saw that it was not forming a pillar at all, but a staff of pure white, like ivory. Upon its length was a spiraling line of carvings, fine runes etched by no hand, but imbued with the truth and knowledge of the destiny of all things. At last, the staff was drawn from the sands and its height was equal to that of the once-god, but surely it had been taller when he was in his full power. She noticed the base of the staff was blemished with a dark crack that ran a tenth of the way up its length, and she wondered at it.

Tavenji, seeing her gaze said, "I saw the crack in the staff too, but didn't ask, and brother never spoke of it." The old man turned and looked at Tavenji, and with a wink he was gone. "Brother!" Tavenji called to the sky. "He vanished and I didn't know what to do... Brother where are you?" He ran to the top of the dune and looked frantically in every direction, his voice echoing across the white sands.

He turned back to Lelonetha, dropping his panic like a mask. "I thought I had done something really bad, letting him reclaim some of his old things. I didn't want to get in trouble and have Father banish *me*. A god can't return like that, can he? Just come back and grab some old cloak and staff and," he snapped his fingers, "Poof! Return to power? It didn't make sense. He was still weak and frail or I would have sensed his power in the realm. But the realm felt empty, that is, except for a trembling in the sands." He knelt and put his hands to the ground. "Do you feel it?" He asked Lelonetha, who knelt and felt the sand.

Of course she *would* feel it, because Tavenji had felt it, and it was his story after all; she was about to say as much when the sensation in her fingertips distracted her. It was very faint, very subtle, but it was there; she felt tremors in the sand, like the movement of a deep-burrowing creature, or the ripples in the Ether when a god stirs in wrath.

She felt the rhythm of the trembling, and the power it spoke of, greater than the fallen god who wandered over his home of old. Some energy had seeped into the Sands of the Ages and been absorbed, spreading itself thin over many centuries. It could be felt now as a disturbance, something aberrant vibrating in the very fabric of the realm, tainting every grain of sand with its pulsating cadence.

There was only one answer, only one thing that could cause such a deep stain in the endless white sands. A fragment of the power of a greater god was buried here, hidden for all eternity. It could not be destroyed, so it was allowed to bleed into the abandoned realm of an abandoned deity.

A new realization came to her, and a cold fury sparked in the goddess's heart. *Was this why Epoch was banished, so that his home might serve as a dumping ground for the corruption of Chaos? Endless sands used to swallow an endless threat? We knew it was hidden here, but was it Father's plan all along?*

Tavenji took her anger as impatience, and quickly tried to hurry things along. He jumped to his feet and said, "Eventually he came back and I was very relieved..." They were standing before the figure of their brother now, having returned from his sojourn looking haler than he had before. He was a little taller now and his clothing was almost as white as it had been in ages past; his silver hair and beard were long and lustrous under the deep blue sky.

Lelonetha smiled at the change, for it was almost as if he had found a bit of peace at last. He was no longer master of this realm, but he seemed more at home here than anyone could.

She wondered if mortals felt like this when looking upon the remains of a loved one whose soul and vitality had departed. Her once-brother was not suffering anymore, but he was so diminished and profoundly changed that she felt the loss of him very deeply, though he stood before her.

The fallen god said in a deep voice, "I am ready to return to exile, brother. I have what I need, and I am ready." He smiled and held his staff before him, and his cloak was wound about his shoulders, enfolding his other arm. Tavenji nodded and took the old man by the shoulders, hugging him close, and said, "Very well then, brother. We will go."

He stamped on the dune and a sinkhole opened up, swallowing them all in a vortex of harsh rasping white. Lelonetha found herself hurtling towards the old gate with Tavenji leading the way, carrying their brother in his arms. The old man was becoming frail again as the power of his realm was left far behind; he was shedding his godly persona, along with what strength he had left, preparing for passage through the gate.

Lelonetha caught up to the trickster god and asked in a quiet whisper, "Epoch has the Dark Heart with him, doesn't he?"

Tavenji looked at the old man withering in his arms and replied, "I think he does. I felt so strange taking him back. I felt guilty, sad, angry, but also... *wrong*. I didn't know what to make of it, until Father called us together."

He shed tears as he gazed into the weary eyes, once

again awash with pain, "To think that he called to me, begged me to help him, so that he could betray us all! I helped him to do it!" Tavenji sniffed and cried to the old man, who could not respond, "Why brother, why did you use me? Was it revenge on Father? Was it to punish us for not questioning him and letting you go?" Lelonetha put an arm around the young god as they hurled towards the dim light of the gate. "It could all end because of this!" Tavenji looked scared and the tears streaked his face in the ethereal wind. "Because I was stupid, all of creation could be destroyed... what will happen to us? What have I done?"

Mother Mercy looked into the pale, passive face of the old man who grew frailer as they approached the end of the story. She looked for malice in his eyes, looked for the twinkle of deception or cruelty and saw none. She was not Valdak, who knew the hearts and minds of all and acted as their judge, but she knew a face that needed mercy's touch, and this was one such face.

How many years of suffering had their brother faced in the mortal world, unable to die, but no longer a god? What horrors had he seen in the centuries since he was banished? Did he still have the gift of sight, knowing the future but unable to change it for himself? Or was he truly blind to all possibilities, only able to see the Terrible Now that passed from one moment to the next in an endless, irreversible march?

Again she grieved that this was only a memory, only a story, and she was unable to help him. She yearned to give him some sign of hope, perhaps an omen for his worldly eyes to show him that he was still loved and missed, to let him know he was not alone. Would it be enough to ease his pain, or would it only remind him of what he had lost?

What of the Dark Heart, the fragment of the Lord of Chaos that he had stolen away to the world of elements? It could only destroy him or drive him further from sanity. It was anathema to Order and had brought ruin to entire kingdoms in its time on Jayde, and now it had returned by the hand of Order's eldest and forsaken child.

Lelonetha watched as Tavenji remembered the rest of his story, holding the portal as the old man's strength seeped away into the Ether, seeing the odd ripple as the stolen relic, weakened by its imprisonment, bled into the fabric of the world beyond. She saw the shadow of an old bent man fall to the ground in a circle of standing stones, cloaked in tatters and holding a crooked staff, while clutching his chest with a free hand. His beard covered his face on the windy mount as the vision faded into the dark of the Void, which then became the cozy draped walls of Tavenji's little tent-realm.

They were sitting opposite each other; the little god looked spent and dejected as he pondered the future of all things and his hand in the affair. The goddess went to embrace him, flooding him with hope and comfort while he clung to her like the child he was, youngest of the gods, most naive and most foolish, innocent in his own way even after eons of making mischief.

For taking pity on their eldest brother, she could find no fault. Just hearing his cry was far more than she or the other siblings had done since his exile. Tavenji went even further, as was his nature, and tried his best to help.

She felt a wave of shame wash over her. *Merciful Mother indeed!* Since the portals were shut, she had unwillingly turned her back on the mortal world, only helping the spirits of the dead find peace on their journey. Unable to channel her healing gifts through her priesthood, she turned inward to make Haven all the greater.

Even Selvina sends her butterflies into the world on little missions now and again, approaching defiance of the Law. Would it hurt so much if Lelonetha, Mother of Mercy, sent a little ray of hope into the lives of mortals once in a while?

They called it the Age of Omens on Jayde because they eagerly awaited such signs, clinging to a faith that had deserted them. She swore to herself, as she held her little brother in her arms, that she would do all she could to let the world know that Mercy still cared for them and that hope had not abandoned Jayde.

As the tent shook again and lightning flashed beyond the drapery, she thought, *Just as soon as brother Balkon goes away...*

Chapter Six

Hopeful Tidings

    It was late in the evening when Drahn the Dweedragon left the library on the upper-most level of the Tower of the Silver Moon. He had been researching the many volumes of work on the study of omens by both religious and wizardly scholars, and had come to the conclusion that neither party had a firm grasp on the subject. For over eleven hundred years, the devoted had been watching for signs from the gods, hoping to glean the future or find meaning in unusual events, but none had managed to come up with a formula that could be used repeatedly to the same end. Some gave meanings to the flight patterns of birds, or the shape of clouds on a given day, others rebuffed such claims, or gave them different significance entirely. Most scholars and seekers of omens had remarkable hindsight however, able to connect signs and portents with events that had already occurred. No one had thus far been able to use such omens to make accurate predictions of the future, even when the signs were similar.

Popular reasoning was that each omen was different and meant for the eyes of those who might glean their meaning; only time would tell if such readings were correct. To the dweedragon, it all seemed as nebulous as reading entrails or scattered bones. If the gods wanted to impart foretelling of the death of kings, famine, or war, they might use a language that could be interpreted before the fact. Otherwise, what was the point?

He thanked the library assistant who had helped him with the heavier books, for Drahn's cat-sized body could not heft the large tomes. He made for the lower level of the chamber where the windows overlooked the city; opening one, he stepped out onto the sill and sniffed the night air. No rain tonight at least; rain made his aerial patrols too difficult and there was always the threat of lightning.

The towers and spires of the city were prone to lightning strikes, and although there were spells placed upon them to reduce the risk of fire, Drahn took no chances. He had seen a pigeon in the path of a lightning strike once, and there had been little remaining but charred feathers. Drahn greatly disliked pigeons, but he had pitied the poor creature.

Closing the window behind him, he leaped from the patina structure and out into the dark sky, extending his wings and catching the cool ocean breeze as he flapped off over the canal. Master Ildric had returned over a month ago from his journey to the north, and after a day of rest, he set himself to spending long hours in his study, suspending his time with his pupil until further notice. Drahn had wanted desperately to ask about the Lady Cindra's fate, to learn what Ildric had found out in the village of Syngmore where the boy Nixy had lived, or to just talk to the old wizard. There were so many things that had happened, and Drahn had been at such a loss for perspective that he'd wasted the day in the Order's library trying to learn about omens and divination, hoping the gods had left clues for him to find. Frustrated, he flew towards the cathedral, his purple scales iridescent in the starlight.

It was only this morning he had seen the birds around the temple roof. A murder of crows had flocked over the spires, making what seemed like an ominous omen to Drahn's inexpert eyes. Upon investigating, he was horrified to find the headless body of a man draped over the buttress supporting the spire of the goddess Hwessa, the Eternal Wind. The man's clothing was tattered and shabby, but that might have been due to the persistent birds feeding on his flesh.

Drahn had landed on Hwessa's outstretched arm, wrapping his tail about her stone neck for support as he looked over the grisly scene below. The corpse was barefoot and filthy, and had nails like claws on his fingers and toes. The smell had been appalling, though the body had not been there long. Drahn was no carrion eater and had no experience with such things, but the eye-watering stench told him this person had not been much of a bather in life. If such a scene did not warrant the name 'omen' then the dweedragon could not imagine what might, and if Ildric was not already informed of the bizarre event, then Drahn would do so this evening.

Casting Guild wizards had unceremoniously removed the body using a combination of spells to dislodge it without damaging the temple. Drahn flew low over the roof of the cathedral, checking for other signs. There was no blood on the roof, no trace of a struggle, and no sign of how the man might have gotten up so high to begin with. There was no head to be found either, not that Drahn was inclined to look for one very hard.

Turning towards the Tower of Sight, the little dweedragon resolved to see his master. The doors and windows were not shut to him, but then, he had not been called back either. If the wizard wanted to be left alone after more than a month in solitude, he should post a sign; Drahn cared too much about the old human to simply pretend everything was as it should be. Besides, what if something had happened and Ildric needed help?

Ildric had called him a fussbudget on more than one occasion, but the dweedragon was incorrigible; it was in his nature to worry about the people and things he cared for. It was why dragons were such good parents and why they horded treasure, among other reasons. Landing on the oft-used sill of the wizard's library, Drahn spoke the password and opened the checkered pane, snuffling at the stale air inside. He hopped in and closed the window with his tail, noticing the fireplace was cold and the only light came from a solitary wizard lamp at the ceiling. Dust had settled on the tables and books, and a nearly empty goblet was the only sign that the room had been recently inhabited. Drahn padded about the floor like a wary cat, sniffing and calling in a small voice, "M-master? Hello?" There was no response.

Heading for the door of the central stairwell, he felt ill at ease, as if he might discover the old man lying dead at his desk or burned to a crisp by a misfired spell. He banished such thoughts before they took hold, reminding himself that one can never be ready for the worst of times, so there was no sense in being over-prepared. Bravery and optimism were much better emotions to nourish. He stretched up on his toes, opened the latch, and began climbing the stairs to the wizard's study. The spiral led up and around until a door came into view and Drahn knocked with all the bravery and optimism he could muster. There was no answer. He knocked again, this time calling out, but still no reply came. He opened the door and peeked inside, sniffing the remains of a fire in the hearth. The room was empty but smelled of the wizard's robes, making Drahn's nose wrinkle. *He must have spent many hours in here*, he thought. The desk was littered with notes and sketched images, and the scrying crystal was sitting in its ornate cradle, well-polished from constant use. The wizard was not present however, and the little dragon sighed and continued his search.

Heading further up the stairs, he came to the trap door of the tower's observatory, a room at the top of the tower capped with a large dome of clear crystal, which was supported throughout by a twisting lattice of sculpted metal and held together with many enchantments. In the center was a raised platform where the wizard wove his most difficult spells, but the room was empty. Ignoring the dazzling view, Drahn descended the stairs and kept looking for his master.

Ildric's bedchamber was small and frugal by the standards of an arch mage, but warm and comfortable nonetheless. Drahn had only been in there once before when the wizard was sick, and his ancient house servant had been unable to make it upstairs with a tray of bread and soup. The old servant had since died, and Ildric had not been sick for some time, so Drahn had not been back to the bedchamber, though there was a lovely collection of blankets in a chest that he often dreamed about snuggling in. He knocked on the door and called out to his master, putting an ear to the wood to listen. There was a mumbling from beyond so Drahn worryingly took that as an invitation and hastened inside.

The wizard was propping himself up in bed, looking worn and disheveled but not unhappy at the intrusion. He had laid his robes aside and wore a long nightshirt, but he still could have used a bath, judging by the aroma that hung in the air. The fire was going, the room was cozy, and everything looked rather ordinary. Drahn smiled with his toothy draconic mouth and perked up immediately, happy to find things so un-tragic.

Ildric hoisted himself out of bed with some groaning and moved to a chair by the hearth. There he sat for a few moments, looking into the fire as Drahn climbed onto a cushioned footstool and waited. Finally the wizard spoke.

"I apologize for my appearance, but it seems I've spent

the last several days sleeping," he said as he attempted to straighten his mane of white hair and short beard, "I decided to rest from my labors, taking some time from my divination, and I misjudged how draining the experience was." He rubbed his eyes with his left hand of flesh as the right hand of metal twitched and squeaked with fatigue. "Since returning from my journey, I learned of Lady Cindra's... incident, and I set myself to unravel the threads of fate binding her and the boy, Nixy." He rubbed his temple, squinting at the throbbing pain behind his eyes. "I believe it was more than chance that brought them together on that winter night, as if destiny required her to save him." Drahn cocked his head, confused. Ildric explained, "If Lady Cindra had not met Nixy that night, if their paths had not converged, then the attack on her ship may not have come to light until it was too late."

Drahn blinked and said, "Do you mean that she died because they met?"

Ildric shook his head, "I mean that I may not have foreseen what happened to her if they had not met. No one understands how the threads of destiny are woven, but I think the attack on Lady Cindra's ship was no random incident." He leveled a gaze at the dweedragon, "and by the by, she is not dead."

Drahn's scales flashed a shimmering blue before returning to their natural purple sheen. "She is not dead? Then your gift worked! Oh, we must tell the count and countess at once!" He danced about happily on his hind legs, clapping his fore claws.

Ildric smiled and said, "We shall, we shall, but this news is not for the public." He wagged a warning finger at the dweedragon, "Not a word of this must get out, and I shall advise the count and countess to keep it a secret as well. I fear she is still in danger from those who wish this alliance to fail."

Drahn could not easily contain his glee, for the news of her death had struck him heavily, and he felt guilty for not doing more to prevent it. *Now she is alive and all is well!* he thought.

"All is well with her, isn't it?" he asked, "Wherever she is?"

Ildric nodded, "She is safe enough, but I fear the Minozhians were only pawns in this; someone is working against the count and the king, but being careful not to reveal their part. There have been too many suspicious events related to this marriage." He stared into the fire for a long time until Drahn spoke up again.

"What did you learn on your journey to Syngmore?" he asked, fiddling with his tail.

"Ah," Ildric said, revitalizing a little. "That was an interesting week. I had not been to that village in nearly thirty years. It is not a common thing for a wizard of any stature to pass through Syngmore village, but there are those who remembered me from when I was there last." He sat up in his chair, preparing to tell the story, "Thirty years ago, before I acquired my... new appendage," he lifted the metallic right hand, embedded with the artifact known as the Eye of Omithys, "I was entreated by the villagers to search the Shadowood for a lost child who had wandered within. The villagers were afraid of the deep woods and never ventured there; they had reason to fear, for there is a power in that forest that has little patience for intrusion.

"Nevertheless, I agreed to find the child, braving the dark gloom of the Shadowood. My powers were tested; dark things barred my path, the undergrowth pulled at my feet and snagged my robes, fear griped my heart from an unknown source, but I would not be thwarted. I voiced a challenge to the darkness, telling it that I would not leave without the child. I was bolder than I was wise, but it seems my challenge was heard. The shadows soon relented, and before long I found a trail in the woods where one was formerly hidden. I followed it and beheld the child, sitting in a clearing that was alive with magic."

Drahn perked up, "A spiwit well? There is a spiwit well

116

in the Shadowood?" The little dragon knew that such places were jealously sought after and guarded; indeed, wars had been fought over the larger ones. There were three small spirit wells in Portshia and Ildric's tower was built on one.

Ildric nodded, "More than one spirit well, I am sure. I called to her and she smiled, waving at me, as if nothing were amiss. I asked her 'Why did you come into the woods, child?' She replied, 'I followed a bird.' Indeed there was a large raven in a tree nearby, watching us.

"I asked, 'Were you not afraid?' and she shook her head. I told her I was there to take her home. She stood..." Ildric looked into the fire, a frown on his brow as he relived the moment. "...She stood and I saw she was holding something in her hand: a knife of ancient craft, with a black handle carved with a raven's head."

Drahn blinked and sat up. "Like the one the boy had? You examined it with the Eye of Omithys that day; what did you learn?"

Ildric flexed his silver hand, looking to the artifact embedded in the palm, bound with glyphs of power. "The Eye showed me glimpses of a storied past shrouded in shadow. The knife is made from a shard of another blade, forged in the days when mankind was young. It was carried far across the sea and saw much use before it came into the possession of that little girl. She grew, bore a son, and left it to him."

"Young Nixy DuQuayne," said Drahn, scratching his chin. "But where did the girl get the knife? Did she find it in the woods?"

Ildric shook his head, "This I cannot see, for it is hidden from me, much as the boy himself is hidden. As I said, there is a darkness surrounding him that is becoming more difficult to see beyond. But I learned more from the villagers that might shed light on the subject. Nixy's mother, the girl I found in the woods, was named Kirana; by all accounts, a young woman of surpassing beauty, nearly twenty years old. Her parents had died of a sickness a few years earlier, and she was left in the care of her uncle's family, who had little knowledge of her uncanny childhood adventure. They knew not of the bird she had followed, or the strange knife she had acquired, only that she had been lost in the woods and found again by some 'wandering wizard.'

"She was married to a local farmer named Mathen DuQuayne, and they settled on his farm near the Shadowood. Within a year, she was with child. I spoke to the midwives who were involved in her care. It was... an unusual and difficult pregnancy. Nine months came and went, and three more after that; many in the village thought it an ill omen, and some wanted to turn her out into the woods, fearing what the strange birth might mean. Cooler heads prevailed and the child was born that summer, but at a terrible cost. Poor Kirana was all but spent and did not survive the birth." Ildric paused as a twinge of pain stung his eyes, making him wince and rub them.

Drahn lowered his head in sadness, recalling his own loss; his mother and clutch-mates had met an unknown fate before he had hatched, leaving him orphaned.

The old wizard continued, "There are fewer stories after the death of young Kirana. Mathen gave the boy to a relative to raise until his fourth year, at which time the lad went to live with his father. The man had become bitter with grief over the loss and rarely spoke to others. He had the habit of drinking to excess, especially on the day that marked the birth of his son and the death of his wife. Nixy was often seen in town running errands, but the adults mistrusted him and the other children would not befriend him. Some said that there were ill omens about the lad; people claimed that ravens would seem to follow him, lurking on the rooftops as if waiting for a meal. Others swear they saw terrible black wolves watching him from the edge of the woods."

"Wavens?" Drahn raised his head and his tail swished thoughtfully, "Kiwana followed a waven into the woods, and a waven's head adorns the handle of the knife! What could it mean?"

Ildric smiled, "Perhaps nothing, perhaps much. Once again my visions were thwarted and I had to rely on the memories of farmers, chipping away at the layers of embellishment that had grown on the tale. The last that was known of young Nixy was that he had gone missing two years ago without a trace. Some said the woods claimed the boy; that he had finally fallen to the waiting wolves and ravens. His father was accused of murdering him and was driven from his farm rather than hanged, for lack of proof."

Drahn did not like farmer Mathen very much by the picture the stories painted, but he could feel badly for his loss. That the man had been driven away for murdering his son was unjust and regrettable. "What did you tell them? Did you let them know he is alive?"

Ildric nodded, "Eventually I did. I had been wrestling with the decision since I began the journey, wondering if it might do more harm than good. But seeing as the boy was already in mortal danger here in the city, I judged that it would be safe to divulge his whereabouts."

"Did you speak to the father? Were you able to find him?"

"If you mean farmer Mathen, then yes. I found him living in a small shack by the edge of the woods. He was a wreck of a man; pain and sorrow was etched upon his face, and his eyes held no joy, but only reflected the dreariness of his existence. He had no fear of me or my silver hand, which so often evokes awe and wariness from the simple folk. It took some time to convince him to speak of his past and his son. He bade me go into the village and purchase food and drink for him, which I did more out of pity than concession. Once he had eaten, and the drink loosened his tongue, he spoke of much that you have already heard. What was news to me was his tale of the last night he saw his son."

Drahn waited patiently as Ildric poured himself a cup

of wine and drank to ease his throat.

The wizard continued, "It was the night of the dreaded anniversary, and he had been drowning his sorrows in the pub. He made it home around dusk and found the boy preparing their supper as usual. He was bitter and angry and said many things that he now regrets, as he had done for many years before. I was not there to absolve him of any wrongdoing, so I took no pains to counsel him. Instead, I tried to focus his thoughts on the events of that night, a difficult task, since the man was now drunk, trying to remember another drunken night two years hence. He finally came to it, when he had grabbed a switch to beat the boy. Nixy had ducked into a dark corner to hide, and Mathen went straight for him. Yet somehow the child was gone, only to return the next morning to steal some food and take the knife his father had hidden in the roof thatch.

"The men of the village searched for days, scouring the woods as deeply as they dared, recalling when the lad's mother was a girl and had gone missing in the forest. 'Another omen' they said, 'as ill and foul as any could be.' It was only when the sober Mathen kept repeating his tale of the boy 'vanishing' in the farmhouse that people began to suspect foul play. They accused him of murdering the boy and dragging him into the Shadowood.

"He felt great pity for himself, for indeed he has led a tragic life, though much was of his own craft. Still, he felt regret for his actions, so I told him that his son was alive and living in Portshia."

Drahn waited for a few breaths before finally blurting, "Well, what did he say to that?" Ildric liked his dramatic pauses too much.

"Very little, actually; he stared at the table and the walls for a while, as if letting it sink in. Finally he asked after the boy's health and wellbeing. I let him know that he was safe and living in the service of the count himself, working in the stables."

Drahn's head and tail drooped a little. Ildric had asked

120

him to watch over the boy, and Drahn had flown by the keep each day, looking in on the stables. It was only ten days ago that the boy had gone missing, and the little dragon had spent his days combing the city for a sign of him. That is, until the rain came, and the crows, and the body... Clearing his throat, Drahn said in a meek voice, "Em, about that... The boy is no longer in the care of the count. It seems he, eh, left over a week ago. I have been twying to find him; I think I've seen him on a few occasions but I'm not sure." His wings wilted as he saw the alarm on the wizard's face.

"He *left*? Does he not remember that there is a demnox after him, after his blood? Fool of a boy!" Ildric stood and began pacing.

Drahn then told him about the storm and the crows, his fruitless study of omens and his theories about the body on the cathedral. Ildric listened patiently, for he knew that to interrupt would only fluster the dweedragon. After much consideration, he came to agree with the little creature's thinking.

"It does sound like the workings of a supernatural power, I concur with you there. I cannot perceive Nixy in my divinations most of the time, only shadows. Yet I think he might still live, and perhaps whatever force is concealing him from me has also come to his aid at the cathedral. If it was indeed this Black Will that was made a feast for crows, then the boy might be safe for a while. Besides, I am far too weary to look for him. I must ready myself for an audience with the count and countess, and decide how to handle this most delicate of news."

Drahn hopped off the stool and made for the door, giving the wizard his privacy. Before leaving, he offered, "You might want to take a bath, master." The wizard snorted a laugh as the latch clicked shut.

It was early the next day when the wizard made the trip to the castle for his audience. He had not sent word in advance, hoping to avoid any more attention to his visit than necessary. Ildric had his doubts about the confidence of his lordship's house; if the hidden enemy had done all that he suspected, then it was possible that they had eyes and ears in the count's home. There was much to risk by giving the grieving parents this happy news, for even a slight change in their manner might inform the observant of a shifting of fortunes. For all his powers of sight, Ildric had no means of reading the hearts and minds of others, no way to tell friend from traitor except by their actions. Such power was reserved for the gods alone, it seemed.

He presented himself at the gate with no special flourish or effect, without the thunderous, magical proclamation of his last visit. He requested a private audience with the lord and lady, this being his first visit since hearing of the death of their daughter. Nearly an hour passed before his wish could be granted, and he spent the time in the same study where he had interviewed the children just a few months before. He was served tea and biscuits while waiting; the servants were quiet and swift, no doubt wearied of the long succession of official condolence visits. He so wanted to tell them all the good news, to lift them out of their misery and gloom, but discretion was the rule of the wise, and this was a matter of gravest delicacy.

Constable Fingelm, who had to cut short a meeting with the count to accommodate the wizard, finally sent a servant to escort him to the lord's study. Ildric took up his staff and followed, climbing the grand stair and proceeding around the circular hall that overlooked the courtyard. Seated within the study were the count and countess in their house robes and cloaks, an empty chair before them for their guest. They looked groomed yet haggard about the eyes, as if sleep had become scarce for them both. The emerald eyes of the countess were rimmed with red and the count had dark circles that made his already deep-set eyes take on the hollow visage of illness.

"Lord and Lady Casselvane, I thank you for seeing me on such short notice," he began, "I regret that I had not come sooner, but I have recently returned from a journey and..."

The count raised his hand for silence, a weary look in his eyes. The countess held her chin up but her eyes downward, her golden hair concealed under a veil. "There is nothing more that can be done, my friend. Perhaps if I had asked for your foresight before our daughter departed..." he took his lady's hand and she took a breath as though it were the first in a while. "Perhaps we might have been better prepared to safeguard her voyage." His bottom lip trembled slightly and a muscle in his jaw twitched after he spoke, divulging the bitter emotion beneath.

"Your lordship, please!" Ildric entreated him. He had raised his silver hand to reassure them, forgetting the strange limb with its lidless dragon eye often made people deeply uneasy. "I have not come to stir up sorrow and regret, but to give hopeful tidings that might ease your suffering."

The count and countess looked into his eyes; a glimmer of anticipation was there now, tempered with a pragmatism that kept the best of hopes at bay. Neither could imagine what news might ease their suffering, save that their daughter's remains had been found and given proper rites, or those responsible for her death had been punished. Even then, the comfort would be little.

Ildric took a deep breath and began, "Before I tell you what I have learned, I must ask that you keep this all in the strictest confidence, and the news of it must not leave this room. I have reason to believe that there are forces working against House Corrina and the crown, and what I have to say might threaten the security of the kingdom if it falls upon the wrong ears." That part he had practiced on the way, for in his mind it was the most important advice he could give to the noble couple. The lord and lady gazed at each other nervously and nodded in agreement, too bewildered to speak. Ildric continued, "I have spent the last month in my tower trying to search through the puzzle of events that have unfolded recently. It was no small feat that your lordship was able to secure an alliance of marriage with Rokvynnar, and certainly no coincidence that their young duke died thereafter by nefarious means. Poisoning, was it not?"

The count nodded, "Though it is not widely known, that is the belief of the ducal household. They have yet to find a culprit in that most wicked crime." He was not overly surprised that Ildric knew, for Sight was the wizard's specialty, yet concern creased his brow as he gleaned the direction of the man's thinking.

Ildric continued, "That you were able to make alternate arrangements was another unlikely achievement. How then would the assassin move against the new duke, now that all were on guard? If the goal was to stop the wedding and the alliance, they would have to adjust their strategy."

"Cindra," said the countess quietly, almost murmuring the name. She knew as a noble-born that her children might be the target of assassins, yet what could be done when the girl was far away at sea, beyond watchful eyes? Even poor Mineth had not been spared.

Ildric pressed onward, trying not to let them fall into misery again, "I reviewed the testimony of the commander of the *Wesvyyn Gull*, the escort ship. The heavy anchor line was severed in the night, allowing them to drift away long before the morning attack on the *Indisputable*. This speaks of planning many hours in advance, not a chance meeting with pirates at sea."

The count rubbed his temple, becoming impatient. "Arch Magus, this has all been discussed among our advisers and generals; I am afraid your month of crystal gazing has yielded little we have not already pondered and acted upon."

Ildric sat back in his chair, letting the slight to his abilities slide by. He gave a measured stare at the countess and said, "Your ladyship, do you recall the day I visited last? When I spoke to Lady Cindra and Master DuQuayne? I had a belated gift for her that day, a bracelet of gold with silver inlay, set with a sea-stone."

"Yes, I recall," she answered, suddenly apprehensive. "She showed me the gift."

"I told her it would bring her luck on her journey, but I was not wholly truthful. The bracelet was imbued with enchantments of water and air, and gifted with the grace of Obesh, God of the Seas. It was one of the many treasures I had collected in my travels, and I felt she might have need of it." Both count and countess were fully attentive now, neither expecting this turn of fortune. Ildric went on, "The bracelet would have allowed her to breathe beneath the waves for a time, and would call for the aid of the animals of the sea to spirit her ashore." He had to motion for silence as real hope kindled in their faces. "What I tell you now must not to be shared, and make no change in your manner, so that none suspect the truth! Lady Cindra *lives!* She is in the care of those who will protect her, but she is surrounded by peril..."

Upon the pronouncement, the countess nearly fell from her chair as she extended a shaking hand to her husband. Tears of joy and relief flowed from her as she gave thanks to the wizard for his intervention. The count too was overcome, holding his wife's hand and shaking with happiness, life slowly returning to his eyes. Ildric was tempted to cast a spell of silence upon them lest they cry out for joy and ruin his precautions, but the lord and lady were trained to be reserved in the presence of company. They regained their composure to the wizard's liking and allowed him to tell on.

"The less I share the better, but I can tell you that I have seen her alive in my visions. I focused my seeking upon the bracelet, which was in my keeping for many years and is well known to me; she has it still. She travels with friendly folk who will hide her from searching eyes, but I ask that you not seek her out for fear of alerting our enemies. If they think the marriage will still take place, they will do everything in their power to stop it."

"But what of the alliance?" said the count, "If nothing is done to find her and proceed with the marriage, the alliance will be foiled just the same. Is that not what our enemies want?"

The countess pleaded, "She must be brought home! We can protect her here in the castle, and if they want the marriage, they may send the duke to us! Let them sail home with an armada this time, not two ships!"

The wizard shook his white head, stroking his beard in thought, "I think perhaps an alternate plan would be best. If we can devise another way to proceed with the alliance, we might be able to flush out the villains without endangering Lady Cindra further. Besides, her dowry was lost to the Minozhians, so delivering her to Rokvynnar would not alone fulfill the agreement."

The countess expressed immediate interest in the alternate course, thinking only of her lost daughter's safety. "We have lands and holdings we might offer in place of a dowry, perhaps they would even assent to foregoing the wedding entirely..." The count shook his head to disagree, but Ildric was not going to entertain this conversation now.

"Your lordships, I would advise to take time in making any plans. You must not appear to be wholly renewed in your efforts or it might arouse suspicion. Continue to grieve, in manner only, make inquiries with weary resolve, take small steps and watch for counter-steps. Above all, do not betray these tidings to anyone! Secrecy and deception will see her safely home, for we must use the tools of our hidden foes against them. Continue the year of mourning and let the black banners fly. They will help to blind our enemies until they reveal themselves."

It had been two days since Arch Magus Finnael made his unexpected visit to Casselvane Keep, and the household was abuzz with the usual gossip. There were many who whispered of the wizard leading a search for the pirates, using his powers to track them across the sea. Others told how the lord count had sent for the wizard to rebuke him for not foreseeing the poor Lady Cindra's fate and preventing it. Constable Fingelm was happy to be away from it all; he had enough intrigue to focus on without the whimsy of servants cluttering his mind. His own villa was in the Highcourt, just a trot down the hill from the keep itself, and it was his sanctuary of peace and clear thought. The only official duties he needed to worry on here were those he had scheduled and arranged himself. Today's duty was more of a social occasion, as well as a means of keeping good relations with the Merchant's Guild. His weekly lunch with Kobus DuChat was something he looked forward to.

The powerful merchant sat across the dining room table from the constable, dabbing the corners of his mouth with a linen napkin. Though not of noble birth, DuChat was wealthier than most of the nobles in the city, Fingelm included. It was easy to envy the man for his luck and fortune, but something told the constable that such wealth was not without an equal or greater amount of toil and bother. Fingelm was no stranger to mental labor, but he preferred to let his station provide for him, rather than his ingenuity.

DuChat was dressed in a modest suit of silk and velvet, adorned only with a finger ring; he was not here to impress, after all. He took another sip of wine, savoring it before swallowing in tiny gulps. "My compliments on your wine stock, milord constable. It rivals my own, I think." DuChat smiled charmingly. "So you were saying about the other day?"

"Ah," said the constable, continuing his story, "The Arch Magus Finnael stopped by the keep two days ago, quite unannounced. Interrupted a meeting I was having with his lordship about the tariffs you were concerned about. It seemed he finally got around to giving his condolences."

"Finally? Had he been holding off for some reason?" DuChat sounded amused.

"Who knows the ways of wizards? He had been away for a time I think, but had returned over a month ago if my information is correct. I think he might have been embarrassed not to have seen the tragedy coming." He waved his hand dismissively, "It might have been best if he had not come at all, stirring up the lord and lady as he did."

DuChat took another sip and asked, "How did he stir them up? Did you hear the discussion by chance, constable?"

Fingelm laughed at the audacity of the question, choosing not to take offense at the commoner's presumption. "Ha! It was a private meeting and I do not listen at doors," he shook his head, "It was the way they acted upon leaving the meeting. They were restless and talking with heads close, glancing about. I asked them what was the matter, and they were a bit terse with me for my troubles. I've no doubt that wizard put some idea in their heads about some plot or another, seeking their favor again by trying to seem useful."

DuChat considered silently and asked, "You do not trust wizards I take it?"

Fingelm retorted, "What's to trust? They act as if they have some greater power and wisdom, but they make mistakes like the rest of us. If this Ildric Finnael has such powerful Sight, as they say, why did he not see and prevent the lady's death? What good is a master diviner who cannot see something like that?"

DuChat finished his wine and smiled, an unpleasant thought forming behind his eyes, "What good indeed?"

Chapter Seven

Berries and Smoke

It was the best year of Cindra's life. She traveled with her adopted family for many, many leagues, learning something new each day; she saw parts of her country that she had only heard about in stories or seen on maps. New experiences were opened to her that would have never been a part of her old life, though some were frightening, difficult, or painful.

She was more active and busy than she had ever been, helping with daily chores, foraging, sewing, and cooking. In her first week with the caravan, Cindra learned to make a fire, milk a goat, scrape hides, and boil water to use for drinking. She was taught which plants to avoid, which to gather for medicines and body care, and which were safe to eat.

Yet thoughts of home intruded on these happy times.

Cindra missed her mother and father dearly, not only for the parting of ways, but because they believed her to be dead and lying beneath the Emerald Sea. No attempt had been made to tell them differently, for Cindra and her protectors did not want to invite disaster from the mysterious masked priest or his Minozhian allies. It was a certainty that the conspirators had eyes and ears in Portshia, and the last thing Cindra wanted was to bring trouble down on the Galindri. She was hidden among these people, though she was fooling no one in their camps. The Outlanders who saw her were none the wiser however, thanks to some clever thinking and a curious old legend.

One of the first stories she had heard from Haani, who was learning the ways of a tribal storyteller, was *T'emeko'a Tol'ózh,* the Infant Son of Arathus. Cindra had heard Luka utter the words once before, when her true identity had been revealed.

Haani explained, "You know of the Dark King Orthicus, and how he learned of the birth of a holy child destined to rule, and how he hunted the child and his mother?" Cindra nodded. "What is told among our people is how he escaped the Dark King and grew to manhood.

"Kraal was his name, and his blood was of mortal woman and immortal god. His mother fled from the hunters of the Dark King across the broken land for five dances of the moon, until the messengers of the Forest King told her to seek the *Gatéth-sho'a* deep in the woods. They had been told of Kraal's need, and it was given to them to keep him safe and see him to his destiny.

"Kraal's mother knew he would be safer without her, and so she led the hunters away from her son, fleeing the forest upon a swift horse. Infant Kraal wailed for her until nightfall, and then never wept again."

Cindra was fascinated, for the story of Kraal she had grown up with left suspicious gaps in his early years. Her people's version told of the noble Lady Ashimae LuLelova perishing amongst many women and children in the village of Wen, after the hunters of Orthicus the Tyrant tracked her down. Tradition taught that she took one of the women's infants to her breast, protecting it like her own. The hunters thought they had slain the mother and her holy child.

Haani continued, "Kraal was Outlander and pale as fresh milk. To hide him as one of our own, the women gathered *b'ámava* berries, crushed and strained them, and bathed the infant in the juice. The berries stained his flesh golden brown, and the hunters of the Dark King saw him only as a *Gatéth-sho'a* child. He thus grew to manhood and learned our ways, and the tribes called him one of their own, and rode to his aid in the Great Battle where he met his destiny."

It seemed that Haani and Luka had been cooking up a similar scheme to hide Cindra from prying eyes. She was quite a bit bigger than the infant Kraal, and they could not find a tub large enough to serve, so Haani and Luka made do as best they could. Haani and Cindra gathered a great many *b'ámava* berries, and Luka mashed them into a dark juice. Deer tallow and some kind of chalky clay were added to thicken the mixture, and it was boiled before being applied to Cindra's skin with a wooden knife, making her feel like a cake that was being frosted.

"We use the berries to dye clothing and make paints," Luka explained as she carefully handled the mixture. "It also stains the skin for many months, and cloth, wood, or leather will hold the color for a long, long time."

When the odd blend of vegetable and mineral matter dried, the excess was dusted off and the girl looked at her body with wonder. Her skin was now many shades darker where exposed; the flesh covered by her skirts was still the same, but to unknowing eyes she looked like a Galindri. *No,* she corrected herself, *I look Gatéth-sho'a.*

Her scalp and auburn hair had been washed in the berry juice and her locks were braided, but were not bound up on her head like she expected. It seemed that having bound hair in the manner of the other adults was a rite of passage that neither she nor Haani had attained. The first time Teya had returned from a hunt and was presented with the new Cindra, she had burst out laughing at the sight of her. Cindra was upset, but it was later explained that if the disguise had been poor, Teya would have probably been angry and critical. Nevertheless, it was the first and only time she had seen Teya laugh so, and it became a happy memory despite the embarrassment.

One of the things Cindra learned was what it was to be *Gatéth-sho'a* in the Outlander world. As they passed through villages and towns, it was not uncommon to see parents ushering their children indoors and casting evil glances at the caravan.

Navo explained, "For some reason, Outlanders think we steal children, dip them in berry juice, and raise them as our own."

They both had a good laugh over that, but the idea bothered Cindra, for she had heard many tales about these people that proved untrue. It made her angry but she dared not express it, seeing that the other Galindri bore the scorn with a weary endurance. It was safer that way, she was told. King Kraal had given them freedom to move with the herds and hunt as they needed, which was more than the citizens of Calilon could do without a lord's permission, yet they were resented and mistrusted. Even the poorest of the nation's peasants looked down on the Galindri as a lower-class people.

Hunting the herds of furdeer was a way of life for many tribes, for the beasts were plentiful and ranged from one end of the continent to the other. The one saving grace that kept them for the Galindri alone was not so much the edict of Kraal, but a secret Kraal had learned while living among the people who ate them. Outlanders did not eat furdeer unless there was nothing else, for the meat was slightly poisonous. The Galindri perpetuated the idea that only they could stomach the meat, thus saving the herds for themselves. The truth was that the furdeer diet included a few specific weeds that gave their meat its toxicity, and the Galindri added the antidote to their own meals. The meat still took some getting used to, and Cindra went through a time called 'the spots,' while the herbs that countered the meat's effects were building up in her body. Purple spots danced behind her eyes after each meal for about a week, but thereafter she was able to digest without incident.

The great furdeer hunt was something to behold; the artistic renderings Cindra had seen did it no justice. Late in autumn, the Galindri gathered to the south of the Mydwood Forest in Kelgavane Province, preparing for the yearly event. The herds were moving down from the early snows in Kiron and Shylith-Dromah, heading for the fertile plains of central Calilon. The signs of their coming were heralded by scouts after weeks of waiting.

It was the biggest meeting of *Gatéth-sho'a* tribes Cindra had seen since the spring gathering outside of Woodcourt earlier that year. Close to a hundred families and their livestock were camped along the forest's edge, preparing for the hunt. Majii's clan had arrived from Cenlind Province to the southwest, accompanied by a herd of horses. Teya's black mare, *A'lanóka*, was among them and their reunion was happy and family-like, with many hugs and nuzzles.

"She has been foaling with the herd for the last year," Teya explained, as Cindra admired the steed, "She gave birth to a fine young filly, I hear. Now she is ready to race the wind again." Teya patted the mare's muscular neck, "Aren't you?" She whispered to the great beast in her own language, showing affection Cindra had seen her give to no human.

After days of scouting their prey, Teya rode to the hunt with dozens of other warriors, chasing the vast herd of shaggy deer for miles while shooting bows or throwing spears, bringing down many animals. The families followed in the path of the stampede, collecting the meat and hides; sorting the bones and antlers; gathering the stomachs, bladders and intestines for later cleaning and use. Little was left in the wake of the hunt but bloodstains in the grass and scraps for the crows and buzzards.

Cindra could not hunt, but she accompanied Luka and Haani to the fallen prey. She had never so much as plucked a chicken, so the butchery of the large animals was quite an education. She had no problem with the sight of blood, but the smells that came with it were more than she was prepared for. She felt sick the whole time, but the smiles and chuckles of the women and children were just enough to help her persevere through the gruesome job. Horse-drawn litters bore the meat and other remains back to camp where the industry began in earnest.

To the other *Gatéth-sho'a,* she was known as Menika Majii-Ama, but to her immediate family she was called Lelóndi, or simply *saya*. The name *Menika* meant 'cat', in secret reference to her family coat of arms, and *Majii-Ama* described her as an adopted daughter of Majii. *Saya* meant 'little sister' and Cindra was happy with that, but when she asked what *Lelóndi* meant, the others had a hard time relating the concept. Amid smiles and uncertain Calilesh, she learned that it was a big joke among those who knew her noble heritage. *Lelóndi* translated roughly to 'she who is lofty,' and Haani imitated the flight of eagles high in the sky. Cindra pouted a bit, but accepted it in the end.

Other Galindri would give her strange looks, noticing her odd features, hazel eyes and clumsy manner. But word spread quickly that she was of Majii's family and her life depended on their open hearts, and that was enough for most.

The family spent that winter outside the walls of Mydwicks, a city that sat at the junction of the Regala and Ani rivers, where they merged into the Great Regala and flowed to the northern sea. Galindri were not permitted inside the city walls, so there was a semi-permanent zone called the Outwalls (a term used in many cities) where Galindri and other 'undesirables' would camp away from the general populace. Trading posts were set up so that if citizens chose, they could browse the wares of the Outwalls and sell supplies that the nomads sought. Most of the people who came to the trading posts were practiced and wary, having made a living from the arrangement for many years, but Cindra could spot the newcomers easily. They had wide, darting eyes and kept their purses close; they had a habit of looking down their nose at the goods for sale, as if they might carry a taint that could be seen with a discerning eye.

She caught many a man giving *her* discerning eyes, and blushed at it beneath her stained skin; though she was used to being admired in a cultured and respectful way, she was quite unaccustomed to being examined like a tavern menu. Many did not even have the shame to stop leering when she caught them. Luckily, she was dressed more heavily for the northern winter, not wearing the light summer or spring garb that required more skin dye and less fabric.

That winter was cruel and passed more slowly than any she remembered, for she was raised far from what northerners called 'true winters.' There were snowstorms almost every other week it seemed; as the white blanket began to pile up, Cindra asked Navo what they would do if things got too cold and the snow too high.

"Well, we simply scoop out the horses and live in their carcasses until spring," he replied, and this time even Luka was put off by his coarse humor enough to smack him.

The answer, as she found, was to dig and dig. They dug trenches in the snow between caravans and campsites, packing up walls of snow and spraying it with water, making it icy and firm. Each area had room for people and animals to move about, but they could not leave with their caravans even if they wanted to. The roads were choked with snow, and horses pulled sleds in and out of the city walls instead of carts. Now Cindra understood why they had spent the last of the autumn months gathering firewood and preparing the furdeer meat for storage. The new cloaks and blankets of furdeer hide were lifesavers as well, and she treated her fur-lined leather boots as prized possessions. In all her years Cindra had never experienced a winter without the grand fireplaces and cooked meals in her father's castle and the season's lessons were harsh.

Makeshift tents served for sleeping on the cold ground when the snowfall was lighter and the ice walls blocked the wind. When things were harsher, the family slept in the caravan in very close quarters, using canvas and rope to make a hammock, like the ones Cindra had seen at sea. After a few nights of sleeping in the hammock, she found she preferred the press of warm bodies to being suspended in the freezing air. Nobility called it 'sleeping like the poor,' but she didn't mind at all.

The 28th day of Kraamoth came and went without much recognition; birthdays were not celebrated among the *Gatéth-sho'a,* and Cindra was not going to make an affair of her fifteenth year if it meant extra work for the family. Majii remembered however, and marked the day as the first time they met, asking Cindra to tell the story of how she came to be in the Market Square on that winter evening far away. She was happy to do so, since she had only told the story twice before, and had been punished by her father the first time. Her new family found it very entertaining, thrilling at the chase that led to the encounter with Black Will and the children's harrowing escape. After the story, her thoughts flew back to Nixy. She wondered how he was doing, working in the castle and learning to read and write. He would no doubt be sad for her death at sea, but he was at least safe and secure within the castle walls. *Funny how things change*, she thought, remembering how she had felt about being enclosed in walls of stone.

Spring came and the walls of the camp began to thaw, exposing more and more of the surrounding community. People would stand on tiptoes and wave to each other where once they had to trudge through halls of packed snow. Fires were harder to maintain because of all the runoff from the melting ice, which turned the campsites of the Outwalls into a quagmire of mud and slush. This was the worst time to Cindra's mind, for snow at least had a kind of order to it once packed and pushed into place. Mud was slippery, stuck to everything, and made everyday activities a challenge.

For much of the winter there had been no need to dye her skin. Besides, there had been no berries to use, so she was fading in color and would need to maintain the disguise before long. It suited her to stay in the caravan when Outlanders started coming around and checking to see if everyone survived the winter, bringing food and ale in exchange for the winter gear the Galindri would not wish to carry through the coming year. She desperately wanted to go into town and sit indoors by a fire with a mug of mulled wine, but such luxuries were beyond her new life. Besides, if her Galindri family could not join her, it would give her no comfort or pleasure.

As the roads became manageable and the fields of snow gave way to fields of flowers, the caravans began to disperse. Majii's caravan, and those of several of his kinsmen, took the northwestern road over the rising river at the Mydwicks Bridge. The path wound through the forest and up the High Road that ran between the cities of Safegaard in the north and Highseat to the south.

The Crownswood Forest bordered the western road as they journeyed towards Highseat, the royal center of Calilon. The Crownswood was full of evergreens and aspens, and was not nearly as dense as the woods farther south, but the game wardens kept the forest stocked with prey for the royal hunt. Natural predators were driven out as best as possible; big cats, wolves, and the horrid *zéh'noka* or 'dread wolves' that Cindra was so familiar with, were forced to find other hunting grounds so the nobility might enjoy their sport.

One day, as she was gazing towards distant Highseat, Cindra said, "I wonder if the king spent this last winter in Portshia." She said it to no one in particular, but Luka found it curious.

"I have not seen or heard of a royal caravan heading there for some time," Luka remarked, "Is that great white palace truly empty all through the year?"

Cindra nodded, "There are servants to keep it in readiness, but no one else lives there."

"Why keep it empty?" Luka asked, "Such a house could hold many without shelter, if the king is in the west."

Cindra shrugged, "They would only be turned out in winter if the king decided to visit. Besides, not even my family is allowed to reside there."

Luka thought on this, "It seems a great waste of stone. Does the king never share his lodgings?"

Cindra replied, "Once, I asked my father why we could not live in the Winter Palace during the rest of the year, and he told me that 'the king would not wish us to become too comfortable in the palace.' It makes sense, I suppose." She sighed, "The provinces to the east of the Cassel Range are almost in a state of rebellion. It wouldn't do for House Corrina to forget who truly rules."

She shook her head as she tried to drive out the first political thoughts to enter her mind in the last year; they were nearing the capital city and all of the responsibilities of her former life were returning to haunt her. The wedding, meant to secure an alliance with neighboring Rokvynnar, was long past due. The king himself had sanctioned the marriage, and was depending on it to secure their naval support, among other things. Now the blushing bride was sneaking about in a Galindri caravan, just a few days from the Rokvynnar border, and tossing everyone's hopes to the wind.

She felt a pang of guilt and wondered how things had changed since she disappeared. Had rebellion broken out in the east? Was her father fighting a civil war against the king's disloyal barons? Surely she would have heard something, for as long as there were ember swallows, there was a way to speed news of importance. The last such creature she had seen was Gavagul on the day she sent him home with her final, desperate message. She had no idea how many of the magical birds existed in the land, but she was sure that if war *had* broken out, the sky would be crisscrossed with their smoke trails, and armies would be gathering in their wake. No tidings were fair tidings, as it was said.

The procession of caravans camped outside of the walls of Highseat on the fifth day of travel, and Teya left with several other riders to find grazing land for the many dozens of horses in their herd. A few of the mares were heavy with foal, promising some new additions to the family soon, and Cindra longed to see one born. One of the joys or her younger days was caring for the kittens born in the castle, watching them crawl about blindly, searching for their mother's warmth. She heard that foals could stand shortly after birth and wanted to see it for herself.

Last summer she had resumed her riding lessons, learning to straddle a horse like a man while wearing trousers, or with special split-skirts that women of the *Gatéth-sho'a* made to suit both fashion and practicality. Saddles were not commonly used among them, so she had to use her thighs to steady herself on the animal; it was not pleasant for the first few weeks, and Luka had to collect herbs for all manner of pains that Cindra suffered until she began to develop what they called *doma-jo-áman,* or 'horse-legs.' She was very happy when she was able to walk normally again, and people stopped calling her *lá-k'o-kus*, the old woman.

The caravans planned to stay outside Highseat for a week and trade for supplies, and Cindra learned that it was permitted for *Gatéth-sho'a* to enter the city walls, so she decided it was time to work on her disguise. She accompanied Haani, Luka, and an elder kinswoman named Tavika to gather *b'ámava* berries, venturing out into the woods to look for laden bushes. Haani was relieved that there were no bears in these woods, for they had a taste for the bitter berries as well, and noisemakers had to be carried when harvesting them in the wild.

Tavika made noise enough as she carried the day with stories of people and places that Cindra could barely recognize with her grasp of the language. The older woman was graying and wrinkled, but lively. She was a younger sister of Majii from another mother, like Haani's relation to Teya and Navo. It was said that Majii's mother had a wise head and Tavika's mother had a wise mouth, but Cindra knew enough not to repeat this in her presence. Still, the woman was pleasant and friendly, retelling jokes in thickly accented Calilesh if Cindra did not laugh at first. Though she did not always understand the humor, even on the second telling, Cindra smiled politely as if she did.

There was one comment that piqued her interest because the subject had been avoided before. Tavika nudged Haani and said in a chiding voice, "So girl! When are you going to put up your hair? Waiting for your father to pick someone for you?" Haani was abashed at first and laughed nervously, then smiled and shook her head as she suffered the old woman's humor.

Cindra looked questioningly at Tavika, hoping she would elaborate; the woman obliged, for elaboration was her defining characteristic.

"She has not yet picked a man," said the old woman, as Haani hunched over a bush to hide her blush. "When she does, she can wear *ó-ki-jéshola*, woman's hair." She indicated her own topknot of falling gray braids. "You are about of age too, Menika, though you are not *Gatéth-sho'a* by birth."

Cindra herself began to blush in understanding, "So it is a sign that one is married?"

Tavika laughed, "Married? No not always so. It is a

sign of experience, that one is ready for marriage if they wish." She picked a berry and crushed it between her fingers, laughing loudly. Luka shook her head and made a clucking sound with her tongue, like she was scolding a child.

The visual was not lost on Cindra, for it was something that concerned nobility in particular. A young bride was expected to be a virgin on her wedding day; a priestess would examine her maidenhead before the ceremony and examine the bed sheets after the wedding night. It was a rather humiliating prospect, but it was demanded by society to insure that another man had not 'deflowered' the bride before her husband could. As far as she knew, there was no such requirement of the groom, who might be the father of a great many bastards that could not inherit his estates and titles. The idea of publicly wearing one's 'experience' as a hairstyle for all to see was awkward at best to her mind.

"*Wá-shad!* Look at how she blushes!" Tavika was laughing so hard, she was in danger of spilling her berries.

Luka stepped in to explain, "The act of love is not binding among our people, but marriage is a life-bond. Navo was not my first, but I was his. We are both happy together and may have children one day, but the marriage does not require it. Nor do children require marriage, since the rearing is shared by all."

Cindra sighed, "So different. I was to be married with my virginity intact and expected to bear as many children as possible."

Tavika chuckled and said, "Not likely now with *doma-jo-áman*. Many women who ride horses are not 'intact,' as you say. The lack of blood on the wedding sheets means nothing among *Gatéth-sho'a*."

The woman was plainspoken; Cindra had to give her that. Haani and Luka had a way of dancing around a subject and making mysteries out of everything. She had the feeling this elder woman might blurt out anything she

141

was asked about, and decided to test it.

"So Teya is not married, but she has taken a lover?" Cindra ventured, wondering at the love life of the stern huntress. A noble woman lived on wine and gossip, it was said.

Tavika's face grew more serious as she continued picking berries, "Ah, Teya *P'inika-do*. She has had a hard life, that one." The other women looked at Tavika as if she was about to do some harm by speaking, but they knew the stories were important and Teya would not speak of them herself. They picked berries in silence as the old woman continued.

"She had a man once, young and strong, from another tribe. He was called Vakii and was a fine rider and hunter. Six winters ago he went into the village of Oba to trade for supplies and never came out alive. There was a crime and he had been blamed, and the Outlanders hung him in the middle of the village. Teya's heart froze that day, and she has been so full of anger." The old woman shook her head at the memory.

Cindra said, "That's horrible. It's no wonder she hates Outlanders so."

Tavika replied, "Oh that was just the last of it. Her hatred for them began when she was younger than you, Menika."

She did not speak for a time, and Cindra thought the subject had been dropped, but the wrinkled woman finally took a deep breath and went on, "When she was young, not eight winters old, she went with her mother, Haana, and other women to gather wood. They were discovered by Outlander brigands, who forced themselves on them, but Teya was hidden." Her voice grew angry and her eyes were sharp as she recounted the tale, "The men laughed and tore the women's clothes, bloodied their faces, violated them; Haana fought back the hardest and earned a brigand's knife for it. The other men left before he was done, and it was then that Teya came out from hiding. She took up a bow and arrow, sat on the ground and pulled it with her hands and feet, and killed the man who murdered her mother." Cindra was struck dumb.

"She took the man's knife, cleaned it on his clothes and took it for her *lok-shíneh*. Then she helped the other women take her mother's body back to camp. Warriors went out to take revenge on the brigands, but Majii forbade Teya to go with them, though she had blood in her eyes."

"D-did they find them?" asked Cindra quietly.

The old woman nodded solemnly, "Yes, they came on them that night and killed them. Still, Teya was not sated. She learned to shoot a bow and fight with a knife, and it was not so she might hunt deer. Majii's heart was broken for his wife, but also for his daughter's need for revenge. He has tried to keep her on a peaceful path, but it is difficult."

"Teya *P'ínika-do*," Cindra intoned, "Teya Two-Knives." She remembered the weapon with the wire-wound handle and brass pommel, the one the huntress never seemed to use. It was the very blade that killed her mother. Cindra wondered if she could ever look at Teya again without her eyes wandering to the knife, imagining an eight-year-old girl taking a life in vengeance over her mother's body. The sun was warm but Cindra shivered nonetheless.

The preparations went faster with Tavika helping, and this time Cindra was presentable in only a few hours, plus drying time. The dye covered her head, arms, torso, and lower waist, since the blouses she wore for spring and summer left the midriff bare, and the *l'lash* wrapping beneath was sometimes all she wore on top. She was painted from her upper thighs to her toes below the waist, since her skirts covered all else that anyone would see. Only a strong updraft could expose her secrets now, and the weather was nice and calm. She accompanied Luka and Navo into town while Haani stayed with her father and extended family; Tavika had many fat grandchildren that needed watching, and Haani loved to tell them stories.

The palace of Highseat was set on the top of a high hill surrounded by twisting roads and buildings that hugged the steep sides, all but obscuring the rock they were built upon. The whole city looked like it was made of buildings set upon buildings in a huge mound, topped with a spectacular castle with high walls. Many gates and fortified structures surrounded the palace itself, so that an enemy would have to fight the entire way up the hill, street by street, until reaching the main entrance. It was built in the days before black powder cannons, so the defenses might not be so relevant now. Cindra knew this much from the history of her father's keep and the reason it sat so low behind the walls of the Highcourt.

The guards at the city gate were checking everyone for weapons and requiring them to either leave them or secure them with 'peace knots,' leather thongs that bound the blade to the scabbard or otherwise made the weapon impossible to draw in anger. Peace knots were checked often by the watchmen in the city, and if found untied or cut, the weapon's owner could face a stiff fine. If involved in an altercation where weapons were used, the person might face death or other serious punishments, depending on the circumstances. Cindra gathered all of this by glancing at the posted notices, realizing afterward that she should probably not make it obvious that she could read. Regardless, the only blade she owned was a Minozhian *Kos* knife, and she had yet to start wearing the brutal thing.

Highseat was a city built in the old Norsican Exodus style that differed greatly from the Celvestrian proportions of the Old Empire, and the subsequent 'enlightened' design that formed her native Portshia. Some of the streets were so narrow they could be considered alleyways, barely wide enough for two horses to pass one another; some alleyways were barely traversable at all. The buildings were clustered together in a frantic bid for space, often joining together over the street level with extensions that seemed more like architectural afterthoughts than structures intended for human use. Most of the buildings had wooden frames with wattle and daub walls: mats of woven reeds sealed with a thick white mixture made of goose droppings and straw, among other things. The radiating wooden support timbers were exposed to show off the skeleton of the structures, creating beautiful building faces of a kind that were lacking in the plastered brick walls of the south. The gutters that lined the streets were the only means of sanitation it seemed, and one had to be mindful of shouts from above that would herald the disposal of someone's chamber pot onto unwary heads. The reek was close and intense as animals and people shared the streets, and the wind had fewer avenues to carry away the combined odors. Casting Guild wizards were employed to deal with the worst of the filth, freezing it into hard chunks or slabs that could be more easily dealt with by the city muck-men.

Navo led the way down a crowded street with Luka and Cindra in tow, edging towards an open plaza where most of the city's commerce was done. It was very different from the Market Square in Portshia; the space was wide but uneven and stretched around the skirt of the hill upon which the city was stacked. Trees took up much of the central space, making for natural shade and shelter, while shops with open fronts or wide windows faced the street, presenting their wares with large painted images for the unlettered. The air carried the smells of cooked meats and baked goods for sale, though some of the meats looked rather suspect. Cindra had eaten already so was not tempted into distraction, but she was in her element and the thrill of the hunt was something not easily quelled. Shopping districts across the land had attracted her; the fact that she had not a copper to spend was beside the point. Many a shopkeeper had shooed her away like a pest or potential thief, but she loved to look at goods both simple and fine, whether she needed them or not. In fact, the less she needed them, the more she mooned over them. Perhaps it was a result of her noble upbringing, or perhaps it was something deeper.

The shadows protected patches of snow that clung to the cool darkness, refusing to melt until late in the spring. There were green buds on the trees, and the call of birds was heard over the murmur of the crowd. It was a fine spring day, better suited for strolling through a field rather than a crowded street, but there were things to be purchased and they had some coin from the winter's trading. Cindra practiced her new language as they walked, knowing that any mistakes would go unnoticed by the townspeople.

"What are we buying?" she asked Luka in the Galindri tongue, approximating the accent.

Luka turned, answering in kind, "There are spices that we cannot gather ourselves, *saya*. Cinnamon and peppers from over the sea, and ginger. They are not customary, but they are welcome."

Not extravagant tastes to Cindra's mind, but she understood. 'Spice gives variety to life' went the saying or something like that. She continued her practice.

"Navo said the horses need shoes, are we getting them here?" She was getting the flow of the *Gatéth-sho'a* speech and was rather proud of herself.

"No," said Luka, "there are smiths in the Outwalls that serve our horses; it is better than walking them through town, where the streets are so narrow."

"*Sheja jezhónk'a noko*?" Cindra said in the Galindri tongue as they passed a small herd of goats.

Navo stopped and turned, making Luka bump into him. He had a peculiar look on his face and Cindra wondered what she had said wrong. She pointed to the goats and repeated her question.

Luka and Navo both burst out laughing and Cindra knew she had misspoken. When they finally settled down, Luka said, "*Neko* is 'goat.' *Noko* is 'brother,' *saya*. You asked if 'maybe we can get a husband for brother."

Navo continued to laugh as he led them through the crowd. "Our little *neko-le* is past her bearing days, and I am already happily married!"

Annoyed that she had provided such amusement, Cindra followed on in petulant silence. *Enough practice for today.*

Trumpets sounded from behind and all turned their heads to look towards the far end of the street. A pair of horsemen was riding towards the market, clearing the way with blasts from their horns and shouts of 'Make way, make way for the prince!' Cindra and the others pressed against the crowd as the horsemen approached, followed at a distance by a dozen mounted riders bearing banners of purple and gold, knights in armor with lance and sword at the ready. In their midst was a young man of perhaps twenty years in a resplendent coat of black velvet and silver thread, with a cape of deep purple lined with sable fur and embroidered black eagles along the hem. His skin was tanned and told of a love for the outdoors. His hair was dark gold and hung about his shoulders, and he wore a bejeweled coronet that caught the afternoon sunlight with flashes of blue and red. His bearded jaw was set, his face grim, and his eyes fixed straight ahead when they were not glancing up at the palace on the hill. His white steed was draped in black with white trim, also with the black eagle symbol emblazoned on the hem. The procession moved past with haste, careful not to trample anyone but taking little heed beyond that.

It took Cindra a moment to realize that she had just met her royal cousin Galen, Prince of Maylione and Crown Prince of Calilon. Known as the Black Eagle, Prince Galen was the only son of King Galen II and his first queen, the late Rosetha LuAurielain. Cindra and Prince Galen shared a great-grandfather through their maternal lines; House Corrina had royal blood from many generations back as well, when a royal Cordobal princess had been married to Cindra's great-great-great grandfather, Amos Corrina. Therefore the prince was both a close and distant relative. Family history was a large part of her education, and it stirred the noble pride within her as she watched the procession vanish into the distance. She wondered if it was a special occasion or a family matter, for the prince seemed worried about something. If the king was very ill, it could be bad news indeed for the Loyalists. It had been a tragic time for the royal family in the year before Cindra's engagement, when Queen Velaina had died in childbirth, and the poor infant Princess Kaithen had passed a week later.

"Bad omen, when the prince comes rushing in like that," a peasant said to his fellow, "There's an air of death about the palace these days, you mark me."

"Don't talk like that, lest you call down extra trouble on yerself," said the other man as the crowd filled in the wake of the procession.

"The whole city's talking like that, if you haven't noticed. First the queen and child, then His Majesty takes ill; it's not just a spot of bad luck, but a curse, I tell ya. It bodes ill for the rest of us too." The peasants moved on and Cindra had to stop eavesdropping and follow her friends.

The day in the city was exhausting and Cindra was happy to head back to the caravan and the campsite at the Outwalls. The outer city was crowded in places, spreading over hills and vales, but there was a strong breeze cooling the air as the sun fell. Luka had bought more than she intended and Cindra had to carry many of the goods, which was a strain on her back and arms after several hours. Nobles did not carry their *own* shopping, much less someone else's, but she did not resent it. Not only was it part of her disguise, but it also made her feel... common? *Normal*, she decided. She had no great purpose, no responsibility to king and country, no need to look beyond the next moment. It was a kind of freedom she had never imagined. It was freedom of the mind, freedom of the spirit.

The next morning she was awoken early, before the sun rose. Teya had come and rousted her from her spot by the campfire and bid her get dressed quickly. Cindra was only wearing her *l'lash* and a pair of short trousers, so she pulled on her skirts and a coat after rolling up her bedding. Teya pulled her onto the back of her horse and together they rode into the dark morning towards a copse of trees north of the city. The huntress would not speak and Cindra was too tired to press her for answers; besides, she had a vague notion of what was going on.

There was a light amongst the trees as they rode towards the fields where the Galindri horses were grazing. The herd was under the watchful eyes of blue-clad keepers, who waved to Teya as she and Cindra passed. Teya brought her horse to a trot and headed deeper into the trees, making for the glow of a campfire. As they neared, a member of Majii's extended family stepped out and hailed them, taking the reins of Teya's horse and leading it away after they dismounted. The huntress led Cindra towards the fire where Majii, Tavika and several men that wore the blue shirts and headbands of Galindri horse-herders stood waiting.

Majii motioned them over and walked towards a nearby shelter where a lamp hung from a branch. There on the ground was a dark bay horse named Le-t'ósha, one of the pregnant mares, her head being held and stroked as she whinnied and panted.

"She is foaling," said Teya, and she smiled as Cindra's wide eyes glittered up at her in the lamplight. "I knew you wanted to see."

"Thank you, Teya!" she said in a hushed voice as she watched the mare give birth. With the assistance of the horse-herders and fair amount of noise and mess, a newborn foal was brought into the world, shivering and covered with afterbirth and blood. The mother nuzzled it and licked it clean, and the men who acted as midwives helped her as much as she would allow.

One of them announced, *"Jo-áman t'menéko."* The little foal was a male, a colt. Cindra was on her knees so she could look the little wonder in the face as he tested his spindly new legs, trying to stand. His coat was glossy and moist, with hints of red from the afterbirth. His black eyes gazed at the audience beneath long lashes.

"If he is like his mother, he will be fast too," she said, "Little T'ózha." She wanted to touch him, but the men had motioned everyone back.

Majii came and stood by her, putting his hand on her head. "It is a good name. T'ózha. May it bless him as he grows. As for you, Menika, it will be your task to see that he grows strong. I give him to you, a gift fitting my newest daughter, and in thanks for the life of my eldest daughter."

Now Cindra felt like a new foal trying to stand on spindly legs. She got to her feet and swooned, hugging Majii for support and crying with joy. *"B'á-ja, ló-poh!"* she sniffled and laughed. *Thank you, father.* The words almost surprised her.

He hugged her in return, his old frame not too fragile for affection. "Teya will teach you what you need to learn. You cannot ride him for the next year or more, but his training must begin soon."

Within the next half hour, the little bay colt was standing on wobbly legs, testing his strength. His coat was a dark auburn, much like Cindra's natural color, and his mane and tail were black, like his hooves and the lower portion of his legs. He was altogether the most beautiful thing Cindra had ever seen, and he belonged to her.

The next week was spent in the horse-fields where she could be close to her little T'ózha. The foal could walk about and follow his mother, nursing when needed; with the supervision of the herdsmen, Cindra was able to pet and nuzzle him, creating a bond between them. The caravan would move on soon and the herd would follow, so the little colt had to be able to keep up.

Cindra was determined to walk with him when possible and keep him safe, and she had even taken to strapping on the *Kos* knife in case a wolf or big cat happened along looking for a snack. Teya told her much of the thoughts and feelings of horses, about their ways of family and how they spoke with their eyes and ears, as well as their voices. She told the girl of all the things a young horse must learn, for they had good memories and would keep their training all their lives. Cindra would teach T'ózha how to wear a blanket in preparation for riding one day, how to have his hooves handled so he would be patient with trimming and shoeing, and how to be groomed. The colt very much liked being groomed, and learned to recognize the bristle brush Cindra carried for the job. He was rambunctious and would caper about at times, but Cindra only laughed and clapped with joy at his play. She took to sleeping in the fields until the caravans were ready to depart on their long journey south.

Teya had decided they would take the King's Road along the western trade route. It passed through Ashenmon, Jathicton, and many smaller villages and towns, finally reaching the city of Pinikal at the edge of the Piniwood. It was a journey of eighty leagues or more; the King's Road was well-kept and as safe as could be managed, and the towns saw many Galindri travelers year-round.

The road also passed through the Highwood Forest, and Cindra longed to see the fabled trees that grew higher than the towers of her home, and were so wide that a dozen or more people could join hands around their trunks. Supposedly one of the great trees had fallen across the road, and a tunnel had been carved in it that a caravan could pass through, and that alone would be worth the trip. There were also stories of elves that still lived in the Highwood, some as old as the trees themselves; other stories told of men with the wings and heads of eagles that now roosted in the abandoned elf tree-city. Some Outlanders believed elves never existed at all, but some said that about the gods too, and they were fools.

She and her Galindri family had visited Pinikal late last spring after the tribal gathering at Woodcourt, but by a different route. Cindra had not yet been disguised, and it was not long after the evil priest's murder plot had been revealed, so Teya had decided they should avoid the northern Wood Road that passed the Highwood Forest. They had instead cut east across country to the King's Road; both roads met at Pinikal, where they camped and gathered the berries for her first coating of color. Now that they would be meeting with the tribes for the summer gathering, there would be much to see and do, and good weather in which to do it. Teya had promised to take her hunting again, when game was plentiful and the family's survival didn't depend on it. Haani was also going to teach her dances that were a part of the summer celebrations, and Cindra was determined to do better than her previous attempts. Dancers wore bangles that jingled as they moved their arms, so Cindra began wearing her gold bracelet that she suspected was responsible for saving her life at sea. She would add to the collection along the way, as she was able, until she jingled appropriately.

On the day of their departure, Cindra gave T'ózha a reassuring hug and patted his mother Le-t'ózha on the neck, walking with Haani behind the caravan so she could keep the foal in sight.

She had wanted to walk with her pony, but one of the herdsmen had ridden up saying, "You must walk ahead of the herd, Majii-Ama. If they become afraid, they will trample you."

She answered, "What about my T'ózha then? Shouldn't he stay with me if it is so dangerous?"

The herdsman laughed and said, "He is far sturdier than you, Majii-Ama! He will not come to harm with the herd."

Cindra had relented and joined the wagons ahead, making do with furtive glances over her shoulder every few dozen steps.

The caravans passed beyond the outer city before noon on their long journey to warmer lands. Cindra kept her eye on T'ózha and fretted when she lost him in the herd, but Haani kept her occupied and calm. As they passed the last of the outlying houses, Cindra turned to take one last look at the capital city and stopped in her tracks, seeing something amiss. Haani stopped as well, thinking the girl was worrying over her pony, but Cindra was looking at the palace where a thin column of smoke could be seen rising from one of the towers.

"What is that?" Haani asked, "I have never seen smoke of that color before." It was purple and shone strangely against the blue sky.

Cindra felt a tingle go down her spine as she looked in dismay at the thin amethyst cloud dispersing in the air. The tolling of a temple bell echoed across the fields, but could barely be heard over the noise of the wagons and horses; the call was soon picked up by other temples and before long, bells rang out all over the city.

"Purple smoke over the palace," Cindra said, her mouth tightening into a line as the noble in her stirred in alarm, "It means the king is dead."

Chapter Eight

Melee and Mud

It was the worst year of Jaron's life. He had left Portshia in shame to begin his two-year exile, heading out of the Low Gate and over the bridge, towards the teahouse and the road where he had taken the Lady Cindra on her first ride out of the city. The trees were showing buds, yet most were bare, with only the hardiest of them showing early leaves. He took the west road towards the Joshian River proper, from which Portshia's canals flowed farther upstream.

There was a strong stone bridge that spanned the Joshian's dark waters, and Jaron paid the toll-keeper a few coppers to cross. The Low Bridge was not really low; it was high enough for a barge or small vessel to pass under, but was named so because it was farther downriver. It was free to cross for knights on the lord's business, but he was not going to compound his shame by pretending he was in good standing. He was dressed as a knight, with his blue beret, blue and gold trimmed tabard, and House Corrina coat of arms, but he did not feel like one at all. His brown hair was neatly bound in a knight's *tipok* knot and his beard was trimmed in the current style, yet he felt bedraggled and out of sorts.

Once across the river, he followed the road to the west until he reached his home village of Wellgate. The device on his shield was the only thing to identify his family, but no one seemed to recognize it if they looked. Heads were kept low and the peasants avoided his eyes, as all peasants should, though he disliked the custom greatly. The last time he had passed through with his father, there had been a gathering to welcome them, but his father visited often and was well known.

He stopped at the village inn and put himself up for the night, making no issue of his family's meager holdings or reputation. He was not in a position to go very far on his own reputation after all.

He woke early and checked his supplies for the journey northward. Wellgate was a crossroad town where the road to the south led to Cordoshome and became the Red Coast Road, and the road to the west turned north through the Shadowood and was known as the Joshian Way. Either path led out of Casselvane Province, but he had no desire to ride by the sea where he might witness Cindra's ships pass or be reminded of her.

The Joshian Way was cut through the middle of the dark woods and roughly followed the river where its tributaries fed the currents on the long passage to the Emerald Sea. The next few weeks of travel on this road promised to be full of gloom and scant sunlight, for the forest canopy grew thick over the road, trying to heal the scar that was slashed through its span so long ago. The leaves came early in the Shadowood, rushing to block out the sun from the creatures below. The dismal setting

155

suited Jaron's mood and the discomfort of his campsites were no more than he deserved, in his thinking. There were few travelers in the late winter and the loneliness was palpable. His ears stung from the chill air and his joints stiffened each morning.

Four days along the road he came to the outskirts of the town of Breega, a pleasant enough community built on a hill above the riverside, with a fortified manor house overlooking the expanse. A high palisade surrounded the town, shielding it with a curtain of deep ashen bark. A large gate could be closed against the threats of the night, but were currently open to allow passage through the town that sat astride the Joshian Way. Despite the pleasant setting and the welcomed reprieve from the murky woodlands, Jaron was loath to stop here because it was the home of House Greenfellow in exile and their *Maurbrik* fighting school. Nevertheless, there were no outlying houses where he might stay, at least none within sight of the road at dusk. He sighed to himself and urged his horse to enter the gates. For a moment he was tempted to cover the device on his shield, but that would be cowardly and he scorned the thought.

The watchman at the gate asked him his name and his business, to which he answered, "I am Sir Jaron of Wellgate, on errantry." There was no need to share the details of his misfortune. "Where is the best place to stay for the night?" he asked.

The watchman answered, "If you're looking for finery, there's little in these parts, sir knight. But the Graybough Inn is the only place for a man of quality to rest; got private rooms, even. It's up the main road on yer right, by the large tree."

Jaron thanked the man with a nod and rode into town as the lamplighters began to move about their tasks. These were men with a covered flame and wicks, not the wizards of Portshia that used arcane power to do menial tasks for exorbitant fees. There was either insufficient money in the town to support the trade, or there were no spirit wells in the area to maintain the verges used for spell casting. To Jaron's understanding of the magical arts, a spirit well was to a wizard what a forge and smithy was to a warrior. He didn't grasp how they used the power there, only that without it they could not make a verge, and without a verge they were no different than anyone else. He had never before faced a wizard in combat, but it seemed that drawing a wand was much like drawing a blade; the fastest were often the victorious.

The Graybough Inn was easy enough to find; the sign was a large painted branch with leaves sticking out over the door, although in the low light it appeared as part of the large tree nearby. The place was small and cozy with a hunter's sense of decorum. Antlers were mounted over the fireplace and the heads of various game beasts leered over the common room. The innkeeper was a wizened old man with a pipe that dangled from his mouth, forming a sag in his lip from its constant presence. It was currently unlit and had not been smoked in a while from the lack of pipe leaf aroma in the air.

"Be needing a room I expect," said the innkeeper without looking, talking around his pipe.

"And stabling for my horse," said Jaron as he slung his shield and saddlebags over his back. He was traveling light but for the mail shirt he wore and the armor pieces packed in the bags. There was enough leather and plate to protect his arms, shins and knees, plus a formed headpiece to guard his face from a slashing blade; it was the most he could manage without a squire to assist him and he had to be self-sufficient. He could never afford a squire at any rate, so it was rare that he traveled with baggage at all.

The innkeeper looked the knight up and down and squinted hard at his face. "You'd be Sir Fedrick's boy, wouldn't you? You're the same about the eyes, but you've got two that work, where he lost the use of one." The man went behind the desk where he looked for a room key in a drawer. "Best hide that shield device if ya plan to walk about in the day."

Jaron was surprised, for he didn't think his father was known in these parts, lest it be by foul reputation spread by the Greenfellows. "You know Sir Fedrick?" he asked, looking at the old man anew.

The innkeeper took out a small iron key and handed it over the desk, "I was in the war with him, knew him when we was but a footman. After the Battle of DuKort he rose in the old count's favor and others fell out of it," he looked about the room as if there were ears listening besides those of the trophies. "My home was here, so I came back. Had to bear all manner of talk from those who knew him only by the tales told by the schoolmaster." He shook his head in disgust. "You'd best be moving on boy, 'afor they find yer in town."

"I don't plan to stay long," he said, taking the key and following the bent old man down a hallway of a dozen doors, "Leaving in the morning, I expect."

"Good. I'll have my boy see to yer horse, and I'll bring a loaf and ale within the hour."

The man showed him into the modest room furnished with a cot and blanket and a low table with an empty candle holder. There was a shuttered window without glass and an iron brazier at the foot of the cot, dusted with ash from former use. Jaron gave the man a copper for his trouble and another for the kind words for his father. He dropped the saddlebags and shield in the corner and placed his father's sword within reach before lying back on the creaky cot.

The room was cold and drafty, and smelled of smoke, but it was better than the chilled, hard ground by the roadside in the gloomy forest. He slept lightly until the innkeeper brought him a tough loaf of bread and a mug of warmed ale for supper, finding himself unable to sleep afterward.

His head was spinning over the secret reasons for coming here, secrets his heart was keeping from his mind. Why did he wander into the den of the enemy after killing their favorite son? Why had he taken the Joshian Way at all? Was being reminded of Lady Cindra really worse than facing death at the hands of the vengeful Greenfellow clan? Maybe he had come here on a secret mission to undo his shame once and for all, to meet the fate he should have met on the day of the festival for the disgrace he brought to the count's house and his own. Maybe he had delivered himself to his own death, trusting the Greenfellows to finish the job that he could not bring his own hand to accomplish.

The guilt had doggedly followed him from the field that day, like a stone hanging about his neck. His friend and mentor, Sir Cord Freekirk, had delivered proof that vindicated Lady Cindra and himself, yet he knew that in their hearts they were guilty of a forbidden love, one that would have gone farther had either of them had their way. The spell upon the roses was just a means of making it public.

To his mind, the plot by Sir Earnold to expose this fact using illicit means was perhaps just and fair in light of the wrong Jaron had done to him. It was another poetic justice that Deliah, Earnold's erstwhile betrothed, had been the one to unwittingly help Greenfellow by providing the roses for the spell. Jaron had stolen Deliah's affections many years ago, leading to the dissolution of the betrothal and a nasty duel. It seemed all of his past misdeeds had returned to punish him. Sleep was not forthcoming and he rolled about on the cot.

There was a whooshing sound outside the window and a pale light shone between the shutters, glowing like embers. Jaron turned at the sound, hand on his sword, ready for an attack from an unknown enemy. A strange bird-call sang out in the evening air just on the other side of the shutters, and Jaron rose cautiously. There was a scratching on the windowsill and the light began to fade slowly as he reached for the latch, sword at the ready. As he pushed the shutters open, there was a fluttering of disturbed feathers and a wash of warmth; the yellow and orange plumage of the ember swallow glowed in the night as the bird avoided the shutters and flew back on the sill, chattering at the inconsiderate man.

"Message," it said in a feminine voice, "for Sir Jaron Dunlorden." The bird was hopping expectantly on the sill. Jaron only blinked at it.

"A message from whom?" He had never received an ember swallow before and had no idea what to say.

The bird blinked back at him, as if taken aback by the foolish question. Was his voice not perfectly pitched and measured? Surely it was. "Lady Cindra Corrina," said the bird in his own voice, and waited lest the man have another question.

Jaron came to his senses and offered the bird the handle of his sword to perch upon, closing the shutters behind him for privacy. "Lady Cindra sent you with a message? For me?"

Gavagul turned his head sideways to look at the man with one of his large black eyes. It was really too much. Ember swallows didn't sit and answer questions, they delivered messages. Correctly.

"Dearest Jaron," he began in a perfect rendition of Cindra's voice and tone, "I regret that I could not see you before you left the city, and I fear we shall never meet again. But I shall always hold you dear as my first love, and I will carry the memories of our time together into the lands of my new home. Should you ever sink into despair, use the remembrance of my love to bear you up, for I shall do the same. Had we more time and fewer obligations, then the world would have been ours to share, and the gods themselves would have envied our happiness. I bid you farewell and send my love, so that it may guide you as a ship that follows a star."

The bird stretched and ruffled his feathers, his task completed.

Jaron sat back in silence, the strangeness of hearing the lady's voice compounding with the emotions of hearing her tender words. He pondered the message and pictured her speaking, her eyes looking up into his. Gavagul fluttered from the sword handle to the table, helping himself to some breadcrumbs, since none were offered as a reward.

She wanted to remember their love fondly then. Not for the shame it had brought to their houses and the scandal it had caused, but for the joy they had felt together, however briefly. It was almost enough to lift him from his gloom; he was in exile for his crime after all, serving a sentence of two years of wandering beyond the bounds of his home province to pay for the indiscretion. He could not clear his conscience or shed his dishonor if he kept such feelings in his heart, pining for that which was forbidden to him, and carrying a torch for a married woman. He had to purge these feelings from his heart, to wipe his mind clean of disgraceful thoughts and desires; he wished he had heeded Sir Cord's advice, and cursed himself for following his emotions into ruin.

He wanted to give the lady a similar message, to return her sweet sentiments, but how could he? To do so would doom him forever, for she would be bearing a torch for him whilst in another man's house, living a lie in matrimony while presuming her love for him was returned from afar. If he looked upon their love with fondness and the dreams of what might have been, then it would not die so long as he lived. Was that what she wanted, to hold his heart prisoner for the love of her? Did she not understand how they had transgressed?

He spent an hour thinking of a suitable response, something that would force her to move on as he knew she must, something that would allow him to break free of his feelings and reclaim a semblance of his pride. He wanted to return as a true and loyal warrior of House Corrina, to be trusted with matters of great import and substance, to serve with honor for his father and his family name. He wanted to look in the eyes of his peers and see the respect he used to see. Greater, even.

He turned to the bird eating his bread and asked it, "Can you deliver a message for me?"

Gavagul perked up and fluffed his feathers. The man was asking foolish questions again. "Who to?" said the bird by way of answer.

"Lady Cindra Corrina," said Jaron. He was waiting for the bird to say whether it could or not, but all it said was "Ready," in a squawking voice, as its black eyes went a bit distant and stared past him.

Jaron cleared his throat, hoping the bird would not convey that as part of the message, "Milady Cindra," he began, keeping things formal, "I wish that things might have been different between us, that I might have been of nobler lineage or greater fortune; as I am, I fear that I am not enough. Our feelings were those of the young and foolish, and we must grow beyond them."

He took a deep breath. "I cannot carry my love for you and still retain my honor as your father's knight, and you cannot carry your love for me and be wed to another more fitting. You have a bright and grand future before you milady, but mine is dim and unknown. I beg you to forget about me, to leave behind the old shame of what could not be, and I shall do my best to put it from my mind also. To live for what cannot be is to not live at all. I hope you understand and forgive me."

He nodded to the bird and said, "That is all," hoping again the firebird would not make that comment part of the message. Could he ask the bird to repeat it and change things if they sounded wrong? Best not to push his luck, he decided.

"Please take that message to Lady Cindra Corrina, who is leaving on a ship for Rokvynnar."

The ember swallow whistled and chirped, fluttering to the floor before the window and looking back at the man. Jaron watched it a moment until realizing that the creature was waiting for him to open the shutters. He rushed to the window and opened it wide as the bird beat its wings and leaped out into the night air, leaving a trail of heat and smoke as it soared above the rooftops and far-off trees. Had he done the right thing? It was a little too late to think about it now. He closed the shutters against the cold night and lay back on his cot, not bothering to undress. He was not going to be in town that long if he could help it.

When he next opened his eyes, the room was alight with the blue of early morning and his fingers were numb with cold. He might have done well to light a fire in the brazier, or at least bundle up with the blanket, but he had been more exhausted than he realized. Groaning as he rose from the cot, he gathered up his things and made ready to leave as soon as he was able. Hopefully the innkeeper or the stable boy was awake to ready his horse while he had a quick bite to eat.

Strangely, he did not feel anxious or afraid of being seen by the wrong eyes, but he intended to continue his journey regardless. He no longer wanted to end his misery here, but to do as he had said in his message to Lady Cindra; he wanted to put his past behind him and return to honor and service. He strapped on his sword belt and took up the shield and saddlebags, making his way to the common room.

The innkeeper was indeed awake and moving about, a curl of smoke coming from his pipe. He did not act surprised to see Sir Jaron up so early, for indeed he was thinking of waking the knight himself if he had slept in. Things were stirring in town and time was growing short.

"Glad you're up sir knight," he said, his morning voice rough and wet. "There's been a man or two from the school, asking about who was staying at the inn."

"Are they always so nosy?" asked Jaron, annoyed at his luck, or the lack of it.

"Seems a firebird messenger was seen coming and going last night, but I expect you know that," he croaked. "Odd enough for these parts, so they wanted to know who might be in residence. I told them it were none of their affair and whoever it was would best be left alone." He went to the door and looked about the street, "My guess is they'll be watching."

Jaron paid with a silver mark and said, "Thank you for that." A friend in this town was more than he had expected. "When will my horse be ready?"

The innkeeper replied, "He's ready now if you are. Had my boy Jack get him ready when I heard you out o' bed." He took the key from the counter and pocketed the silver without comment.

Jaron left the inn and met Jack with his horse. The innkeeper's 'boy' was perhaps older than Jaron and rather large, but had a simple face and foolish grin. "Milurd," he mumbled and bowed his head. Jaron set his gear in place and mounted up, steering his steed towards the north gate out of town.

He looked over the rooftops towards the dome of the temple of Balkon and the tall square tower that overlooked the Greenfellow *Maurbrik* Fighting School. The school grounds were on the main street, but the buildings were set back behind a row of trees. Men in yellow and green tabards stood about under the trees and watched him pass, talking amongst themselves. They were all between eighteen and twenty-five years and looked like capable fighters, carrying the bravado of the town's elite. They all wore black armbands as well, for the news of Sir Earnold's death had traveled fast.

Jaron had not covered his shield, but had hung it on the other side of his mount to face buildings opposite the school. *No need to announce myself*, he thought. He kept his horse at a steady pace.

Before he reached the north gate, a group of men in the colors of the *Maurbrik* School moved to bar his path. They had no weapons drawn and did not look unfriendly, but they seemed intent on knowing his business. It was possible that someone had seen his shield and recognized the device of the brown stag's head against the green field. That standard would surely be known by reputation all over town if the Greenfellows had their way. The men motioned him to stop and the largest of them called out.

"Hail there, sir knight! May we speak with you?"

"It seems you intend to whether I like it or not, else you would not bar my way." Jaron said with annoyance.

The big man raised his hands, "Apologies, we did not mean to be impertinent. It's just that we had word of an honored guest in town, a knight from the south. Perhaps you might be so kind as to honor our school with your presence." There was something a little too sincere in the man's voice, and he was the only one smiling. The man on Jaron's right had moved to get a better look at the shield.

"I doubt I would do your school much honor," he said, as he watched the man examine the shield and nod to the others.

"Still, our master might wish to meet the man who put his son in the ground." He motioned to the watchmen, who closed the north gate, trapping Jaron. "It's not often a Dunlorden pays a visit to our school." They moved in as more came from behind, surrounding him.

The floor was polished by years of training and had seen bloodstains before, but never Jaron's blood until today. He mused on this thought as he received another gentle welcome by way of a kick in the stomach delivered by one of the school's zealous students, doubtless fed on stories of the Great Dunlorden Treachery and the unwarranted fall of Good House Greenfellow. He had to struggle not to take it personally as another student, or perhaps the same one, kicked him to the floor again. He had lost track of who delivered what blow.

There was a shuffling of feet and a murmuring amongst the gathered throng as the master entered the training hall. He was escorted by one of the senior students who gave his arm for support while the frail Waliss Greenfellow made his way to the chair that overlooked the combat floor. Jaron raised his head to watch him as his attackers relented, showing respect to the master as he came to preside over the scene. The old man was bent from age and weak health, if his pallor was any sign; his eyes were sharp however, and his face was pinched in a scowl as he turned to glower at the son of his old rival.

He seated himself on his chair as if he were a lord in judgment, his bent spine giving him the look of a vulture as he leaned forward. The man's hair was once dark but now bore silver streaks; his face was long and drawn with all of the pride that his heritage deserved, and Jaron could find no trace of the coward that had been described in the old tales. The man had deep-set gray eyes, and gray teeth that stood between his lips like the rotting remains of an old forest, tall and crooked.

"So *this* took the life of my son," he spat in a powerful voice that reverberated about the hall, "The last and proudest of my issue, slain by a *farmer!*" His hands shook and balled into fists as he bored his dark eyes into Jaron, seething with hatred. "What *impudence* would bring you to cross into this province, into my home, to flaunt the blood of my family upon your hands? Speak!"

Jaron raised himself on his elbows, determined not to grovel before the man regardless of his current predicament. "With all respect, I was just leaving when your students dragged me here."

"Ah yes, just passing through," the old Greenfellow took on a mocking tone, "On errantry, I suppose. Doing good deeds in the country at large, and bearing this..." he motioned to someone behind Jaron, who stepped forward and presented the master with a sword in an ornate leather scabbard. Jaron bristled as Valdiroth was unsheathed and brandished by the old man like a toy.

"That is not for you to wield," said Jaron as his ire rose. "That is Valdiroth, one of the Corrina Honor Swords."

The old master's eyes flashed with anger. "Whelp! This sword used to be mine to wield, before your wretched birth! Do not seek to lecture me about the honor of House Corrina. As I heard it, my son..." his eyes fell in sorrow before resuming, "...my son fought to preserve that honor which you so predictably sullied. Death was his reward for upholding *Corrina honor*," he sneered as he spoke the words. "Yours, it seems, was to bear this." He held the sword up to the morning light that spilled in through the high window slats, then replaced it in the sheath and laid it across his lap.

Jaron thought to tell him of the plot that had been uncovered, of the enchanted roses and the spell to make him and the Lady Cindra lose their control, of the real intentions of dear Sir Earnold. It would be pointless however, telling such facts to a grieving father. At best it would seem like a desperate lie to save his skin; at worst, a plot to further discredit the Greenfellow name by the lackeys of House Corrina. He kept silent.

Master Greenfellow sat back and sighed, "No answer? You Dunlordens always have an answer for everything, if I remember correctly. Or perhaps your father's gift for quaint peasant wit was not passed on?" He stifled a cough, leering down at the knight. "You will tell me one thing before we deal with you. Why are you here?"

Jaron rose to his knees, thinking that much more would earn him another kick to the floor, "I was banished for the shame I brought to House Corrina, and I chose to leave by the Joshian Way. The road passes through your town, nothing more."

This news seemed to amuse the old master to a small extent as he said, "Banished... perhaps you stole the Honor Sword on your way out? Perhaps if I return it, I will earn some clemency from the dear count, hmm?"

"Perhaps," Jaron said. If the old man sought to gain favor by turning over the sword of a knight his students killed, it would serve him right.

Waliss Greenfellow leaned forward again as if to spear Jaron with his rage. "I do not *need* the clemency of House Corrina and its feeble count! I have learned to do without the good will of the Lord of Casselvane for some time." His eyes seemed to rattle in their sockets as he spoke;

spittle flew from his lips and speckled the polished floorboards.

He handed Valdiroth to his elder student and proclaimed, "Let the blood of the Dunlorden stain this floor and remain forevermore as a reminder to our enemies. Let the shame of House Greenfellow be washed away by the death of farmer Fedrick's lowly seed. Let his father suffer the pain of loss, wither and die." His voice shook at the last and he motioned to the student, who drew the honor sword and approached Jaron, his intentions clear.

There was a sound of doors opening, and footsteps, and a deep voice filled the hall with consternation, "I hope I'm not interrupting anything?" Jaron turned and saw a servant trailing in the wake of a large man in a black robe with red trim. The symbol of a spiked mace was embroidered on his breast and an ornamental mace hung at his belt. The man had a ruddy face and bushy brown hair that seemed to have migrated from his head to his beard, which was dyed red. His eyes were clear and bright, though it was early in the morning for a Balkonitte priest before Massday.

The servant announced with exasperation, "Deacon Rime, of the temple of Balkon. He insisted on entering, master."

The deacon strode forward to stand next to the man with the sword as he examined Sir Jaron kneeling on the floor. "Is this a training exercise then, how to execute a man? Or is this your idea of justice, Master Greenfellow?"

The master motioned for his servant to leave and leveled a stony gaze at the intruding priest. "This man, if you must know, is the murderer of my son. He has been banished for his crime and has delivered himself into my justice. There is no place for you here, unless you wish to give him his last rites and pray for honorable service on the Field of Strife in the hereafter."

The deacon walked around Sir Jaron, studying him. There was no pleading in Jaron's eyes, only grim resolution. "How interesting," said the priest, "One hears so many stories; I recall the messenger from Portshia told of a fair challenge and a duel, and how both fought honorably. Hardly what I would call a murder."

"Nevertheless, he deserves his fate!" Master Greenfellow exclaimed, "My son fought for the honor of the count's daughter, and was killed by this... this lecher! I demand justice!"

"I agree," said the priest, "There are things to answer for, but I hardly think you are fit to judge, considering your family history, which is well known here. If you wish for a trial by combat, I can ordain a formal battle between Sir Jaron and your school's champion." He waved his hand about as if he were making it happen as he spoke, "Or if you wish for a more traditional trial, I can call upon some of my brotherhood to convene a hearing..."

"You cannot interfere in this affair!" raged the old master, "This is a family matter and not a province of the faith."

The deacon smiled as he stood next to Jaron saying, "This is a fighting school, and *our* faith is the province of the warrior class. All who enter here honor Balkon and his teachings, or so I presumed. If this knight is to die, it will be on the field of battle, or at *least* with a sword in his hand. If a crime was committed, a court must decide his fate. He will not be executed by an angry mob."

"How dare you?" shouted the old master as his students stepped forward in resentment.

The deacon cut them off by raising his ornate mace over his head, thundering his voice like a cannon at the assembled throng, "I dare because I am the servant of the gods! They have grown silent, but their teachings remain! Let any who dare the wrath of Balkon come forward," he looked around at the men, who were cowed by his authority, "Let them strike down an unarmed knight of the realm and call it justice! I tell you they will be damned to join the ranks of the Dishonored, to do never-ending battle on Balkon's Field, hacked limb from limb, only to be raised again at the next dawn."

No one stepped forward, so Jaron decided it was time to rise to his feet. His body ached but luckily nothing was broken; he could not have ridden to the next town with a cracked rib or shattered jaw, and this town was no place to recuperate. Still, he was not out of the woods yet, as they said in the cities.

"Now," said the deacon to the crowd, "Do you choose a champion from your ranks to fight a duel?" The men looked at each other, and then expectantly at the master, who shook his head ever so slightly. Some of the students, the wiser ones, seemed relieved, while others were frustrated. This knight had defeated Sir Earnold, who was the best the school had produced and was to be the master upon his father's death, once his duties to the Count of Casselvane ended. No one would have wanted to challenge *him*, so no one stepped forward to challenge his killer. The man holding Valdiroth sheathed it and set the sword upon the floor before Jaron, sensing there would be no beheading today.

The old master stood shakily from his chair and looked the deacon in the eyes, his expression unreadable. "Take this scoundrel from our midst. Let the will of the gods be done here. Let him leave our town and not return." *Maurbrik* Master Waliss Greenfellow strode from the room, anger giving strength to his frail limbs.

The students slowly filed out of the training hall, casting deadly looks at Jaron as they departed. Before long, the knight and the priest were alone.

"Of course, this only means you are safe until you leave town," said the deacon with a jovial voice, "We cannot be everywhere, sir knight." He patted Jaron on the back, making him wince in pain.

"I want to thank you for this," said Jaron, but the deacon raised a hand to stop him.

"It was the innkeeper who alerted me to this predicament, so save your thanks for him," said the priest, leading the way out. "But I suggest you gather your belongings and not dawdle in town overlong."

"It was not in my thoughts," said Jaron as he stretched his back and felt his bruises, "I shall leave immediately; please convey my thanks to the good innkeeper." He took up Valdiroth and buckled it to his belt.

"Certainly, Sir Jaron. Now if you will excuse me, I must arrange a mass for the students of this school, to beg the forgiveness of Balkon for their shameful behavior. That should give you at least a few hours' head start." He smiled with a twinkle in his eye.

"With all respect, deacon," asked Jaron, "why did you intervene? After all, you must live here when I am gone."

"I intervened because the law of Balkon was being thwarted, nothing more. I do not care for the particulars of your families' feuding or who killed whom in a duel. Greater men throw their lives away over lesser matters. We of the church are here to maintain society and uphold the divine laws; besides, there is no room for this madness in a fighting school. Students come here to learn the warrior arts and increase their worth on the battlefield, not to become a vengeful mob."

The deacon opened the door that led out to the yard, where Jaron's chestnut stallion was tied and waiting, gear mostly intact. The shield was defaced and smeared with manure, but that could be dealt with later. Jaron untied the reigns and mounted his horse.

"I am in your debt," he said, as he settled in the saddle, getting ready for a hard ride.

"Give your thanks to Balkon instead," said Deacon Rime as he waved to the knight, "Now be off with you, and watch your back, sir knight."

Jaron rode off at a gallop, daring anyone to get in his way.

It was midday in the forest when he reached a roadside teahouse, permanently shaded by the massive boughs of the dark trees. He stopped long enough to water his horse and himself and then resumed his rapid pace, heading north along the Joshian Way. He had been formulating a plan as he rode, thinking of a way to throw off his pursuers, who were surely behind him. Stopping at the teahouse was a fortunate break, for it allowed him to be seen heading north in a hurry when his real plan was to move in another direction. Once out of sight of the teahouse, he turned west and entered the Shadowood, intending to cut to the southwest and meet the road that ran between Breega and Waynwell. With any luck, he would reach the road before dusk, but it was more likely that he would have to camp in the woods for the night. It was not a pleasant prospect, for he knew of the forest's reputation among those who lived near its borders.

The first hour of travel through the forest was slow and confusing, for many times he found himself within sight of the north road instead of heading away from it; the shadows were throwing off his sense of direction and making it difficult to read the position of the sun. The trees were dense and allowed for few choices of a path; the further he headed into it, the thicker the trees became. Undergrowth was another problem and often his horse stopped, seeing no way to continue. Jaron had to dismount and lead the wary animal for several miles. The terrain was uneven as well; many a clear path led to a drop-off several feet deep, or a wall of mossy rock would block his progress, making him have to find a way around. The shadows were darker than seemed natural, and visibility was poor. The foliage appeared to devour the light around him, hiding the source of ominous sounds in the distance.

The night was miserable and rather sinister; the first Sir Jaron had spent in the woods so far from the road. Campsites by the Joshian Way were open and usually maintained, with a fire-pit and fuel ready, if the last camper had any courtesy. Out in the woods, he had to forage for firewood among the close trees, and there was scarce little just lying on the ground. Being nearly a month until spring, he had expected to find much deadwood about, but the forest seemed to horde its scraps from intruders. He gathered enough for a small fire by nightfall, and it took him close to a half hour to light the stubborn kindling, an effort which seemed excessive. By the time he had a little warm campfire going, it was nearly freezing and his fingers were numb. He slept little and huddled over the flame, his horse staying close as the nightly noises closed in on them.

The distant howling of wolves snapped him out of a stupor late in the night and he kept his sword drawn and at the ready, trusting his horse to warn him if a predator got too close. *With my luck he'll just bolt and trample me*, he thought as he looked up at the worried animal.

"Easy, Vortigras," he said to his chestnut stallion, "It's just a pack of vicious wolves out for blood, nothing to worry about." His words were spoken soothingly and that was all Vortigras cared about.

What sleep he got was full of fitful dreams; wild animals danced across his mind, and the shadows held nameless dread that he could neither escape nor confront. Waking in the early morning light, which was dim but enough to see by, Jaron noticed that the fire had gone out and that his sword, once firmly in his grasp, had been moved to the other side of the fire pit, just out of reach.

Had he tossed it away in his sleep? Was there some nightmare that had made him fling it from his hand? He quickly stood and recovered the blade, feeling unbalanced and wary as the trees groaned in the distance. A wind was blowing over the canopy, making the dark boughs creak and whistle, and chilling his skin as he gathered his gear and readied his horse. The stories of the Shadowood were not undeserved, it seemed. This would be the last night he would stay in its dark embrace if he could help it.

The new day proved better for traveling as he moved towards the border of the dark woods; the gray trees gave way to more open woodlands of oak, beech and maple trees, and the much-welcomed sight of blue sky and sunlight were enjoyed by man and horse alike. The brush was sparse and easy to pass through; there was even some new grass for Vortigras to graze upon, and a spring in a small valley that fed a nearby field. After letting the horse drink his fill and refilling his water-skin, Jaron mounted up and rode to the southwest by his best estimate, avoiding signs of civilization when he could.

By noon of the next day he came upon the Waynwell road, a well-used and unpaved expanse that ran along the northern border of the Shadowood as the forest stretched its arms to the west. It was an easy journey from there as the sun set before him, making him lower his eyes when the trees did not block the fiery rays.

He soon came upon a campsite that was occupied by five riders, all settling in for the evening. They turned to look at him and started shouting, drawing their weapons and moving to block the road, and it was then that Jaron realized they were students of the Greenfellow School; they had been sent along the western road, just in case he might try such a trick. He spurred his horse into action, drawing his sword and charging the enemy's flank. He clashed swords with a man and deflected a blow to his leg as he galloped by, cursing himself for walking right into their grasp. The men quickly mounted and pursued him, spurring their horses hard to catch up.

After the brief self-recrimination, Jaron focused on his current dilemma. If he had an advantage, he was sitting on it. Vortigras was a fine and powerful steed with a superior lineage that traced itself to the desert horses of Rasha and Rakaal and the best Galindri stock. With his family's limited funds, he could have chosen either a suit of second-hand armor, or a good horse upon his knighthood, and he had chosen the latter. Vortigras was a spirited and fast courser, but also had great endurance and willpower, making him superior to the rouncey pack-horses of his pursuers. They might follow him hotly for a time, but eventually their steeds would tire and slow, while Vortigras could maintain his pace for almost half a league or more. Another advantage, if it came to it, was that *Maurbrik* fighters were mostly footmen and fencers; bodyguards and duelists trained in a style to be better at fighting close. *Daerbrik* style was for knights who also fought on horseback with weapon and shield. He was moving too fast to try and unbuckle his shield from where it hung on the saddle, but he had no need of it at the moment. *At least it's clean now,* he thought with a smile.

The last he saw before the light failed was a milestone marking fifty-five miles to the city of Waynwell. His pursuers had indeed fallen back, never getting closer than two horse-lengths of Vortigras's tail. Since they had no bows or throwing weapons, they could do nothing but hurl insults.

He passed several campsites in the night; travelers were resting on the way to or from his destination and gave him strange looks for riding by at a quick pace after sunset. The moon was nearly full and shed light enough to see the road where the trees weren't too thick, and the wind was cold but at his back. His horse had tired and Jaron decided to lead him, ready to get off the road at the first sound of approaching riders.

It was nearly midnight before he made camp a distance from the road, with no fire to attract attention and the trees for shelter from the wind. He was getting low on food and had expected to resupply before now, so he briefly considered his options. He could reach Waynwell by tomorrow night and try to lose the vengeful students in the city, or he could cut northwest across country to try and meet the Kelgar Highway heading north to Kelgerton, where he had intended to arrive before spring. At the rumbling of his stomach and the dryness of his throat, the answer became obvious; he was not meant for wandering in the wilderness. He was a fighter and a man of the city, regardless of his roots.

The next day he set out for Waynwell, intent on getting back to civilization. The road was free of pursuit but he kept looking back nonetheless; he was ready for a fight this time, with his shield on his arm and wearing what armor he had. At least he would look a bit formidable when entering town.

Waynwell was a large, walled city that sat on a prominent rise in the terrain; the expanse covered a long, wide hill that stretched roughly north to south, and beckoned with lights and whitewashed walls of stone. The outer city was sparse and made up of farmland and orchards, while the inner city rose gently up the slope to meet a curtain wall that ran almost a quarter-mile long and protected a large castle. The roofs were thatched instead of tiled with red clay like the buildings of Portshia, and as he got closer he noticed the walls of the houses were painted in different earth colors, block by block; whether for function or fashion, he could not tell.

The guards at the East Gate let him pass without question, though they repeated the warning to stay out of trouble, as they did for everyone. There was no restriction on his weapon, for which he was grateful; it meant that he could defend himself without fumbling with leather knots. Cities of the southern part of the realm were known to be more tolerant of duels of honor, though that was changing. Too many young men were throwing their lives away over petty squabbles and insults, drawing blades and blood rather than settle by more peaceful means. Jaron was sure that if they outlawed dueling in the cities, the combatants would opt to choose another location rather than talk it over.

Before long he had made his way deep into the city and found a decent inn to put himself up for a time. If the Greenfellow students wanted to fight, they would have to do it with a modicum of civility, and not an ambush or assault like in Breega. With any luck, they had not followed him into town and were waiting outside the walls, or had turned around and headed home. He doubted they would want to face their teacher with failure, so he did not relax his guard.

After spending some time in the market area and visiting several merchants, he equipped himself better for extended periods in the wilderness or woodlands. He purchased a cloak with a hood and a wide-brimmed hat for the upcoming days in the warm sun. They also served as a disguise of sorts, allowing him to blend in with pilgrims and other travelers.

The students found him on the fifth day while checking out the local inns. Jaron was spending the afternoon in the common room with a pint of ale and a piece of cheese, passing the time away, when the lot of them walked in, glaring at him from across the room. His sword was handy but not drawn, and he stood as they approached, his hand resting on the hilt.

"Gentlemen, you have come a long way for something that does not concern you." He glared back at each of them in turn.

The largest of the students stepped forward with his hand on his own weapon and said, "What concerns our master and the good name of our school concerns us all, Dunglord." The other men snickered at the remark, shifting their feet to be ready for action.

"Dunglord, yes, very clever," said Jaron as he straightened his back, "If you wish for a fight, I think the innkeeper would want us outdoors. There is a courtyard next to the stable that should do nicely."

The men looked at each other uncertainly, not sure if they should let him leave the room. Another student said, "Let you outside so you can run? Not likely."

Jaron fixed him with a glare. "I will not run. I am tired of running and would prefer to fight the five of you than to spend another night in the woods with no fire. Choose who fights first, or will you take me all together like brave Greenfellow men?"

They almost drew their weapons on the spot, but the panicked innkeeper called from the kitchen for them to take their quarrel outside, and they grudgingly did so.

Jaron led them to the rear door, considering it his

foolish act for the day to turn his back on them as he did. Upon reaching the doorway, he ducked to the side, backing away into the open courtyard by the stable. Valdiroth sang from the scabbard, igniting with a dim blue flame as he held it to the side for the best effect. The students, their own blades drawn, paused at the sight of the magical sword, unsure if they wanted to pit themselves against such a warrior with such a weapon.

The honor sword was one of three enchanted weapons made for House Corrina as a reward for service to the crown, and each had an elemental power. Vyzeroth the Bright-blade and Noviroth the Frostbrand were the other two antique swords, kept in the vaults and used for ceremony. The count's personal guard was given the honor of wielding Valdiroth the Firebrand, which scorched flesh and armor and only ignited for the rightful bearer. Sir Jaron was happy that the sword recognized him as the Corrina champion; whoever had forged it or enchanted it (were they the same person?) had given it some means of knowing for whom to function.

"Having second thoughts about your school's precious reputation?" Jaron taunted, "Maybe you'd prefer me to be disarmed and helpless like before?" He recognized one of the men as having delivered a few blows in the training hall. "You first?" he asked.

The students moved to surround him but no one attacked, wary of the flaming blade. Jaron moved to keep them all in sight, altering his stance slightly as the thrill of the impending combat started to build to dangerous levels. He controlled his breathing, willing himself to wait and be patient as he slowly lowered his guard. *If they are serious, they will move in now*, he thought.

Lulled by the knight's relaxed stance, the closest student rushed in from the left and spun his blade in an arc, bringing it across Jaron's neck. Jaron stepped out of the arc of the blow and brought his own sword up in a sweeping cut under the man's jaw, searing across his jugular. The student fell as the vein cauterized, dropping him into a bloodless heap on the ground.

Jaron moved to defend against the next attack as the student on his far right thrust his sword at the knight's face, while the large man with the clever wit struck at his legs. Jaron ducked low under the thrust as he parried the leg blow, then knocked the thrusting sword away and launched himself at the large student, drawing the flaming blade across the man's abdomen. The big man fell as the wind left his lungs with a ghastly moan, and the three surviving students weighed their chances. The smell of burnt flesh was mingling with the odor of the stables.

Jaron kept his breathing steady as he adjusted his stance, maneuvering to keep the wall of the inn on his left, his opponents in front, and the stables behind. His own horse was there but he could not use him to escape just yet; Vortigras was not saddled or harnessed and the stable door was secured.

Escape did not seem necessary however, as the three men were looking to their fallen fellows with expressions of shock and fear. *They must never have seen real combat before*, Jaron realized. Sparring on the training floor is different than application, where a misstep ends a life. The men were young, but not too young to grasp their own mortality; they started to back down and look to each other for support. Now was the time to fight with words, not weapons, as Sir Cord would say. He almost heard the big knight's deep voice in his head and he smiled.

"You don't have to join them," he said evenly, his calm enhancing their fear, "I advise you to go back to your school and finish training." He watched their eyes, looking for signs of fight or flight; if he spoke too much they might take it as weakness. If he was too bold and threatening, they might be goaded into a fight he did not want. He chose his next words carefully, "There is no honor in dying in the street for an old man's grudge. Let him teach you how to fight, not how to live." He kept his guard up and moved towards the door, motioning to the fallen men with his free hand. "Give them the proper rites and leave this city." He entered the inn and left the door open behind him; his sword extinguished as he sheathed it and went back into the common room. He was not followed inside.

The next day Jaron packed his supplies and saddled his horse, making sure Vortigras was in good condition for travel. The steed had not had his daily grooming routine in a while but was holding up well under the circumstances; Jaron swore to give him an apple once they were in season again. He left the city through the north gate and began his journey into the highlands of central Calilon, staying briefly in the town of Oba and continuing northwest.

Ten days on the Kelgar Highway brought Sir Jaron to the provincial seat at Kelgerton, a sprawling city that spread over many hills and vales, with clusters of wood-framed buildings surrounding temples that dotted the terrain. There was a tall castle with many towers that overlooked the charming countryside; it was the home of Lord Mamfett, one of the more powerful Loyalists that stood with the king against the Dissenter Houses.

Jaron found a stable for his horse and a room at an inn by the Balkonitte Temple, paying the innkeeper for a few months in advance. He then set out along one of the radial streets that spread from the temple towards the renowned Lockvale fencing school. They taught the *Haevrbrik* Style of two-weapon fighting, which was more focused on dueling with a long and short blade. It was good to expand one's horizons, especially when one had as many enemies as Jaron could claim. He reflected on his recent adventures as he had done many times on the road, imagining how he would tell them to Cindra, if she were there to listen.

His thoughts had flown to her many times since leaving Portshia and he wondered what she was doing on her voyage, more importantly, how she had reacted to his message. Had it been cruel to try and end their affections so abruptly, and through a talking bird, no less? He shook his head. There would be so much more for her to experience in her new life.

Her ship had left port two days after he had fought that duel in Waynwell, and she must be a quarter of the way to Rokvynnar by his reckoning, eight days at sea against the wind. There was to be a new moon ten days from now, and he envied her the chance to see the ocean lit only by the brilliant stars from horizon to horizon. Would she think of him under that tranquil mantle of night? Or would she have moved on in her heart, eager for a new beginning? He hoped it was the latter, though he knew he would be thinking of her regardless.

The fighting school was more welcoming than the last he had visited; no one wanted him dead here, which was a marked improvement. The students had never met anyone from as far south as Jaron, so they made jests at his accent, and were good natured and mocking in the manner of young men. Jaron took no offense, remembering the camaraderie he shared with Sir Cord Freekirk and the way their speech would shock those who did not know they were friends. It almost made him feel at home.

The master of the school was a good-natured man that seemed, at first-glance, to be a bit too portly and unconditioned to be on the combat floor, much less teaching others. But Master Lockvale was nimble and quick, and while he did not have the endurance of his students, he could match anyone in short contests. Jaron learned that it was not uncommon for the master to take his students drinking after each week, which explained his girth to some extent.

The months went by and Jaron improved greatly in both mood and skill as he focused on learning the new style, leaving the memories of Lady Cindra to inhabit his dreams and weaker moments only. It was not until the late summer that he heard any news from Portshia.

Merchant caravans made their way north from the spring trade festivals and brought goods and tidings from far off lands into the interior of Calilon. It was during a walk in the market of the Obamitte District that Jaron came across a merchant cadre from his home city. He was admiring some of the new jackets when he asked the garment seller a friendly question.

"What news from Portshia, friend?"

"Ah, I could tell from your speech that you were from the south," the man replied as his face fell, "Dark news mostly, I'm afraid. It was to be a cause for celebration, but it all turned to evil."

Jaron became concerned immediately. "What has happened?

"War, or word of it; war with Minozhia no less, if talk's to be believed." The merchant scratched his chin when gossiping, as was seen often among southerners when speaking of rumors and hearsay.

"Minozhia? Was there an attack?" Jaron was worried now. The Minozhians were not to be trifled with and the count was better at choosing his battles.

"Oh, it's a sad tale," said the merchant as he recited the story once again for a captive audience, "The poor count sent his daughter to be wed to a foreign duke, to secure an alliance, and I might add, a lucrative trade with those insular Rokvynnar types; alas, there was a tragic end to that voyage." He shook his head miserably to enhance the weight of his tale, unaware of the reaction it was causing in his listener. Jaron's nerves had gone from tense to raw in seconds at the mention of the count's daughter, and he was not in the mood for the man's theatrics.

He clapped a hand on the man's shoulder and shook him, "What happened to her? Speak!" The merchant was shocked out of his narrative and stammered to give the facts he knew.

"S-she was waylaid upon the sea by a Minozhian ship, and all was lost!" he said frantically, "They say she was cast overboard and drowned, spared the torments of the beast-men at least. She had the mind to send a firebird with her last message, telling who was to blame. The count sent his fleet to hunt the coast and beyond for vengeance, it's all I know!"

Jaron let his hand drop as he stared unbelievingly into the man's eyes.

"There's a year of mourning declared in Portshia; the black banners fly there now..." the merchant said, seeing the pain in the knight's face as Jaron stumbled away. The merchant knew he had lost a sale, but let it be.

Jaron's world was no longer real. The people around him were phantoms, the sunlight was dim and cold, and the pavement under his feet seemed to rush up to meet his boots as he walked, jarring his legs. She was dead? It could not be. She was young, so young and full of life, with a grand future before her. How could she have fallen to such a fate? Were the gods so uncaring that they would turn their backs on such a one and let her fall to a cruel end at the bottom of the sea? A thought struck him like a blow to the chest; *was this to be the cost of our sin?*

His head was spinning as he walked the streets, plodding towards his room at the inn like a trail horse, unthinking and locked in monotonous routine. He wanted to lie down, to lie down and maybe never get up, not until the world changed back to the way it was. She was dead. It could not be.

The days began to merge together until he could not remember when he had last slept or eaten, when he had gone outside or when he had bathed. He had ceased his training at the school. Once or twice a fellow student had asked about him at the inn, but he would not see them. He spent his days in his room and his evenings in the tavern where there was a fire. He was not so much interested in warmth, for the summers were not overly cool at night, but the fire was something he could stare at and lose himself in, consuming his pain in its crackling heat.

He ordered ale, then another, and that too became a habit as the drink dulled his senses and made him feel light and carefree for a time. Each morning was a lesson in excess and throbbing pain that he refused to learn, and he repeated his mistakes again and again each night. Summer changed to autumn and he marked it only by the dwindling of his funds and the heaviness of his clothing when he ventured outdoors.

It was in the ninth month that Kelgerton saw its first snowfall, early for the year, as it was sure to be a hard winter. The paved streets were slippery and iced over, the unpaved streets were a mixture of slush and mud that made it difficult for carriages and carts, and worse for those daring to walk them. Chattering teeth and curses accompanied the sucking footsteps as striders made their way home to warm fires and dry beds.

Jaron was out of sorts as he walked the street towards the inn, having spent the evening at a tavern down the way. He was becoming a nuisance at his regular spot and decided he would not waste another night there. He had donned his cloak and belted on his sword, noticing he got better service while wearing it, and had consumed a bit more than usual this night, since the tavern maids were unfamiliar with his limits and he was uncaring.

The way home was difficult and tiring; he was sure he would sleep well enough tonight, though the morning would be horrific. The wizard lamps illuminated the muddy streets, casting puddles of yellow light that he used to navigate. He counted the lamps to the inn out of habit, too tired to read street signs or look for landmarks.

There was a man up ahead on the roadside, looking down the way as if he was waiting for a carriage, though his clothing was too poor to suggest it. Jaron squinted at him in the low light, wondering briefly what the man was about, but paying him little mind. He was far too intoxicated to care about other people's problems and the lone man was not his concern.

Not, at least, until the man lunged and knocked him into the nearby alleyway where a second man was waiting. Jaron shouted in drunken anger, flailing his fists in vain as he pitched face-first into the mud. He felt hands rifling his belt and vest for a coin purse, finding it at his waist and cutting it free.

There was a hissing voice saying, "The sword! Get the sword!" and he felt himself liberated of his weapon.

He tried to stop them from pulling it from the sheath but only managed to cut his left hand through his leather glove. He grabbed for the foot of the nearest man and tried to bring him down, but a kick to the head ended the dispute. Jaron lost consciousness as he rolled over on his back, white stars dancing in his vision.

When he awoke it was morning, the pale blue light of dawn painful to his eyes. He was chilled to the bone and caked with mud, his back soaked and numb, and his face half covered with muck. He groaned and tried to stand, but it took all the effort he was able to muster and he spent the next several minutes leaning against the wall of the adjacent building.

After resting and regaining his balance, he staggered out of the alley, unsure what had happened. *I was attacked and robbed, damn it all!* His hand went reflexively to his sword and he fumbled about at the empty scabbard for several seconds before the realization struck him. Valdiroth was gone.

Jaron fell to his knees at the roadside, the pitying gazes of passersby only adding to his disgrace. He could not return home now, not without the Corrina Honor Sword. He had fourteen months until his exile was over, but it might as well be a lifetime. Finally overcome and unable to bear his shame and misery, he collapsed in wracking sobs.

Chapter Nine

Dark Answers

Things had gone well for the little thief. When he returned from his breaker test almost five months ago, bearing a bejeweled dagger with Clavemont's seal on the hilt, Dexer had been struck dumb. Daymi and Cricket were just struck however, after Dexer learned that they had given him the one house to break that no one ever returned from, and they fell out of favor completely. Nixy was elevated in the ranks as a 'made brother' and he said goodbye to his family name of DuQuayne, which he had never shared with the other lads and now never would. It was a reminder of his former life and he was happy to put all that behind him, even the good parts. His time with House Corrina had been bittersweet and the pain of Cindra's death had driven him from the count's service and back to the brotherhood of thieves. They were his family now, and no one would give him any trouble. Not even Black Will.

He had to remind himself that Black Will was dead, that he saw him killed. The night it happened was like a blur. He remembered the breaker test and how he got into Clavemont Manor, but there were things that he had to struggle to recall, as if they buried themselves deep in his mind and he had to dig them up.

Vemlok.

The word hung over his head like an ax ready to fall and he saw the bright blue eyes in pale flesh. It was a vemlok that saved him that night, but saved him for what? Lord Clavemont had not called upon him yet, and that was just fine, but what did the mysterious man want from him?

Vemloks were supposed to be people raised from the grave; he knew that much from stories. Sometimes people came back possessed by the thirsting spirits, horrifying monsters with gray skin and fierce eyes that clawed their way out of the ground and drained the living of blood and vitality. They would leap on their prey like wolves, tearing with their teeth or burying their fingers in the victim, leeching their life away through their hands. They didn't throw dinner parties or live in mansions.

He wanted to ask the other lads about vemloks, maybe even Dexer, but something always stopped him from saying the words. Was it the warning Clavemont had made? He wanted to ask, but he dared not. It wasn't like the man could hear him in the Warren, could he? Whenever he told the stories about breaking Clavemont Manor, he always omitted things like the fact that he saw Clavemont at all. It was as if the lord was a forbidden subject in Nixy's speech, though he thought about him often when he was able to remember.

He thought about the troll too, but he hated those memories; there was nothing pleasant about the troll. The creature had said some horrible things that made little sense, and the vemlok had frightened it away, so

Nixy knew he was safe for now. *Safe from the troll at least*. For all he knew, he could be in much deeper trouble than before.

After he was made a brother, Nixy got to choose his digs, his chores, and his name. 'Digs' were sleeping quarters that, in the Warren, meant he could have a cot off the ground and a space that wasn't so drafty. Chores were the type of work he would do for the Circle, like picking pockets (his favorite) and moving packages, which were small items to be fenced. The name he chose would be his professional name by which he would be known to most of the Circle of Gold; more than a nickname, it was a moniker that could mark a thief's career.

Nixy's new name among the brotherhood was Shadowskipper, a name that would hold his reputation and deeds in a way his own name could not. It was an obvious alias, not real-sounding like some people's fake identities, but he liked the sound of it and Dexer seemed to as well. It had a ring to it and told others that he was the best sneak there was, or would be someday.

It was after the first day of autumn that Dexer sent Nixy on a special package run; it seemed someone had found a buyer for the jeweled dagger, or letter opener as Dexer called it, though it bore Clavemont's family seal which made it difficult to fence. The buyer arranged to pay twelve gold crowns for the item, a fair sum to be sure, and wanted it delivered to a place near the North Wall Walk, near the theater.

The address was given to Nixy to memorize and he went on his way, strolling around the Temple Walk and towards the theater. Before long, he felt a pull to go down a side street, and he followed it despite his job to deliver the dagger, curious to see what was so darned interesting down that way. He turned down street after street, following the feeling that pulled him like the smell of dinner, like the call of a sweet voice.

He soon found himself before the door of a

nondescript apartment in the courtyard of a small block of modest houses. It was a newer part of town but was not kept up like the wealthier neighborhoods; the walls needed plaster and the paint was fading after decades of neglect. There was lush ivy bushes growing unchecked up the walls, making the doorway seem like a living thing that had been cultivated instead of built. He reached for the door to knock, but it opened before he could touch it. All very strange, he thought to himself. The smell of earth and growing things filled his nose and he felt at ease.

The room was simple and elegant, with no decoration but for the paint on the walls. An open window let in the afternoon sun and gave the place an airy breeze. There was a round table in the middle of the room and a man was seated at one end; an empty chair waited across from him and he motioned to Nixy to take it. Nixy sat down, curious to know what had brought him here. Was this the address he had memorized? He had no idea. He looked blankly at the man.

"I am pleased to see you again," said the man in a silky voice, cultured and polite.

Like the snap of a dry twig in his mind, Nixy recognized Lord Clavemont sitting before him, his pale skin and hair shining in the ambient light as his burgundy coat gave the room its sole touch of color. A tingle of danger ran down the boy's spine as he realized he had been led here, relieved of his wits as he wandered right where Clavemont wanted him. He tensed as all of his survival instincts came rushing back in a flood.

"H-hullo milord," Nixy mumbled, unsure how to address a nobleman who was also a horrible monster but looked so nice, if a bit weird. He could not help but look into those pale eyes that were much less piercing today than they were that night in the rain.

"I have arranged to buy back my keepsake, but I trust you will not tell anyone it was me?" he asked, as if it were a question and not a powerful suggestion that nestled deep in the boy's mind. Nixy shook his head. "Good," he said with a smile. His teeth were as white as his lips.

"I have been thinking about you often since our last meeting, and I have many questions for you." Nixy squirmed. "Don't be afraid, child. I mean you no harm." Clavemont said, and Nixy relaxed a little, still getting over the shock of just wandering here so unthinkingly.

"Are you really a... vemlok?" Nixy asked despite himself. It may have been rude to interrupt the nobleman, but Nixy was not in his right mind anyway.

Clavemont smiled, enjoying the audacity of youth. "You heard that from the Guadim, did you? I see you have questions as well... So be it." He touched his fingertips together, elbows on the arms of the chair. "It is only fair, after all."

"Guadim?" Nixy asked, "You mean the troll?" He was going to learn about monsters today, right from the source.

"Ah yes, the troll, the *T'drall*," he intoned. When Nixy just blinked at him he explained, "The Guadim were a very ancient evil from the early days of man, but they are few now." Nixy liked hearing that. *"T'drall* is an old word that meant 'monster.' Only scholars read that old language anymore, for it has not been spoken since long before my time.

"And to answer your question: yes, I am a vemlok." He paused and recollected, "I was born in Aurilon over one thousand and one hundred years ago." Nixy's eyes went wide, his jaw dropped and Clavemont smiled at his reaction. "I know, it amazes me as well sometimes. To my knowledge, I am the oldest one. Though to be specific, the vemlok is the thirsting spirit that gave me this second life; it is not my identity. I am the same man I was in many ways, but that is not true of most who succumb to the thirsting spirits after death."

Nixy had one nagging question, "So, are you really *dead*?" He wasn't sure he wanted an answer, especially from a dead person.

Clavemont tilted his head and said, "If I were dead, I

190

could hardly be so chatty, could I? To be dead is to be a body without spirit. I have two, I think, the vemlok and my own. Perhaps I am more alive than most?" He smiled at the idea. "But like all... hosts, I had to die for the thirsting spirit to take me. Think of it as a second birth."

"Do they all look like you? I mean, are they all so... pale?" Nixy didn't know if it was a touchy subject, but he had to know. It would help to know who to avoid.

Clavemont laughed and looked at his hands, white and hairless like those of a statue. "Never have I seen another who looked as I do, for though many are pale, they are not unnaturally so. The unfortunate ones are more ghastly and corpse-like, and they don't last very long in polite society."

He grinned, "My condition was strangely convenient as it turned out, though it was the curse of my family for many generations. I was born an albino, like many in my line. The sun hurt my eyes, burned my skin and relegated me to a life indoors. Later, after I... died," Nixy flinched at the comment, "the vemlok that took me could not withstand the sunlight, not for many centuries." He looked out the window at the street beyond, the rays of the sun casting shadows on the walls. "No one noticed when I took to living by night and hiding from the day. Everything was already in place. Perhaps that was why I have lived so long, in part."

"So those pictures in the house, who are they?" Nixy regretted the question as soon as he spoke it, for it was a reminder of the crime that had put him in this situation.

"They are my portraits, for I have portrayed many generations of my family. Splendid, are they not? I painted most of them myself." He smiled. "You know, only my household staff is aware of what you now know," he leaned forward and Nixy sank back in his chair a bit, "I only reveal myself to those on whom I feed, but with you it is different. I have touched your blood, that night on the cathedral, and I hope to have the strength to never do so again."

Nixy was shaken as he remembered the man's warm touch against his cheek, the way he had reacted afterward. Clavemont had taken blood through his skin! The vemlok had fed on him!

Nixy stammered, "Y-y-you *don't* want to f-feed on me then?" This was good, wasn't it?

"Oh, but I *do*," said the pale lord, "I do, but I shall not. The last time..." His eyes went distant and his face became drawn. Finally he straightened and sighed, "I will not let it happen again, let us leave it at that. Now I have questions for you, child. It has been liberating to share some of my past with you, but now I must know about yours."

Nixy could not imagine what this thousand-year-old, blood drinking, monster nobleman might want to know about him, for he was just a farm boy of eleven years. "What do you wanna know?" he whispered, almost afraid of the questions.

"Tell me of your parents," he said. Nixy blinked. Was that all?

"Well," he began, "my dad lives near Syngmore and my mother... she died when I was born."

Clavemont waited for more, but the story seemed complete. He prodded for details. "What were their names?"

"Dad's called Mathen DuQuayne," He realized with shock that he had just used his family name, just blurted it out. Had he put his father in danger? Regardless, he was compelled to continue. "My mom was named Kirana," he said, adding quickly, "She was an orphan and she died when I was born."

Clavemont thought quietly for a moment and changed the subject; "Tell me how you disabled the alarm spells in my house. There was one on the cellar door and one at the study."

Nixy remembered this, for it was a proud moment. "Oh, I felt something strange about the door and I didn't know what to do, so I just wished to be safe; I said a little prayer and wanted to not get caught, and I felt the danger go away." He sat up and smiled.

Clavemont was surprised, "That is all?"

"Yup!" said the boy happily. He thought himself very clever for figuring out the trick.

Clavemont looked at him shrewdly, "Have you ever been around magic wards before? Have you learned of wizardry from someone?" The boy shook his head and Clavemont pressed, "Has anything ever happened that you could not explain?"

Nixy could think of dozens of things over the last several months that defied explanation, including how he arrived at this meeting. He thought for a few moments and said, "I was sure you saw me that night in the manor house, at the top of the stairs," Clavemont looked puzzled, "When the lightning flashed I was right there, but you laughed and ignored me."

The pale man's eyes went wide as he remembered the night in detail, saying, "You were *there*, at the top of the spiral stairs?" Nixy nodded innocently. Clavemont declared, "I thought I was seeing things in the storm light, for I saw only a shade in the corner, though I can see perfectly well in the dark." He clapped his hands in delight. "Marvelous."

Nixy was confused. "You mean you *didn't* see me?"

"I saw only a shade, a ghostly figure. There are many in this city. I did not see a young boy in my house. If I had, you would not have left alive. As it was, it was only the interference of the demnox that gave me pause. I had to learn why he violated my sanctum to reach you." He touched his chin thoughtfully, "The Guadim said he needed you for the war..."

Nixy didn't like the sound of that. "What war?"

"The one that is coming, I imagine." Clavemont said, "The Guadim have been trying to undo the world of man since man awakened. The last time they stirred a war, it was known as the Time of Chaos, when my... second life began. What the next war will accomplish, I dare not presume."

"But why do they want me?" Nixy whined. "Talon Finnael couldn't tell me either."

"Ah, the wizard has spoken to you. I suppose it was because the Lady Cindra was involved, gods keep her. You walk in interesting company, child." Clavemont seemed a little uncomfortable as he continued, "This I can tell you, for I have an insight the wizard does not: your parentage is not what you think. You have ancestry more noble than most now living, blood more powerful than I have ever... felt..." He folded his fingers together tightly and his eyes seemed brighter as he spoke; "Now I think you should leave. Keep this to yourself, if you please. Leave the item on the table by the door and take the money pouch there, and be on your way. Forget this place, this room."

Nixy got up quickly and did as he was instructed, uneasy about turning his back on the man all of a sudden. He left the dagger and took up the pouch, and the next thing he knew, he was strolling along the Temple Walk back towards the Warren. The afternoon sun was warm against his back, but the trees shaded him; his feet were light and his mood was happy. His chores were done and he had the money and Dexer would be pleased. He hummed a cheerful tune as he walked, wondering at the strange worry tickling the back of his mind; it was almost like he forgot something somewhere.

Ah well. He'd figure it out sooner or later.

———

Trade Guild chairman Maron Theenix and his wife Madred sat across from Julen Gordon and his wife Lemorea in the carriage. The nervous, balding man and his pinch-faced wife had quite grudgingly agreed to share the ride with the talkative pair, for they also claimed to have business at DuShonmaer, the manor house of Kobus DuChat. It was likely they were simply wheedling their way into his presence like they were known to do in other social circles. The last Maron remembered of the Gordons was at the Lady Cindra's birthday celebration nearly a year ago, where they had both made an impression, especially on Madred, who spoke with great disdain about their fellow commoners. Now Madred was openly scowling at the couple as they prattled on about Julen's most recent travels and business dealings. It was simply to be endured.

"Then of course, in the early spring, I must make for a conference in Pinikal, where I will be meeting with many colleagues from many different provinces. There is talk of a new tax along the King's Road for trade caravans of over a certain number..." Julen Gordon went on as if everyone was interested.

Madred decided to deflate the man if she could and said, "You must have lost a small fortune when the count's alliance fell through with the Rokvynnar. I understand you invested heavily in shipping contracts?" She gave him a wicked smile that, to her mind, was disguised as sympathetic.

Julen was undaunted. "Ah, sadly yes. But I hear the count is proposing a new treaty, so all may not be lost! My other investors and I have great hopes for renewed relations."

Maron perked up. "Really? He thinks the alliance can continue without a marriage? I doubt it will stand." Madred glanced at her husband and raised an eyebrow.

Lemorea Gordon chimed in to support her husband, "Oh, there is talk, much talk. Why, I heard he is sending envoys to discuss the mutual Minozhian problem with that Rokvynnar duke. After all, it was *their* ship that was attacked. The count's poor daughter was only a passenger."

Madred sniffed at the idea that this woman had news she herself had not heard. Was not her husband Maron the leader of the Trade Guild council? She chose to look out the window and scowl, pretending to ignore the

Gordons.

Maron leaned in a bit and said, "Might there be room for another investor in this little scheme? That is, if you were not hit too hard by the loss." He thought to himself, *There might be a way to work this to our advantage without taking the bulk of the risk.*

Julen and Lemorea looked at each other and smiled, "Possibly," said Julen, scratching his chin, "But you sit on the guild council; is that not an unfair advantage? After all, the guild sets the prices and tolls for all incoming goods..."

Maron lowered his voice, though no one outside the carriage could hear, "My involvement need not be known. I could be a silent partner. Besides, who doesn't want to have someone on the inside?" He winked at Julen and the merchant smiled as Lemorea gripped his elbow in approval. Madred, still looking out the window, allowed a sly smile and said nothing. *Fools*, she thought, *so easily manipulated.*

They arrived at DuShonmaer and the couples climbed out of the carriage; Julen offered to pay the driver, much to the appreciation of Master Theenix, and to a lesser degree, his wife. The couples announced themselves at the gate and the servants showed the Gordons to a separate waiting room, while ushering Maron and Madred towards the study of Kobus DuChat. Maron Theenix was happy to have gotten an upper hand so easily, and had much to tell their host. His wife sniffed at the Gordons as they were led away and chuckled to her husband.

"The count is sending envoys and we are positioned to act. That was quite competent, dear husband, even for you." She put on her best smile as they were led into DuChat's study.

Julen and Lemorea Gordon sat quietly in the waiting room where they were served drinks by a pretentious-looking butler. They thanked him loudly and watched him depart, then Julen leaned over and spoke to his wife in a low voice, "That might prove useful," he said, "and I have an idea on how to spend his investment." He folded his arms in thought.

Lemorea nodded, "I hope it does not involve our horned friends again. I do not trust them."

Julen replied, "They came through for us the last time; the Corrina bitch is dead."

"Last time you met with them you were almost killed in an ambush, Ghethas." she said.

"That was just a filthy brownie hunting party. I can handle the Minozhians again if we need to. What about this new alliance with Rokvynnar?"

"It might work to our advantage if they align against the bull-men, but all we need do is delay until next spring. Our agents in Highseat cannot be rushed," she said.

"And the Dark Heart?" asked Ghethas, priest of Llomaak the Countless Lord.

"It shall be delivered, the Mad One promised. He only waits for the chosen scion and he will turn it over to us," answered Maveezh, priestess of Llomaak.

Ghethas frowned, "Why do we trust his judgment on the matter? Should we not choose our own vessel for the Divine Blood? After all, the Mad One is... well, mad."

Maveezh shook her head, "He claims to have knowledge that will help us, but he will only say when the time is right." She stopped as a servant walked past and waited until he was out of sight before continuing. "I do not like it either, but the High Priest trusts him for some reason."

That was enough to quell any argument from Ghethas for the moment. The High Priest was the authority in this part of the world and rightly so, for he was powerful and cunning. Ghethas decided to brood in silence and his wife did the same.

After a half hour, the head servant came to collect them into DuChat's study. Master Theenix and his wife were being shown out, and the Gordons gave them a cheerful goodbye as they passed them in the hall. Once they entered the High Priest's study, they donned their bestial ceremonial masks in case they were disturbed. Disguise was traditional for meetings of the faithful, and served to intimidate outsiders. The High Priest known publicly as Kobus DuChat did not wear such a mask, for as he once told his loyal subordinates, his face was not his own.

Chapter Ten

New Leaves

Jaron was set on revenge as he walked from one end of the city to the other, trying to learn where someone might sell a stolen sword. The thieves could not know the significance of Valdiroth, but it was obviously well-made and bejeweled, inscribed with Celvestrian runes that were the language of magic. If they had half a brain between them, they would realize that the weapon was worth a prince's ransom. Indeed such weapons had been used to ransom nobility in the past, though the Corrina family weapons had never fallen under such times as this before. *All because of me*, he thought.

There were many blacksmiths and weapon sellers in the sprawling city, though none had purchased Valdiroth. Jaron had a stroke of luck when he learned that a dozen or more shops in the Balkonitte district had seen the sword and refused to buy the clearly stolen weapon, though one merchant had tried. He had asked many questions for which the men had no answer; then the shopkeeper had asked how an enchanted blade came into their possession. Once the sellers learned it was magical, they left and never returned.

Jaron spent a week more in Kelgerton searching for the thieves; he came to the conclusion that they were either lying low or had used the coin in his purse to move on, possibly to sell the sword in another town. After giving an explanation and apology to his former master and fellow students, he bade farewell to the Lockvale School, readied his horse, and rode out of the city.

There was only one road of significance and it led either southeast to Oba, the way he had come, or west to the town of Aldrig, the home of the central Mystic College. Aldrig was the obvious choice for someone looking to sell a magical weapon, or at least he hoped that would be the thinking of the thieves.

The Mystic College had originated in Celvestria, where the science of wizardry began, then spread with the Norsican Exodus to the new land of Gartetha. The land was blessed with an abundance of spirit wells so the study of the art had flourished, and the recognized center of learning was Aldrig.

The road marker told of a sixty-mile journey to the town, which would take three or four days by horse but more on foot. If the men were so poor that they took to rolling drunks, then they might not be able to afford a horse. Nevertheless, Jaron could not take much for granted and had to assume that the thieves had a good head start on him. He made a brisk pace, as quickly as Vortigras could manage without tiring too easily. The horse had forgiven him the neglected company rather quickly, much to Jaron's relief.

The highway was well kept, but the early snows made for slow going, and a disgruntled horse was not something he needed. Thankfully the mud was not thick and the ground was becoming harder with the early frost.

There were little villages spaced about a day apart, making for convenient places to rest for the night. Teahouses often doubled as lodges for a small number of travelers, offering sleeping space on the tables or floors. Jaron asked about two men carrying a finely-made sword, for he had no other description, and was pleased to learn that there had indeed been two brothers that looked to be farmers, one of whom had a fine sword wrapped in a cloak. They were just a few days ahead, having brandished the weapon at one teahouse when another traveler took too much interest in their business. *Valdak must be blessing my quest*, Jaron thought, *Justice and revenge will find them.*

Three days' hard travel on the highway led him to Aldrig, though he had seen the high towers from almost half a day away. There were at least thirty towers about the town, many of differing sizes, shapes and styles. Some were simple shell keeps or freestanding square towers, unanchored by walls. Others were built with magical assistance; their sizes and shapes defying the skills of the most prodigious of stonemasons. There were passages between buildings that resembled gatehouses, but no external walls or defenses existed. It was as if the wizards had nothing to be afraid of, and this was likely so, for no one had dared try to take Aldrig in any war.

The town sat upon either one large spirit well, or many smaller ones clustered together, making it easier and safer for the wizards there to cast spells. Someone had explained to him once that the magical energy of spirit wells flowed upward from the ground, making towers best suited to utilize the resource. It also made for an impressive edifice that spoke of power, influence and pride.

The Mystic College took up most of the center of town, with the outlying buildings housing the people who lived and worked to keep the institution flourishing. Artisans, scholars, craftsmen and farmers were all involved in making the town what it was; the wizards were only what it was known for. As for authority, there was no lord in charge of Aldrig. A council of academics and guildsmen made up the governing body and defended their territory, mostly by the power of their reputation, supplemented with mercenary soldiers when needed. It was an arrangement much like the one enjoyed by many religious centers, which could claim to answer first to the gods, then to earthly rule.

Jaron made inquiries in town that yielded the same results: the two men had come through and tried to sell the fine weapon, even lowering their asking price and claiming it to be magical, which many with training had confirmed. It was to no avail however, for the sword was not a mere curiosity or unclaimed treasure. It bore the markings of the royal forge and heraldic symbols that identified its ownership. Also, its glyphs indicated that the blade's power was limited to a specific person. The men had left town before the proper inquiries could be made, for they would surely have been detained for theft. The problem was that no one saw which direction they fled, and there were three roads out of Aldrig.

Jaron thanked the merchants who had refused the thieves, and asked if there was anyone who might be able to help him find the men. He was directed to the Tower of Divining, one of the smaller buildings near the center of town.

The entry to the tower was an oaken door with a large, iron knocker in the form of a dragon claw clutching a lidless eye. A young man who wore the deep blue robes of an initiate answered the door, the twin tails of his yellow cap hanging to the right of his head. He looked at the knight with questioning eyes.

"Greetings," Jaron said, "I am Sir Jaron Dunlorden, and I am looking for the master of this tower." He held his beret in hand and hoped he still looked the part of a knight after the last few months of hard living and neglected hygiene. The boy bade him wait and went to ask for him.

He came back to the door moments later and let the knight inside, leading him up a spiral stairway to speak with the master of the tower. The lowest floor was a simple anteroom with hooks on the wall for cloaks, and shelves for snow boots once winter set in for true. There was also a ledger of some kind and a small desk, probably where the boy had been seated. Closed doors accessed the upper rooms, and voices could be heard behind them, giving lectures. Jaron tried to feel some sort of magical aura about the place, but could not detect any difference. What did magic feel like anyway?

At the top of the tower was a door marked with symbols, some of which were in Calilesh. It read: *School of Divining and Insight, Professor Robben Thortensban.* Jaron tried to straighten his hair, for he had not anticipated having to make a good impression on his quest for justice and revenge. The boy knocked and opened the door, admitting him into the circular office.

Seated at a desk, surrounded by shelves full of scrolls and bound volumes, was a man of late age with long gray hair bound by a single band, and a flowing beard that fell below the desk. He wore a pair of glass lenses perched upon the bridge of his nose with a wire frame, presumably some sort of tool for his chosen study of second sight. The old wizard wore a black velvet robe with purple trim that marked him as a professor, and a twin-tailed indigo cap set to the left. A carved wooden dweedragon sat on the desk, next to a scrying crystal which rested on a wooden mount.

Jaron stepped forward and smiled nervously, "I suppose you know why I'm here..." It was meant to be a joke, but the man was not laughing and only stared.

Jaron cleared his throat, "Apologies professor, I am Sir Jaron Dunlorden, knight of Casselvane. I have come looking for information about a stolen sword that passed through this town not a few days back." He rotated his beret in his hands as he waited for some sign of helpfulness.

The old wizard spoke, "Pleased to meet you, Sir Jaron, knight of Casselvane. I am Professor Thortensban, Arch Mage and head of the School of Divining and Insight. I expect you require my help to locate this stolen sword?" The professor sounded bored.

"Please," said the knight, "It is the Corrina Honor Sword, Valdiroth, sword of flame. It was in my keeping but was taken from me." Jaron still saw no interest in the old man's eyes.

The professor looked at him over the glass lenses, "Are you prepared to compensate the school for my efforts, Sir Jaron?" He folded his hands on the table.

Jaron was taken aback, for he had no more than a few coins to his name and his need was a matter of great importance. "What... kind of compensation professor?"

The wizard looked at Jaron as if he were a slow student and said with an instructor's air, "Divination, indeed all magic, is both difficult and taxing. It is not to be used on request, or as an act of good will. Those who study the mysteries of the Art are like any other tradesman, entitled to fair compensation for their efforts. Have you adequate funds to cover the spell you require?"

Jaron was about to ask after the price, but the look the professor gave him said much. In some situations, if one must ask the price, one probably cannot afford it. His temper flared for a moment as the shame colored his face, but he had little choice in the matter. He could not force or threaten the man to assist him, and it was likely that all within this town held the same view on payment. As a man of honor and duty, Jaron looked down on the idea of not lifting a finger without the promise of coin; his honor was coin enough. As he calmed himself and gathered his wits, for they were nearly at an end, he formed an idea.

"What manner of service can I render that would meet the amount for the spell?" He asked with all the dignity he could muster, disheveled and desperate though he was.

The professor blinked at him, not expecting this turn. "Do you mean to say you will work for the casting? We have no use for a fighting man here, not at this time."

"Another task then," Jaron said, "Whatever manner of work that is needed, it is a big school after all."

The wizard looked shrewdly at him and considered. "I presume, that since you are in pursuit of this blade, you will want the spell first and the payment to follow upon your successful return?"

Jaron said, "I need to retrieve the sword as soon as possible, and I am close behind the thieves. I give you my solemn oath that I shall return to work off my debt; give me an amount of time and a series of duties, and I shall fulfill them."

The professor smiled and said, "There are those of my colleagues who would call me a fool for entertaining the idea, but despite your appearance, you have a certain quality about you. I will find this weapon, though I cannot say if you will successfully retrieve it." He moved the scrying crystal to the middle of the desk, "Now, about the price..."

Jaron followed the western road that ran north around the Piniwood Forest towards the town of Eyorone. It was not the route he would have guessed, for it moved into the foothills of Mount Piniwen as it curved south, making passage difficult on foot. This was fortunate because it meant he could catch his prey faster. He urged Vortigras onward as he scanned the horizon for two specks walking with a bundle.

He passed a few weary travelers on the way to Aldrig who informed him that indeed, the men had been seen on the road and were not more than a day ahead. His anger grew as he rode on, eager to make them pay for the trouble they had put him through and the shame they had heaped on him. He began to picture in his mind what form his revenge would take. The men deserved death for their crime, and a cruel part of him entertained thoughts unbecoming to a righteous man, yet they helped to smother his shame. The men had stolen far more than a sword from him, they had taken his honor and humiliated him, and he would make them pay in kind.

It was that very evening that he caught up to them, just as the wizard had told him he would. They were camping off the road in the trees, their fire giving them away. Jaron brought his horse into the forest and tied him to a tree, then drew a dagger and stalked into the woods towards the light. He approached slowly, watching his steps in the deepening shadows of night, grateful for the damp weather that softened the fallen leaves.

He could hear their voices and smell the cooking of a meager meal. Valdiroth was leaning against a tree on the far side of the fire, its polished blade gleaming in the flickering light and drawing Jaron's eager gaze. Finally, after an agonizingly slow approach, it was within his grasp again. All he had to do was take it and bring justice upon those who had stolen it.

"Not one!" said the younger man, who was in his late teens and had the look of a farmer who had worked all his life, "Not one person wants it! That thing is the most valuable bit o' metal we've ever laid eyes on, and we can't get rid of it."

The other one, probably in his mid-twenties but looking much older, shook his head. "I was for certain the wizards would buy it, magic like it is." He held his head in his hands, "That could feed us ten years, surely." He glanced at the blade as if it were taunting him.

"How much of the purse is left?" said the young one. He was poking the roasting critter with a stick, his eyes hollow and hungry.

"There's enough to cover the family's debts, maybe more. Don't matter much if we keep moving, trying to unload this sword, we get farther and farther away every day. It's getting on winter early and we might get snowed in before we get back."

The young one looked up at him with despair in his face. "We get snowed in and we're all as good as dead. The girls can't provide for themselves yet, and mother..." He threw another stick in the fire with finality.

Jaron had heard enough. It was clear that these men were desperate, but that did not excuse them. He was going to take advantage of their low morale to surprise them and get his sword back. He dashed out of the shadows and leaped over the fire, startling the brothers as they fell backward. He grabbed up the sword and spun on the closest brother, holding the blade to the young man's throat as the older man scrambled away.

"No! Please!" cried the young man, his eyes wide in terror.

The older man spun and saw his brother at the mercy of the intruder as recognition dawned on him. He staggered forward and fell to his knees saying, "Please, don't kill Paddy! He was only doing what I told him! Please sir, have pity sir!"

Paddy recognized Jaron and his blood ran cold. "He found us Renny, you said he wouldn't, but he found us... please, please, please..." He began to sob with fear.

Jaron looked down at the young man; Paddy looked to be Jaron's elder, but that could be owed to a much harsher life. His brother Renny knelt there, frozen in fear with his hands out, pleading. The honor sword was cold in his hand, though his hate burned bright.

He thought of all that had led him to this point; the banishment, the news of Cindra's death, the months of drink and wallowing in self-pity, the sorrow and misery that he could not overcome, that he *would not* overcome because it was easier than moving on.

He had taken neither his own advice nor Cindra's message to heart. He was holding too tightly to her memory, not to the simple happiness and joy of their time together, but to the shambles it became. It had led him to lose his sense of self and his honor, and these men had been there only when he was at his lowest. Yet these wretches were lower than he, poor and desperate in a way that a simple twist of fate had spared him.

Jaron took a step back and raised the sword from the young man's throat as Renny stumbled in to help his brother to his feet. They stood uncertainly as Jaron glared at them, not sure if they should run or if the knight was playing at some kind of game.

Finally Jaron spoke, "When you took this from me, I had no honor to stain; I had done that myself. Now I have recovered Valdiroth..." he beheld the blade and it warmed, bursting into blue flame that danced along its length, making the men recoil. "...and I have a new chance to recover my honor. I should thank you for that."

He sheathed both the dagger and Valdiroth, extinguishing the flame. "Keep what you took from my coin purse. I will earn it back. Steal no more, for your next victim may put you to the sword." He turned and walked back into the forest towards his horse and the long journey back to himself. The brothers could only weep for their good fortune, for they were still alive, though they should not be.

Jaron brought Valdiroth back to the town of Aldrig and placed it in the keeping of Professor Thortensban, who was not as surprised as his fellows at the college. After the care of Vortigras was seen to (including the apple he had promised him, plus interest) Jaron set to work. The list of tasks was extensive but not beyond his abilities, and it rather reminded him of his days as a squire. *Appropriate, for I am training myself again*, he thought.

He took duties cleaning stables, carrying and chopping firewood, scrubbing and cleaning about the tower of divination, even darning torn robes. Through it all he neither complained nor looked down upon any task, for Valdiroth was safely returned and his honor was on the mend. The professors were quite taken by his spirit and humility, a trait unseen in most knights and mercenary warriors. Jaron maintained a sense of humor through it all, making jokes at his own expense as he toiled in their service.

Many of the students became friendly with him, seeing the young knight as a curiosity and pressing him for stories of his adventures, which an academic, were compelling and moving. He had always imagined the study of magic to be one of the more diverting of pursuits, but he was puzzled at how the apprentice wizards found it to be mundane at times. *It must be thus with all studies*, he thought, *spend enough time with the fantastic and it becomes ordinary.*

Jaron stayed in Aldrig into the winter, after three months' worth of duties in service to the school. Professor Thortensban was more than happy to return the sword to Jaron, saying, "You, sir knight, are a credit to your profession. I know of no other who would have kept his word so faithfully and willingly."

Jaron was pleased but a little concerned, "Thank you, professor, but I hope that is not so. Surely there are other knights with similar virtues?"

Thortensban shook his head and lamented, "Alas, no. Those few wandering knights that seek the aid of the college are full of their own privilege and self-importance, demanding rather than asking." He sighed, "Some arrangement is always made, though it may seem more like haggling in the street for a sausage, than an exchange for valuable services. None, and I mean no disrespect by it, mind you, none would have offered to *work* in exchange for a spell such as you requested."

Jaron thought on that a moment. He likely owed his agreeable nature to his relatively poor upbringing. He had never felt the sense of privilege that came with wealth and family titles.

"I am sorry to hear it," he said, "But it was well worth the cost. This sword is a precious heirloom of the house I serve, and it is the greatest honor to bear it." He patted

Valdiroth reassuringly at his hip.

The professor smiled, "We of the Mystic College have been honored by your presence here, and I welcome you to return to us again in friendship, so that we might offer our hospitality."

"I would be pleased to do so, though I know not when that might be," Jaron said, "It is my hope to return to my home in the south after next winter."

"Ah well, I wish you luck with your journey." Thortensban scratched his beard. "I cannot imagine your lord would long wish for your absence, regardless of the circumstances of your banishment." The subject had come up once or twice, and Jaron wondered how much the diviner had learned through his own faculties. Surely it was more than he let on.

"If I may trouble you for one last favor," said the professor, "There is a group of students who must return home for the winter months. It is a two-day journey to the village of Gorshed, and if you are so inclined to escort them, I think it might earn you the goodwill of the townsfolk, that is, if you are heading in that direction."

"That I will do," Jaron said, "My wanderings have been rather lonely, with only my horse for company, fine conversationalist though he may be."

"Excellent!" proclaimed the professor, clapping the knight on the shoulder, "I shall make the arrangements..."

It was a fine, crisp morning when the knight and his charges set out upon the journey south. The early snow had made the roads impassable to carriages, so a sled driver and team of horses were employed to take the five lads to their village. The boys ranged in age from thirteen to sixteen years, the age of a squire's early martial training. Jaron was swinging a sword by the age of twelve, but most of these lads looked too scrawny to heft one.

Though they came from a farming community, their

parents were wealthy enough to send them to the college, so it was unlikely that they had spent their childhoods in manual labor. As he later learned, Gorshed was known in the region for its wool and textiles, many becoming rich by way of the trade routes.

The boys were friendly enough with Jaron, many having spoken to him during his time in servitude. The lanky Ryken Gaddisen, the eldest, was the most talkative. Jaron knew the other boys only by their surnames or nicknames, which were how the lads addressed each other. *Not unlike a fighting school*, thought Jaron. There was dark-haired Mavaard, tow-headed Dungrave, and the younger lads 'Woolly' and 'Jester'. Woolly, it was explained, was fourteen and already had an excess of body hair, owing in part to his mother being a sheep, as the joke went. Jester was, well, a jester. The young lad had a remarkable sense of humor and the ability to mock like no one Jaron had met. *If I only had such a talent for my battle of wits with Sir Cord*, he thought. The elder knight always got the last word. Greaves, the sled driver, was a gray grump of a man who ignored the lads as best he could.

"My uncle's a member of the Portshia Casting Guild," Ryken Gaddisen was saying with pride, "He's the second most successful Gaddisen to ever come out of Alva province, next to old Uncle Dram in Rickshome-on-Joshian. I intend to follow in their footsteps one day."

Jaron nodded, the talk of Portshia making him uneasy. "Perhaps he could sponsor you, or take you as an apprentice?" He really didn't know how such things worked among wizards, but in most professions it was all about whom you knew; family above all.

"That's more likely than you think," Ryken remarked, "Uncle Brom's son Filbert isn't *interested* in the family trade." He said it with scorn, making the other lads in the sled glance at him.

"Not interested in shearing sheep?" asked Jester. The other boys laughed despite themselves.

"Don't be thick," said Ryken, "Uncle Brom hasn't been near a farm since he was your age." Turning back to Jaron, he explained, "Filbert wants to be a *sell-sword*. Got his head full of all kinds of nonsense. He thinks a fighting school will take him."

Jaron was all too familiar with the sentiment to be offended. Glory in battle was celebrated and romanticized, almost *sold* to eager youth; like a night of thrills with a cheap whore, seeking it out was often paid for with a lifetime of pain and regret.

Jaron knew firsthand, he had experience; experience with battle, not cheap whores. *It was perhaps a bad comparison*, he thought to himself.

"Why do you think no school would take him?" he asked.

Ryken smirked, "Because he's a Gaddisen. We aren't the muscled sort. We're all arms and legs, as they say." He spread his robed arms to illustrate, the dark blue fabric hanging as if over a clothesline. Jaron smiled and the boys joined Ryken in laughter that echoed crisply across the snow-laden field that was their road.

They stopped that evening by an outcropping of rock that was a landmark to the boys, rising from the fields like a tiny snowcapped mountain peak against a backdrop of trees. Greaves tended the horses as the boys stretched their legs and made for the trees to relieve themselves. Jaron didn't relish sleeping on the snow tonight. Though the last three months had been full of manual labor, he had spent each night in a warm cot by a small fire in his meager lodgings. Now he only had the bedroll behind his saddle, and the boys had not packed much more for the overnight trip.

They did not seem worried; in fact they looked particularly eager as they set their luggage against the large rugged monolith. Each boy drew forth a wooden rod or wand, carved and decorated in some way to make it distinctive. Jaron realized with a touch of unease that they must be wizard verges. The boys were about to perform some kind of magic, and the knight stepped back warily. They were still students after all.

Ryken waved the other boys back with his free hand. "Alright, let me show you how it's done," he exclaimed with bravado, and the other lads heckled him as he prepared his spell. Jaron watched in fascination as the older boy held the verge out before him, gripping it at the center instead of the end as Jaron had expected. He lowered it to the trodden snow at his feet and muttered some words in old Celvestrian, "*Doshae cuam, thmdii d'thess.*" The snow began to move and fold under the motion of the outstretched arm, as if an invisible plow was pushing it away from the young wizard. Ryken's eyes were intense and his brow furrowed in concentration as the other lads smiled and nodded in appreciation. Soon a small pile of snow was pushed against the rock face, exposing the wet earth underneath.

"My turn!" proclaimed Jester, eager to prove himself. He held forth his verge like a dagger in a guard position, more what Jaron thought 'looked right', and spoke a different phrase, "*Vomaal cun veste n'thnen, thmd'dis!*" He waved the verge to the side dramatically and a burst of slushy snow sprayed upon his fellows, much to their dismay. Vortigras stamped and tossed his head at the sudden explosion and Jaron had to calm him with a pat on the neck.

"What was *that* supposed to be?" Woolly demanded, as he wiped snow from his face. "You did that on purpose, you little turd!"

Jester giggled but shook his head saying, "Honest, I didn't. I mean... it's something I've been working on. It worked better in practice."

Dungrave scowled, "Did you say 'arm of winter-bane?' Was that supposed to be a warding spell? It was crap."

Jester shrugged, "A frost ward with a bit of elemental fire. It was supposed to melt it away..." He examined the patch of wet snow still covering the earth beneath.

Mavaard was not happy. "Elemental fire? Are you

mad? If you had miscalculated, we'd all be steam-scalded, idiot!"

Jester was deflated, his shoulders sagging. He muttered, "It worked in practice..."

Mavaard said, "If you were practicing at the school, the spirit well probably made it more stable. Now I'm all wet." He passed his own gnarled verge over his body and muttered angrily, "*Posthe daasim.*" The slush evaporated away in an instant, but Mavaard teetered and collapsed in a heap in the ankle-deep snow. His friends rushed to his side, sitting him up and slapping his cheeks as the boy regained his wits.

"What happened?" Jaron asked, concerned now. He knelt beside the boy as his eyes regained focus.

Dungrave explained, "He was distracted; too angry to handle the drain. Casting takes a lot of concentration, especially if you aren't used to pulling outside of a spirit well."

The knight nodded as if he understood, not wanting to show his ignorance. It was enough to understand that magic was difficult and dangerous. He had heard that such things could happen, but had never witnessed it firsthand. The lack of anxiety in the other boys told him this was a minor occurrence and probably something they had all experienced.

Once the students cleared and dried the ground under the rock face, the bedrolls were spread out and the boys ate their evening meal of bread and cheese before the modest fire. Jaron had gathered the wood amongst a nearby copse of trees, hoping it would be dry enough to kindle, but then he remembered that such things were probably beyond the cares of wizards. Sure enough, one of the lads used a spell to ignite the wood and they enjoyed a merry blaze for a time as the world grew dark and the stars came out.

It was not long before they were all asleep, and Greaves the sled driver gave a sniff of derision as he lit his pipe. "Foolish boys," he said, "Still have no mind of their limits." Jaron looked up at the unexpected comment. The man had been silent the whole day. "Best hope there's no need to wake them. You'd be hard pressed if there was."

"What do you mean?" Jaron asked.

"Wizards, *proper* wizards mind you, don't go casting spells for little nonsense like this." He indicated the snow pushed aside and the dried patch of earth. "Even the masters can suffer from too much strain. It tires a body out, magic does. It's something we aren't meant to tamper with, but tamper we do."

"What exactly happened to the boy who passed out?" Jaron asked.

Greaves shrugged, "Couldn't handle the pull, most likely."

"What does that mean?" he asked, interested.

"See," Greaves began, "A spirit well is like a... like a fire. It's bright, it's hot... you can use it to cook on, or forge metal, or read by. When you have it, things are easy for you. When you don't, well, it's much harder to do those things. Try forging metal only by the heat you can make by rubbing your hands together!" Jaron shook his head and smiled, still not really understanding.

"Casting a spell takes a tool, a verge. It's a wooden object that holds an amount of silver. The silver lets the wizard 'pull' from the forces around him, and the wood protects him from pulling too much. Follow me?"

Jaron nodded uncertainly, "Go on."

"Well, going back to the fire; imagine you need to cook something, but all you have is a weak ember. Using magic outside a spirit well is like taking that ember and making it grow into a cooking fire, but instead of blowing on a pile of kindling, you're taking the fire into yourself and making it grow, then spiting it out again fully formed."

Jaron could not begin to imagine what that would feel like. He said, "So Mavaard got burned, so to speak? He pulled too much magic through himself?"

Greaves shook his head, "Not quite, no. The verge protects you from pulling too much, but if the effort is too great or the wizard isn't focused enough on what he's doing, the spirit forces try to equalize and..." He held up a burning brand from the fire and blew gently on the flame, making it flicker and wane. When he stopped, the flame was smaller but still burning. "The effort disturbs your own spirit, making it flicker like this flame. It can make you weak, can make you fail... or can blow out your flame if you're taking on more than you can handle."

The knight shuddered, and not entirely because of the chill winter air.

Jaron spent the rest of the winter in Gorshed, where the families of the students took turns giving Jaron lodging. He tried to make himself useful, learning to shear sheep with the men, and spin it into thread with the women, bearing their good-natured laughter and teasing. More than one family he stayed with had daughters that were eager to catch his eye, but his self-restraint was more than he thought possible. It would not do to return his hosts' hospitality by leaving expectant young women in his wake when he left in spring. Besides, he could only think of Cindra with any true tenderness in his heart, and his thoughts of her were bittersweet and tempered by the pain of her loss.

As spring approached, the fields began to blossom with flowers and the trees with new leaves, so Jaron bid his hosts farewell and headed south towards Alvane, the provincial seat. It was a fortified town with a stone curtain about the small castle and a wooden palisade around the bulk of the town center.

It happened that Jaron was lacking funds, and only had what food the people of Gorshed could spare for him, so he made the decision to sell some of his possessions for meager coin that would 'last him on a pauper's purse strings', as the saying went. His shield sold for a silver mark, which was less than he hoped, but his arm-pieces and leggings brought him half a crown. All he kept was his mail shirt, and of course the sword, which besides being priceless was not his to sell.

It was liberating to be free of his family crest, which had brought him nothing but trouble on his journey, though he felt no shame in bearing it. His painted shield marked him as a knight, and a knight was welcomed if he be free with his coin and caused no trouble. A poor knight was to be watched with a wary eye. Jaron still wore his *tipok* knot tied behind his head, but it was in need of rebinding and did not look as it should, so few made note of it or his status.

Alva Province was a quiet and peaceful land, for the lush Piniwood Forest covered half of it and the other half was made up of scattered settlements along the Alva Road, a broad dirt embankment that stretched the hundred-mile length of the territory. Jaron took on many small jobs working for local merchants and tradesmen, sometimes for coin and sometimes only for food and lodging for the night. The hard work agreed with him, and he was happy to see that the ill effects of his earlier binge were wearing off. In a way, having to be frugal was a blessing that he had not considered before; the lack of fine food and comfortable lodgings made him sturdier in heart and mind, allowing him to focus on what was important.

He practiced his fencing in the evening, sometimes using tree trunks or posts as fencing dummies. He woke early and did exercises to loosen the muscles and warm the blood, just as he had done in training at the Freekirk School as a squire. He ate sparingly and drank little, for ale was to be found in every town and village, but moderation was not, and he had to provide his own council on what was appropriate for a fighting man.

Spring brought planting season and Jaron aided many farmers as he rode through the land, taking time to convince the more suspicious-minded peasants that his intentions were honest and true. He made little coin from his labors, but often had at least one meal per day and a warm place to sleep, even if it was in a barn or with the livestock. Bathing was something he did as he was able, making his personal cleanliness more important than he had during his entire stay in more urban locales. He cut his hair to a style more fitting a knight-errant and had the wife of one of his hosts rebind his *tipok* knot with a little instruction. His tabard, which bore the heraldry of House Corrina, was not often worn, mostly because he was still in exile and therefore did not properly represent the count. It also became a kind of reminder of his eventual goal, to return to his home city and don the colors again with honor and dignity.

The hardest part of his convalescence was by far the feelings of sadness and loss that besieged him whenever he thought of Lady Cindra, which seemed to occur every hour of every day. He made an effort to think only of the joy they shared; the night he took her to the theater and dinner, the horseback riding and the peaceful rest under the tree, the kiss.

The kiss was counted among those joyful times despite the shame and scandal it caused, for he could not bring himself to dishonor her memory by thinking otherwise anymore. He began every day by dedicating it to her memory and went to sleep each night with a prayer on his lips for her peaceful rest in the afterlife. Was she a devotee of one or more gods, Selvina, perhaps? He did not know for certain but asked Lelonetha to keep her in Haven, where she would be freed from the suffering of her final moments.

As the year progressed and his travels continued west to Pinikal, he began to see her in the women he met, his mind recalling her frame, her hair, her smile. He would see the lady's likeness in the face of a milkmaid; her figure was brought to mind by a petite peasant girl who crossed his path outside of town; her laughter was like that of a woman in the market. He would look for a moment, wondering if his mind was playing tricks on him or if her charms were indeed universal, though spread among a select few, and not held all at once by another save her.

He began to wonder distantly if he might ever find happiness with another and what combination of beguilements it would take to cheer him and win his heart again. It was not among the things he chose to dwell upon, for he was a knight of House Corrina and his marriage prospects were not among the important matters that he would face in his life. Yet her image remained in his thoughts lest he forget, which to his mind would be like a second death.

Those who are loved live on in memory, his father often said, when remembering Jaron's mother.

Pinikal was a fair city and wealthy, being located where the King's Road met the Highwood Way north from Woodcourt. The Piniwood Forest stretched to the north, and to the south were fertile farmlands and open grassy plains.

The Outwalls were home to many Galindri caravans this time of year, and the inns were full, though Jaron could little afford them anyway. He would spend his days laboring in the city, keeping his horse in a stable while he worked for a number of tradesmen and earned money for his meals and the keeping of his mount. His evenings would be spent about the Outwalls where he would make a camp beyond the caravans and outlying houses. The evenings were warm enough to be comfortable with a small fire, and the insects could be kept away by burning a variety of grasses, which he learned by watching the locals.

Summer evenings were filled with the smell of cooking and the sounds of music and merriment about the Outwalls. The number of caravans had increased each day and sometimes Jaron had to move to another spot when newcomers claimed his campsite; it was not so troubling, for one patch of ground was just as good as another. Still, he found himself edging closer to the northern woods as more travelers arrived with the warm weather.

He would pass by the village homes and the neighboring caravans every night on his way to his camp, pausing occasionally to listen to a melody that caught his ear. His stomach grumbled at the smell of evening meals being prepared, for a fine meal was beyond his means.

Unable to bear it any longer, he scrimped and saved for a dinner in town once per week, finding a tavern in the village that offered simple but hearty fare and ale for a few coppers. It was his one indulgence and he shared it with Vortigras as best he could, bringing him a handful of cooked carrots or whatever he thought the horse might like.

There was one particular barmaid that he fancied, for she was near his age and pretty, where the others were older and on the frumpy side; also she had auburn hair and green eyes, though her teeth were a bit crooked, as was her smile, but charmingly so. She had leaned close while serving him once and he caught the smell of her skin, the scent awakening his memory and bringing back emotions that the day's toils had beaten out of him.

He left for his camp with his heart heavy and his mind clouded. Lady Cindra's memory had overtaken him again; he had seen her face and form in the barmaid and several other women that night, even in a Galindri girl who twirled and danced with her kin, her braided hair flowing with her layered skirts. Save for her dusky skin, the girl was so much in Cindra's likeness that it pained his heart, and he trudged into the woods to be away from all traces of humanity.

Chapter Eleven

Cindra's Fair End

The following months were worrisome for Cindra as she and Majii's family followed the other caravans to Pinikal. The king had died as they were leaving Highseat and that meant only one thing: the Dissenter houses would likely move against the new king's authority. Her cousin, soon to be crowned King Galen III, would be tested by those who believed him weak and uncertain, and he would have to prove them wrong.

She thought of her father and mother preparing for a war on their doorstep, as borders were closed and the barons over the Cassel Mountains declared their lands sovereign. She thought of the troops mustered in the loyal provinces that would fight a civil war to bring the traitors back in line. She thought of Jaron.

He was still banished from Casselvane until early next

year, but he might run into trouble as he traveled the country. Hopefully his status as a Corrina knight would not bring him any problems, but knowing his sense of duty, he might be inclined to join with a Loyalist house if the fight came to a nearby friendly land. Before she left on her ill-fated ocean voyage, she learned that Sir Fedrick had loaned him the Corrina sword of flame, so she knew he would be better off with it at his side. She wanted to see him again despite the foolish message he had sent, especially now that she was no longer bound to wed another, being dead and all. He was still beneath her station, but that only mattered in the society she was born into, not the one she lived in now. It was so liberating to be able to dream and not see so many obstacles.

In the days following the death of the king, long trails of white smoke could be seen crisscrossing the sky; ember swallows were being dispatched bearing the ill tidings. Some were seen by night, blazing like fiery, living comets; omens and harbingers of evil times to come. There were also likely to be summons to the new king's coronation, which was traditionally held at the Cathedral of Arathus in Ashenmon, the heart of the Church of the Divine Court in Calilon. That honor was once held by the cathedral in the city of Wenmaar, far in the east, but the center of the faith moved along with the capital two centuries ago. Only local lords would attend since the kingdom was so vast; Cindra's parents would not be going; she was certain of that.

The journey through the Highwood Forest was amazing, although the road itself passed among few of the giant trees. To the east was the majestic, chiseled peak of Mount Piniwen, and to the west, the tops of the immense evergreens rose like the spires of a wooden city, towering high over the smaller pines that ran on both sides of the King's Road.

It was said that the mighty trees were impossible to cut down, and that a dozen men could join hands around the massive trunks. It was also said that Eagle Men could be seen circling the highest treetops, deep in the forest. Cindra was not sure she believed that, but the Time of Chaos had made many unbelievable things true.

They camped in the forest for seven days, letting the herd graze and drink from freshwater springs while the women gathered berries, mushrooms and other herbs that grew among the ferns and undergrowth. Game was plentiful and Teya took Cindra hunting once again, bringing back a snood hen and a brace of coneys for the meal they shared with Tavika and her family.

The rest of the time she spent with T'ózha, teaching him to be led and grooming him, finding happiness in brushing his black mane and tail. The little pony was growing almost fast enough to see from day to day, and his spirit was increasing with his size. His strength astonished Cindra when he pulled against his harness or bumped into her with his nose; he would be strong yet willful, unless she managed to tame him before his first year.

Teya said that he might even be strong enough to ride by next spring, promising as he was. The huntress was seen to smile more as she taught Cindra to train her new horse, and the company of the tribe meant Teya could lower her guard and relax more often. It was a welcomed change.

The caravans arrived at Pinikal in midsummer and made camp with Galindri tribes that had come from far and wide, eager to trade stories, goods, and marriage prospects. Summer was a time when young men and women would meet, and if marriage was desired, their families would have many weeks to get acquainted, arranging dowries from their herds or flocks.

A few men from other tribes approached Cindra curiously, but they only had to look at her eyes to see she was different. If that did not dissuade them to let her be, her *k'ó-saya* Teya would frighten them off. Cindra did not mind the attention so much, but the ways of courtship and proper behavior between *Gatéth-sho'a* men and

223

women were unfamiliar to her; she had no desire to make a mess of things or have to explain her deception. Besides, the fewer people that knew of her secret, the better.

Instead, she divided her time between T'ózha and Haani, who was teaching her the summer festival dances. The young maid had many offers of marriage herself, but had no wish to leave her father and family just yet. She also had no reason to put her hair up either, though Tavika still prodded her when a fine young man would walk by and smile.

The festival began when enough elders were present to make a *do'aya ayát-sem*, or a ten-hand circle; a ring of fifty venerable men and women from various tribes who would gather around a bonfire and declare the summer celebrations started. Majii was one of the fifty who were so honored, and Haani danced with the other youngest daughters about the fire.

Cindra was his youngest in name, but Haani was his youngest daughter by blood and that passed the honor of dancing to her. Cindra was fine with that, for she was not yet confident enough to get up and twirl before a whole crowd of *Gatéth-sho'a* and curious townspeople. Still she stood with Teya, Navo and Luka while they clapped in time to the music.

After the opening dance there was a feast of spiced meats, nuts, pickled greens, flatbread mushroom pies, berry tarts, and many things that Cindra did not recognize but sampled just the same. Few *Gatéth-sho'a* were farmers, for that meant being tied to the land that was claimed by Outlander lords, but there were enough who traded with the townspeople to supplement the meals with local vegetables and fruits. Honey mead and dark ale added to the merrymaking and Cindra became bolder after the first few cups, dancing around the smaller fires with Haani and the other maidens.

Cindra asked Navo why Teya did not dance, and he said jokingly, "These dances are for girls, and she did not grow up like a girl." His smile was half-hearted though. "It is not her way, not for a long time," he said soberly.

She let it go at that, not asking for more. She remembered the story of the little girl wanting to join a mission of revenge, wanting death and blood for her murdered mother. Teya had seen death and even killed before she was eight years old. The thought made her recall her own blooding, when she saved the huntress from a Minozhian bull-man. She fingered the horn handle of the large *Kos* knife at her hip as she looked across the evening's revelry, sorry she asked. It had dampened the mood considerably.

Morning came with an upset stomach and pounding headache, both of which Luka treated with many cups of water. "It is the price in misery that is paid for pleasure," she had said as she comforted the addled girl. Cindra took the rest of the festival in moderation, using the threat of that pain to keep her from overdoing it again.

Days were spent wandering in town, or with T'ózha in the pastures beyond the farmlands. Nights were spent listening to stories around the fire as Haani spun tales of the olden times in her native tongue, while Navo played the flute for accompaniment, imitating the sounds of birds or the whistle of the wind, enhancing Haani's performance.

They traveled about the many caravans, visiting distant relations and sharing food and drink, telling of news from near and far. The death of the Outlander king was a topic often discussed, for though the *Gatéth-sho'a* did not pay homage in any real way, they knew that it could have powerful consequences. Cindra did not take part in these discussions, though she knew far more than anyone present about what was at stake. Even here, among these warm people in the midst of their celebration, she could not escape her past.

One day, Cindra, Teya, and Haani went wandering about in the woods north of town, looking for the source of a stream that ran by the horse pastures. They had hiked for many miles into the Piniwood before they heard the sound of falling water up ahead. The land was steeper here and they had to trek upwards around a thick cluster of trees and vegetation before they reached the source of the noise. Runoff from the hills, or perhaps a spring, was spilling over the rocks and into a pool of dark water, collecting in the little depression before overflowing into the stream below.

Teya scouted about and pronounced it safe, for there were no animals or people, and the water was clear enough that no hazards could be seen beneath the surface. Haani clapped and began to disrobe, folding her clothes neatly on a dry rock. Teya took off her boots first, shaking her head at her little half-sister.

"Are you even going to try the water before jumping in?" She asked, as the maiden unwound her *l'lash* and stood only in her lovely skin, painted gold and brown by the afternoon sunlight.

Haani giggled and replied, "Brave huntress! Sometimes in life you must... LEAP!" She dove headfirst into the pool and swam a few strokes beneath before coming up, her dark gold hair clinging to her back. "It's f-fine... c-come in!"

She looked invigorated but shivery, and Teya laughed saying, "A bit cold is it? It's running water!" Teya dipped her toes in before undressing and motioned to Cindra to join them. "Is Menika afraid to get wet?"

Cindra was indeed like a cat in that way, for her only experience with water was bathing in the castle and nearly drowning in the ocean. Bathing was nice, but this water was frigid; Haani's teeth-chattering endorsement was fooling no one.

"I'll just soak my feet a bit," she said, and took off her shoes, lifting her skirts and stepping gingerly into the pool. It was not terribly cold at the edge, but the deeper pool might be a different matter. Besides, what if her color washed off?

"Very well, *saya*," Teya said, as she bundled her

garments and waded into the pool. "You may mind our clothes." As the women splashed about in the cool water, Cindra sat and paddled her feet, hoping this place was not often visited by man or beast.

The women followed the stream back to the edge of the forest, then to the Outwalls, having enjoyed themselves in what seemed like a secret, private pool. No doubt others in town knew of it, but were not inclined to visit just for a swim. Nevertheless, Cindra's feet were the same dark color after an hour of soaking, so she decided she might consider going in the water next time. Maybe.

The days were warm and sunny but the evenings got cold, and firewood was running in short supply so close to the town. It happened one night that there was not enough wood to make a cook fire and it was tasked to Cindra and Haani to go and fetch some. Haani was uncomfortable asking at the other caravans, for it was their own lack of preparation that led to this, but Cindra offered a solution.

"We might try the village. There are taverns and inns with much firewood, and they might sell some to us," she said as they walked.

Haani was reluctant and replied, "Oh, the days when the *Gatéth-sho'a* buys firewood from Outlanders. What have we come to?" She shook her head and sniffed at the idea.

Cindra said, "We only need a small bundle for the night and I have a few coppers." She jingled the coins tucked in her *l'lash*.

Haani clucked her tongue in disapproval and said, "If you want to spend coin for what can be found on the ground, then that is your affair."

"Come with me though. I don't want to do it alone." Cindra said.

Haani agreed and together they walked about the Outwalls, looking for an inn with a woodpile behind it. There were a few that looked promising, but the innkeepers shooed them out the door before they could ask. They tried at the back door of the next inn and got questioned before being shooed away.

Haani was ready to quit, but Cindra convinced her to try one more. The place was near enough to the caravans that many campfires could be seen among the trees, and Cindra had wondered at it as she passed on her shopping trips. It was called the Outside Inn, and was built in a peculiar style that was not seen in Portshia. The common room was in one building and the lodging rooms were all adjacent to it, built back to back with their doors facing out on either side; a narrow porch stretched the length of the building, providing a place to stand without getting muddy. The rooms were less discreet, since they opened into the town rather than a hallway. Each had a sliding window set high on the wall, so that fresh air could enter and still maintain the room's privacy. The common room was more like a small office with a fire and a few chairs; the innkeeper smiled as they knocked at the door frame and came over, a questioning look on his face.

"Well now, what have the gods blessed me with this night?" he said with a smile, and the women were both relieved yet wary. "Two dark lovelies at my door."

He was a hefty man with balding head and a mustache that flowed to his jaws and up to his ears. His eyes flicked up and down their figures and Cindra felt like a meal set before a glutton.

Using her best Galindri-accented Calilesh, Cindra asked, "Do you have firewood to sell?" She offered some copper coins so the particulars of the transaction were clear; she didn't like the man's wandering eyes.

"Why, I might just have some..." he stepped outside and walked around the building to a neatly stacked pile. "Here we are," he said; he undid a canvas cover that kept the stack dry. "How much do you need to warm your shivering skin?" He stroked Cindra's arm and she tried not to flinch.

"Just a few logs, kindly," she smiled pleasantly. She

wished Haani would step up and wiggle to distract the man. This was almost not worth it.

He took two good-sized logs from the stack and presented them. "Here you are lovelies," he smiled at them and opened his hand for payment. Cindra quickly dropped three coppers into his hand and that seemed to please him, luckily. "Be safe now," he said as he winked before heading back inside.

Cindra and Haani turned quickly to go and nearly bumped into a man who was walking towards his room. She stumbled and looked up at him, startled. He glared down at her with annoyance but said nothing, a scowl forming under his beard as they moved to and fro, trying to get by one another in an awkward dance. Something about him was familiar and Cindra tried to get another look as he moved past. He wore a dark cloak and traveling outfit consisting of comfortable trousers and a shirt with vest. Upon his head was a cloth hat covering blond curls, and his blond beard was thick but well-kept; his face reminded her of home, somehow. He passed her with no recognition, heading for the narrow porch and his room.

Cindra huddled close to Haani, whispering urgently, "I've seen that man before, Haani. I don't know where exactly, but I swear I recognize him!" She walked adjacent to him, trying to seem inconspicuous while watching his every move. He opened the door to his room, and within she saw a group of men seated near a burning fire pit, the light illuminating fierce snarling maws and rows of teeth. Cindra gasped and dropped the firewood, making Haani jump aside.

"What is it?" she asked, picking up the logs.

She hissed, "Haani, g-go get Teya, tell her the masked priests are here at the inn!" She waited for the door to close and she crept towards it.

Haani blocked her way, "What are you going to do, Menika?" she asked sternly, a fearful tremor in her voice.

"I'm going to try and listen in. They must be up to

229

something and I'm going to find out what. Get Teya, quick!" She darted towards the door and Haani dared not follow her lest she give Cindra away.

"*Me-ni-ka!*" Haani hissed. Cindra was not to be thwarted, so Haani cursed and ran back to the caravan, praying her saya did nothing too stupid.

Cindra stepped on the narrow porch, wincing as it creaked. She trod carefully; glancing back once to make sure Haani was going for help. Padding on the floorboards, she leaned in close to the wall and tilted her head towards the sliding window. She could make out voices and a few words, but nothing clear. She stood on her tiptoes and put her ear as close to the sliding window as she could.

"A special welcome to our agents from Highseat," said the voice, "Well done indeed, brothers." There was a murmuring of approval. "Now that His Majesty is no more, the barons will begin to move. I've also learned from the High Priest that the scion is in Portshia, and soon the Dark Heart will be turned over to us."

Agents from Highseat? Did they have something to do with the king's death? Cindra was aghast. *The scion is in Portshia? What did that mean?*

A question was asked from one of the muffled voices and another was raised, but Cindra could not make out the words. The man answered, "We must tread carefully. He is more than he seems. I will..." the words grew muffled again, "...so you needn't worry." She inched up higher, trying to hear.

A different man spoke this time, "What about Casselvane? We hear there is talk of a new alliance?"

Casselvane! Cindra thought, *He means my father!*

"We will use this new alliance to place blame for the death of his daughter. He will see plots where there are none, and miss the one right under his nose." Cindra gasped as her legs went weak. *They are scheming against my father!* She pulled herself up to the window again.

The window shutter slid open and an arm came

through, grabbing her hair. She screamed as the door flew open, and the blond man she had followed came out, his mouth and nose covered by a hideous bestial mask. He grabbed her by the arm and covered her mouth, pulling her inside, as the man at the window let go. She held on to the door frame with all her might, trying desperately to keep from being trapped within. Seven men in beast masks were gathered in the room, conspiring against king and country, each with murder in their eyes. The man who had grabbed her hair now pulled her arm from the door frame and lifted her bodily inside, the door slamming closed behind.

"Well, it looks like we have some entertainment," said the blond man before her, his eyes looking positively wicked over his snarling mask. "Looking for something to steal, perhaps? Or maybe you came to sell your beauty? We aren't the paying kind."

One man laughed, "Ha-ha, but Ghethas, you're married!" The others chuckled.

"My wife is the understanding kind," Ghethas said.

The man holding Cindra pulled her closer and held her arms. She reached for the *Kos* knife at her hip and had it halfway out of its sheath before Ghethas snatched it away.

"Look at this," he sneered, "she's got a Minozhian knife. Isn't that charming?"

Cindra struggled and cried out in the Galindri tongue, desperate to maintain her disguise, *"Ne, ne! Doha erenáya!"* They covered her mouth again.

"We can take her into the woods and show her how to use it..."

"There are too many other brownies around; best stay in the room until we finish with her."

"Leave a surprise for the innkeeper."

She struggled fiercely but to no avail; her wrists were held fast by powerful hands. The men began to surround her, their masked faces leering like hungry wolves and mythical beasts, fangs gleaming as their breath hissed through the painted jaws, reeking of ale and nightshade chew-leaf.

The door suddenly burst open to reveal three Galindri men with knives, a ferocious gleam in their bright green eyes. They did not speak, but gestured to the Outlanders to return their captive, as more men approached from the campfires.

The masked priests looked to Ghethas for instructions, but he just chuckled nodded to the man holding Cindra, who let her pull away. The blond priest dropped her *Kos* knife, which stuck into the floor with a *thunk*. As she bent and grabbed it, Ghethas her took her by the wrist, saying to her, "I hope we meet again, sweet one."

She wrenched her arm free, her bangles rattling as a few fell away. She turned and ran past her Galindri saviors, shouting back at the masked men, "*Neko-fáche-beh!*" She adjusted her clothing and stalked off to the caravans as the others enclosed around her protectively. As she passed a tree, Teya and Haani stepped from behind it and joined her, hugging her fiercely.

"Teya," she said, surprised that the huntress had not come herself, "Why were you not there, *k'ó-saya*?"

Teya shrugged and said, "If it was the priest from the Minozhian camp, I thought he would recognize me and make more trouble."

Cindra considered this and said, "That was very clever, Teya."

"If I had taken time to be *more* clever, you might have been killed, saya. It pained me not to act." She poked Cindra in the chest and said, "Don't be so foolish again!" She strode on ahead in a huff.

Haani walked with an arm around Cindra, feeling the girl's excitement wear off as her body began to shake with fear and stress. *She will need rest and some mead to calm her nerves, the poor child.*

———————

Ghethas watched the Galindri depart, the dark figures

casting a forest of long shadows from their campfires. His priests did not need to get caught up in any violence tonight, not when a loud cry could bring half the brownie nation down on them. He sneered at their backs, content with the knowledge that they would all be destroyed in the ultimate catastrophe, one he would help to unleash. He reached down and picked up a hoop of gold the girl had dropped, turning it in his hand. *A memento from my brownie girl*, he thought.

Then he examined it further, noticing the delicate silver etchings that looked like Celvestrian glyphs, and the inlaid images of dolphins. It had an embedded seastone and seemed to be of fine craftsmanship, more suitable for a high noble lady than a Galindri trollop. His mind began to spin and he looked again for the girl, but she was gone, having faded away into the sea of caravans.

Into the sea....

———————

It had been a month since the incident with the masked priests, and Cindra was starting to relax her guard a bit. The priests surely didn't wear masks all the time, so they would not be so easy to spot; all strangers were watched closely around the caravans, and Cindra kept her eyes peeled for the man she had recognized, though she still could not place him. He sounded like the same priest from the Minozhian camp, but that might have been the mask muffling his voice. She had not seen that man's face, so why did she recognize him? Was he from Portshia? Did he work in the castle? It was maddening.

The summer festival was winding down and many of the early arrivals were packing up to go. Teya had discussed their departure with Majii, and it was decided that they would head east to the Shadowood and turn downriver at Breega, spending the winter in Portshia. They would then travel in the spring to Rickshome-on-the-Joshian, the richest city of the north, built astride the river running from Lake Lumiras. The Calione Peaks made a stunning backdrop for the lake in spring, and Cindra longed to see it, but something else was pulling her away.

She knew she could not stay with her new family forever, not when there were such forces moving against the kingdom and her true family back home. Assassins, wicked priests, Minozhian pirates, traitorous barons; who would strike next and who else would reveal themselves? She would have to return somehow.

The evenings were thankfully distracting and full of merriment. One evening, Navo invited a few other musician friends to attend their campfire and play, so Cindra and Haani danced, twirling with glee. Their movements were harmonious and fluid, braids whipping and bangles jingling as they spun in time with the beat of drums. All the practice had been rewarded as others came by to see the performance, drawn by the jaunty tune and the beautiful dancers. Even a few Outlanders wandered by, pausing to watch while others clapped in time with the beat.

Cindra was absorbed in the moment as her soft leather shoes tread the grass and leaped about the fire; her skirts flared in shades of blue, yellow and burgundy; her hands and arms wove and bent, making her bangles chime. Sadly she had lost the gold bracelet Master Ildric had given her, possibly on the night of the incident with the priests. It worried her at the time, but nothing had come of it so far; it had been over a year since she was lost at sea and first saw the masked priest with the Minozhians. Her part in this conspiracy had come to a close long ago and she had been in hiding ever since. There was no reason to think someone would pick up her trail now, was there?

Majii's caravan would leave at summer's end after parting ways with Tavika and her family. The Outwalls were emptying slowly and villagers were more likely to be seen passing by the remaining caravans, looking for good deals on trade items that were left over.

Cindra took T'ózha on walks and fed him by hand during the mornings, but the afternoons were too warm to spend in the open of the horse fields, so she would help Luka cook the lunchtime meals under the shade of the trees. It was likely to be a short winter, according to the older Galindri who sat about discussing the weather; the summer had been warmer than usual, and the birds were arriving late, or early, or some such thing. They spoke in their own tongue and drifted in and out of familiar parlance, using terms that made little sense to Cindra. It was interesting listening to them speak with Majii about old friends and family members long gone, using words that might only have meaning among themselves. It was turning out to be a slow, relaxing month.

She had even gone with Haani and Teya to the pool in the forest several times, getting a bit braver each time. The water had warmed a little and there were fewer people about to intrude, although they had once found some local children there first, and had to loiter in the woods until they left. It was otherwise their own secret spot and they enjoyed it while they could. Cindra had learned to swim with a little more confidence, paddling around the pool while Teya dove beneath her, grabbing at her toes. Haani preferred to splash, and she and Cindra would team up on Teya when the toe grabbing got too excessive. Aside from the discovery of the evil priests and their diabolical plans, it was a lovely summer.

———————

The work was tapering off as the season grew late and the Galindri moved on, but still Jaron kept busy as much as he could. He took to training in the woods, practicing for the first hours of the morning and going into town for work, returning in the evening to eat and sleep by a little fire. He would spend some days just resting or riding Vortigras about the fields, keeping the horse fit as well.

His time in Pinikal was coming to an end, so he considered where to go on his way back to Portshia. He figured that taking the King's Road south and following the Red Coast Road all the way to Cordoshome would be the best plan, for the village was a three day ride from Portshia and would be more welcoming than some other towns he could pass through. He had earned enough money to return home; if not in style, then at least with a meal and a room at an inn when he needed one.

He wondered if the brothers who stole his coin purse had made it home and helped their family, or if they had fallen to another fate. He did not dwell on it however, for he could not control the fortunes of others but could only do his part to aid them.

As the summer had brought more visitors, Jaron had moved farther into the woods to camp in solitude. As they moved away, he found that he preferred the solitude at night and continued to sleep in the forest, despite the open spots near the Outwalls. He was growing wiser as the hardships of the past year taught him about the realities of life and how to face them.

All his life he had taken orders from someone, be it his father or Sir Cord, his teachers or commanders, the count... he had never had to rely on his own judgment as much as he did now, and it was harder to steer himself than he thought. Old habits die hard, and his newfound purpose fought against the patterns of a more irresponsible and spoiled existence. He almost longed for a return to a structured and ordered life under someone else's command.

The summer grew late and the heat tested Jaron's endurance, but he was in better shape than he had been in four years, since being knighted. Still, he took his ease more often on the hot days, or made for his camp in the woods earlier than usual. It was on one particularly hot day that he decided to ride Vortigras in the fields, preparing him for the journey home. He watered him in the nearby stream and followed it into the woods, looking for a cool place to nap away the noonday heat.

He found a path leading to the right of a tumbling torrent that came down over a cleft in the hillside, with the sound of falling water beyond. He led Vortigras as far up the forested tor as he could, tying him to a low branch and hiking a short way towards the trees at the crest of the hill. Beneath him was a lovely pool of dark water that was fed from the hills above and brimmed over into the stream below. The music of the water was beguiling him to sleep, and he was ill-equipped to resist. He laid his sword against the tree and leaned back on the cool grass, his eyes shielded by his arm and the drifting shadows of leaves. Within moments, he drifted into a sound sleep, the wind whispering through the branches above and soothing his soul.

He was awakened by the sound of splashing and laughter that, at first, he thought to be a trick of the forest. Then he heard women's voices echoing below, so he crawled to the edge and looked down into the pool. His curiosity was rewarded by the sight of three dark-skinned Galindri women, all nubile and bare, swimming and frolicking in the cool waters. One was stepping on the rocks to collect her clothes; her skin was a lustrous, dark brown; her body was strong and taut, with sinewy shoulders, back, and legs that signified a life of constant physical hardship, and Jaron wondered at her. She was beautiful, but rather fierce-looking, and he watched with a bit of chivalric guilt as she wrapped her breasts in a length of coral cloth, bound up her hair, and donned a short, layered skirt. She watched the others play for a while, then called to them as she strapped on a belt with two knives. She moved behind some trees and out of his view, so he turned to admire the other girls. Vortigras gave a blustery blow as if to scold him.

The next one out of the water was shorter and curvier; her long, braided hair shone like dark gold, and she had slightly lighter skin than the first woman. She picked gingerly among the rocks for her clothing and wiped herself dry before dressing, making Jaron sigh and lean his chin on his hands. She was nimble and graceful, with the body of a dancer, and the young knight felt his pulse quicken.

Wicked man, he thought to himself.

As the curvaceous girl was dressing, the last girl came up out of the pool. She had dark, auburn hair in long braids, and light brown skin that glistened in the sunlight. She seemed to be the youngest of the three, or was not quite as well-grown, but her figure and physique were somewhere between those of the other two women. She was slim and lean but curvy in all the right places, if modestly so. She waded waist-deep into the shallows of the pool, and he waited expectantly for her to expose her other assets.

As she rose out of the water, Jaron beheld a shocking sight; the shape of her bottom did not disappoint, but its color was as light and pale as his own, if not more so. It was the same almost halfway down her thighs, as if she was painted but for what her skirts hid. As she turned and he saw her face more clearly, he recognized the dancing girl he had seen many weeks ago, the girl who had so reminded him of Lady Cindra that it made his heart ache. Now his mind was reeling as he got to his hands and knees, resisting the urge to shout her name. Was he mad, or was this truly possible?

Vortigras whinnied behind him, making the two women turn to the sound and grab for their clothing, rushing for modesty. Before he could think, he heard a rustling through the foliage and was suddenly kicked in the ribs; someone was leaping on him as he rolled towards his sword, blades flashing to his throat. He was now on his back with the fierce-looking Galindri woman straddling him, her piercing green eyes filled with malice as she held a cold steel blade to his neck; another blade was poised to strike him if he moved. His mind and body were not in agreement over the danger; he thought awkwardly, *without the knives, this might not be so bad.*

The blade pressed his flesh as the woman's chest heaved, and she snarled something at him in her language; Jaron could see murder in her eyes and felt a tingle of fear. Voices called from the pool below and she shouted an answer, likely a brief warning. Jaron did not know if she would understand, but he had to know before he died, he had to take a chance and ask.

"Is that Lady Cindra? Is she really alive?" He flinched as the blade bit his neck, drawing blood. The woman hissed at him like an angry cat, her eyes fixed on his. She reacted slightly to the name but he only felt the danger increase. "Please, I must see her." He pleaded with his eyes, praying she understood and desperate to know if what he suspected was true.

The woman called out as the others approached, speaking rapidly to them without relieving the pressure of the knife blade. They appeared from around a thick tree and jerked to a stop upon seeing the man trapped on the ground; their feet were bare, their skirts hastily slipped on, and their tops were held to their breasts for modesty. They looked afraid and angry, but the face of the younger girl registered shock as she recognized him.

"Teya no! Don't hurt him!" she shouted in perfect Calilesh. Jaron gasped at the sound of her voice, a voice he never thought to hear again.

"Cindra?" he asked, as the blade came away from his throat. The woman remained over him however, knives at the ready. "Is it really you?" Tears formed in his eyes as he held his breath, waiting for the answer.

Cindra nodded and ran to him saying, "Yes! Oh, Jaron!" She fell to her knees and hugged him, much to Teya's dismay; the huntress was still deciding if she should kill him, but now it seemed the decision had been made for her. She was still tempted though.

The knight held Cindra close, burying his face in her neck and crying softly; she did the same for an endless, perfect moment, tears turning to laughter and back again.

239

Then she sat up, drew her clothes to her chest again and gave him a punch in the stomach.

"You were spying on us!" she said, as her dignity returned. Teya rolled off of him and sheathed her blades, watching him like a snake eying a mouse.

Jaron sat up and coughed to cover his shame, "I... well, I fell asleep here, and when I awoke I heard noises in the pool. I was just investigating..." He looked apologetically at the women, particularly the armed one. "That was quite an attack," he said to Teya, hoping the compliment would soften her. "You took me completely by surprise. How did you know I was here?"

"Your horse gave you away." She turned and strode back to the pool to recover their remaining clothes.

Jaron looked at his traitorous steed and said, "The blowing, I suppose." He threw a twig at Vortigras.

"The smell," Teya called as she disappeared out of sight.

"At least it wasn't *my* smell," Jaron said as he rose shakily to his feet. He looked happily at Cindra, dying to ask her all the questions that were spinning in his head. He wanted to embrace her again, to kiss her, to tell her he had thought of her each day...

"Turn around, you scoundrel!" Cindra barked, and he noticed the two women were still covering up, not quite dressed. He spun about and faced a tree. He wanted to comment that he had seen everything already, but that would surely earn him a return visit from the knife-wielding woman.

Vortigras whinnied at him, and to Jaron's ears it sounded just like laughter.

Chapter Twelve

Parting Ways

The following days were full of happiness and sad memories as Cindra and Jaron recounted their tales, full of tragedies and triumphs and the pain of longing. Cindra felt the worst for it because Jaron had been told of her death and it had ruined him for a time; she wondered anew at her parents and what had become of them, for the death of her younger brother had been a terrible blow. She knew she needed to tell them she was alive, lest misery drag them down into ruin as well. Cindra told him of the Minozhian attack and how Mineth was killed, of the magic bracelet and her Galindri saviors, of the plot to kill her revealed by the masked priest who worshiped the 'Countless Lord.' There was so much to tell that they sat about the campfire long into the evenings, her Galindri family commenting as their parts in the story came up.

Only Teya sat apart, sharpening her knives.

"The priests were here, in this very town, not too long ago!" Cindra was saying, "Haani and I happened upon them and I listened at the window as they plotted. Jaron, I think they caused the death of Galen II, possibly even his long illness." She leaned forward, her voice shaking as she recounted the night, "They have plans for Portshia too, and they spoke of my father. Jaron, what are we to do?"

They all looked at Jaron for an answer, fearful of what he might say. Majii and his family could see that the time of their parting was drawing near and their little Menika would soon go back to the dangers of her old life. Cindra, for her part, was afraid that Jaron might want to return on his own and take on the danger himself, leaving her to wring her hands in worry over the fate of her family and the kingdom. Jaron stood and walked about the fire, wrestling with his thoughts. Finally it was Majii who spoke.

"You must go back, Menika," he said, and his family looked to him with sad acceptance, "Your time with us was not meant to last forever. Your life is not with the *Gatéth-sho'a*, but your own people, your own parents." Cindra looked at her adopted father with tears in her eyes and saw the old man was crying as well.

She went to sit by him, hugging him close, "*Ló-poh*," she said through her tears.

"*Mén-ko-she*," he said. *Daughter*. The words for her adopted status were for the sake of others and had no place here. Navo, Luka and Haani came to put their hands on her head and shoulders, calling her *saya* and weeping. Teya just stood and walked off, hiding her face.

Jaron watched the scene, only now understanding the bond she had formed with these people during her time among them. It was a closeness he had been missing during his exile, perhaps rightly so, for it was meant as a punishment after all. He had another six months left before his banishment was over, but the time seemed far too long now that Cindra had been found. He knew he must bring her home to her parents, but it was likely she would be in worse danger there. He would not part from her, nor could he enter the city before his term was ended. He imagined that finding Cindra alive might justify an early return, but then what? There was so much to consider...

"I don't mean to interrupt," he said to Cindra and the crying huddle of Galindri, "but I think Cindra would be safer with you for the time being. We are not returning just yet." Cindra looked at him with worry in her eyes and he said, "I intend to bring you home, but if things are as bad as you suspect, then we must be cautious. We need to plan..."

Cindra ran to him and gave him a hug that surprised him, yet he returned it just the same.

The next day it was decided that Cindra and Jaron would travel with the caravan until reaching the city of Waynwell, where the pair would depart, heading south to Ghat and the Red Coast Road, skirting the southern Shadowood. It would take longer, but the quicker road would lead to the village of Breega, and Jaron had no wish to return there, especially with the count's daughter. He did not trust Waliss Greenfellow or any of his students, and would not bring Cindra within ten leagues of the place. He shuddered to think what form the schoolmaster's revenge might take if he had both Jaron and Lady Cindra in his clutches.

The Galindri were happy that they would have Cindra with them for a part of their journey at least. Teya remained moody, for she had expected the pair would leave as soon as possible, the knight spiriting her back to her lordly father and his castle. She was happier about the new plan but still showed little warmth to Jaron. Tavika, however, was a different matter; she had another week before her caravan would depart and she spent the time learning all she could about the young knight and the past he shared with Menika Majii-Ama. Cindra tried to deflect some of her questions or interpret them in a more tactful way, but the woman was relentless. She would elbow Cindra in the ribs and ask Jaron, "She would look better with her hair up, don't you think?" Jaron would smile and nod politely, unaware of why Cindra was blushing so.

After Tavika's caravan departed, Majii's family began to pack things up for the long journey east and say their farewells to the remaining Galindri. The long summer days became shorter and the weather cooled, signaling the beginning of autumn and the time to leave Pinikal. Cindra was concerned that Jaron's presence among them would draw unwanted interest, but no one seemed to care. Besides, he was a knight in name only, for he bore no outward symbols and wore no armor but for the mail shirt under his tunic. Even his *tipok* knot was undone, the excess hair simply being tied back with a leather cord. His sword was too fine to belong to a common ruffian, though few looked at it very long, as it attracted the wearer's attention.

Cindra's skin was possibly more of a problem, since the *b'ámava* juice wore off over time if the disguise was not kept up. It may not be so hard to explain an Outlander man traveling with a Galindri woman, but it would attract some attention, especially if her color faded unevenly.

The caravan departed from Pinikal early, after a night of feasting and stories; Majii's kinsmen took the horse herd with them, leaving Teya's mare A'lanóka and Cindra's colt T'ózha, who was ready to be weaned from his mother. The parting was sad but the little pony soon looked to Cindra for everything, which was as it should be. She was able to lead him with a harness behind the caravan and Jaron walked with her leading Vortigras. As the town vanished into the distance and the forest became all that marked the horizon, Cindra felt more at ease than she had for some time. They were on the move now and any danger could be seen from far away; anyone watching them would be obvious if they got too close. She had felt exposed so near the town with all its buildings and windows.

Jaron and Cindra spoke at length about how to approach Portshia and what dangers they might face. Her arrival at the castle and the uproar it would cause would spread to the far reaches of the city within the day, surely alerting those who sought her life. This was assuming there were no traitors in the count's household who might strike her sooner.

"I think they were only concerned about the alliance," said Cindra, as she reasoned through the problem. "But the priests spoke of a new alliance they could use to place the blame for my 'death'... I wish I had heard more before they grabbed me."

"From what I heard, you were nearly killed or worse," Jaron scolded, "I hope you learn to leave the spying to others."

"Who could I have asked? Haani? I would not put any of them in that kind of danger!" She was irritated with him for even suggesting it and Jaron chuckled to himself. "What?" asked Cindra, frowning at him.

"You would make a dreadfully troublesome noble lady with that attitude." They both smiled as he remembered the girl he knew over a year ago, wondering how much she had changed. She had been brave and foolish then as well, saving the life of that boy in the city after slipping out of the castle. "What am I going to do with you, Cindra?"

She smiled at him. "I like hearing you say my name without my title," she said, as he realized his mistake. He began to apologize but she stopped him, "No, it's all right. I have been just Cindra or Menika for so long now, no servants, no bodyguards, nothing to remind me of who I'm supposed to be."

"I'm sure you'll get used to it once you're in the proper setting and attire," Jaron said as he looked her up and down. His thoughts wandered back to the pool and he blushed, turning to gaze into the distance so she would not see.

"I don't want to get *used* to it again," she said, defiant and resolute, "I cannot imagine being locked up in a castle or married off, when I have seen so much of the world. Jaron, there is so much more to do and see! I want to go where I wish and love whom I choose, I don't want to be moved about like a game piece on someone's board." She was so fervent with her words that Jaron began to fear for her. He had seen this look in her eyes before and knew how she would forsake sense and safety to chase her dreams; it also troubled him that he wanted to help her, though how he could do so without diverging from his sworn duty was beyond him.

He mused, "I often dreamed about what it could be like if you were with me, if we were free from duty and obligation. I imagined where we would go, what we would see together; I knew it was impossible, of course, especially after I heard you were... dead," he gave her a pained look, "But now it seems so dangerously possible. I don't want to see you locked away or married off, but I can't run from my duty either."

Cindra kept her eyes ahead on the caravan, "I can't ask you to give up your chosen life," she said with a hint of resignation.

She remembered 'Princess Moon', the play they had attended so long ago, and how the star-crossed lovers were divided by the warrior's sense of honor and duty. The princess had taken her lover's sword and danced, attempting to rally him into action. The details were not the same between her and Jaron, but she wanted to take his sword and thump him on the head with it just the same.

"Besides, you said we should forget the shame of our feelings and stop living for what cannot be." There, she had said it.

Jaron groaned as he heard his words thrown back at him. "I... forgive me, Cindra. I was distraught when I

246

answered your message. I have had much time to think about and regret what I said." He hung his head in shame and stopped, Vortigras nearly bumping into him.

Cindra stopped as well and T'ózha nuzzled her. "I never took your advice," she said as she placed her hand on his arm, "I never forgot you or how I felt."

"Nor I you," he said, looking into her eyes; the color of her dyed skin made them look so much more vibrant. Without thinking he leaned forward, and cupping her chin, kissed her gently. She closed her eyes and returned the pressure of his lips, so long remembered and relived in her dreams. For an endless moment they were lost in the passion of the memory, feeling the madness and desire of the enchantment that had set their souls alight and brought them to ruin. Then the moment faded, but the feeling remained. They gazed into each other's eyes and saw the love they shared reflected there, like a light dancing between their spirits, rekindled and renewed. They did not speak for a time, but joined hands and walked behind the caravan, basking in the warm sun and in the emotions that fluttered in their hearts like mad butterflies, making the world seem a brighter and more colorful place.

Haani watched from the back door of the caravan and giggled, moving past her sleeping father to part the curtains to the driver's bench and pop her head out between Navo and Luka. "Menika and her man shared a kiss!" she proclaimed.

Luka smiled and placed her hand on her husband's knee, "I think she will follow her heart to whatever end."

Navo chuckled, "I hope it guides her better than her head. She is a reckless one."

"Reckless but brave," said Haani, "She saved Teya's life, after all."

"Teya will not be happy to lose her, I think they have a common spirit," said Luka.

"She sees much of herself in Menika, much that could have been..." Navo looked to his elder sister, who rode ahead on her black mare. "...and maybe she envies her new happiness with the Outlander. Teya needs to find a love of her own, and soon."

Luka said, "I think she fears for her. She will not be able to look out for her anymore."

Haani remarked, "Who really knows what Teya thinks? She never speaks of it to anyone." She ducked back into the caravan to spy on the new couple.

The farms and towns along the road were few and sparsely settled, the villagers mistrusting and wary of strangers. The caravan would often stop by the roadside, out of the way of the townspeople, but they still drew unwanted attention as the village watchmen approached to ask their business and see them off. Jaron was a great help at this point, for he was obviously a man of authority and the villagers saw him as one of their own, though he kept strange company. They were cowed more often than not and extended their hospitality for a night or two, providing the Galindri kept to themselves and made no trouble.

Teya sorely wished to make trouble, for she had been in a sour mood since Jaron's intrusion into their lives. Cindra figured it was partly due to the manner of their meeting, and she herself had a few things to say about his boorish conduct. Jaron stopped trying to plead his innocence long ago, making many apologies to the women when it seemed fitting.

Jaron had made one attempt to speak to the huntress alone, but it had not gone as well; he approached her while she was tending the horses one evening, making sure they were apart from the others.

"Teya? I know we got off to a bad start," he scratched his head nervously, "but I wanted to thank you for taking Cindra in and keeping her safe. She means a great deal to me."

The huntress stopped and stared at him, boring into him with her leaf-green eyes. "She never spoke of you;

she talked of home but not of you." Jaron was struck dumb and only looked back at her. "You hurt her before, yes?" She went back to brushing her horse and said, "If you hurt her again, I will cut out your heart."

He walked away from the camp then, looking for solitude in the fields under the stars. Was it true? Had she never spoken of him out of the pain he had caused? Perhaps her time among these people had been a welcome reprieve, where she could forget all that pain. He considered that the huntress had only spoken so to hurt him, but something told him otherwise. She obviously cared for Cindra and was being very protective of her, like an older sister.

He took the woman's warning to heart, but he was still troubled by the lack of mention. He had not shared his thoughts or feelings with others because he had no one to confide in, not that most men did so anyway. Cindra had been living with three other women, and had never brought up his name or the story of their time together? If that was true, then perhaps her feelings for him were not as great as she had him believe. It was a nagging thorn of doubt that buried itself deep in his heart and turned in his stomach, making him feel queasy.

Jaron was quiet for the next few days, even as Cindra talked about her travels and the sights she had seen. She asked him a few times if all was well with him, but he only nodded and bade her to continue her stories. His mood did not improve however, and Cindra knew something was nettling him, so she spoke to him alone after the family had made camp.

"Jaron, tell me what is wrong. You have been quiet and gloomy for days now." She sat with him on a fallen log that bordered the road. "Was it something I said?"

"Perhaps something you didn't," Jaron replied before he thought the better of it.

She blinked at him, "What do you mean?"

"Teya said... she told me that you never spoke of me." He looked at the ground instead of her eyes, ashamed that such foolishness was troubling him so.

Cindra was taken aback as she tried to remember all of the stories she had told over the past year and a half. "I never... I am sure I mentioned you before; I told Haani about the tournament, surely... or maybe it was Luka." She took his hands in hers to reassure him, "If I didn't speak of you, it was because such things are private to me and I didn't wish for questions or reminders." She looked into his eyes, "There have been many painful things that I've had to overcome, many wounds that needed to heal."

The allusion did not comfort him and he felt a great pang of guilt. "I am sorry, Cindra. I have caused you needless suffering and I am so very sorry." His chest constricted and he felt near to tears as he cursed himself for harming everything he touched, even one he cared for so deeply. Teya had been right.

Cindra saw his torment and stroked his hair, "Jaron, I have forgiven you for the things you said. You were only trying to protect us both from yearning for the impossible," she took his hand, "but now things have changed; we are free and can live our lives as we wish, at least for a time."

He was not convinced. "Free? We are hardly free, Cindra. We are still bound by our station and duties, though we may pretend otherwise."

"Then let us pretend while we can!" She said, "You may bow to me and call me 'milady' when I am back in my fine clothes and castle walls, but now I want to be your Cindra. The Galindri marry when they find love, not when they are told to do so. I wish for that freedom, even if only for a few months."

Jaron heaved a heavy sigh and said, "I have spent the last year trying to regain my honor and sense of duty so that I may return to your father's service as a better knight, a better man. I do love you, my dearest Cindra; I have since the night we met, but..."

"But what? Do you think I would tell my father that we are lovers, that I would expose us once we return home?"

"No, but the truth would live with us. We would be lying with every glance, every action."

"So it would be better to deny how we both feel?" Cindra was becoming more frustrated with him, "I was raised with the teachings of Selvina, who says that to deny love is to live in darkness. I don't want to live in darkness anymore; I want to know love, Jaron." She leaned forward and kissed him before he could speak, pressing her lips to his and sharing breath, caught up in the burning of her heart and the desire to feed that flame, though all may burn around her. She did not want to be bound any longer; she wanted to be free of all care and obligation, living only for the moments that might never come again. She looked ahead to the paths her life might take and found she did not care unless he was with her.

Jaron took her in his arms and kissed her deeply, all the barriers in his mind breaking away like twigs before a flood; all that mattered was her touch and the pressure of her lips, the beating of their hearts as they shared a moment in time as one. His thoughts became a meaningless blur and his wits grew mute; a tiny voice in his head convinced him he would learn to live with the conflict, to find a balance between honor and impossible desire. If it was the beginning of his undoing, he refused to see it.

The caravan passed the orchards of Waynwell as a summer storm was rolling in, and Jaron was annoyed to find that he could not take the caravan into the city walls; Cindra also refused to part with her adopted family to have better lodgings for herself. Reluctantly, he helped set up a camp in the Outwalls where the trees were thinner and the only shelter to be found was under the roof of the wagon. The space was cramped, but he was grateful that they extended their hospitality to him. Haani was still shy around him, but at least Teya had stopped looking at him with daggers in her eyes. The married couple was the most open and tolerant, and Navo often made jokes to lighten their mood.

The rain lasted for many hours before letting up enough to go outside. Cindra took a blanket and wiped the rain from T'ózha's coat as the pony stood patiently by, nuzzling her for reassurance. Vortigras was less than happy, for he was used to being stabled in a deluge and he let Jaron feel his discontent with rough nudging and biting. The Galindri horses were not bothered, for they took such things in stride.

Jaron intended to get Cindra some suitable clothing for the rest of the journey and wanted to take her to a few local shops, but her current attire and skin color proved to be a problem. Galindri were not allowed the freedom of the town or shops, and it would be foolish to explain her disguise, for it might compromise her safety. Jaron had no sense for buying women's clothing, especially without the woman present, so it was decided both for ease and practicality that Cindra would dress as a young man after leaving the caravan with Jaron. She was curiously inclined to the idea, for she had always wondered how her life would have been different with another gender; surely her family life would have been happier. Jaron bought her a selection of trousers and shirts, with a few simple jackets and hats to complete the illusion. He was surprised to see that, apart from her darker skin, she looked the part of a young local boy to the casual observer, though he could well imagine the soft curves he knew to be beneath the loose clothing. Cindra mistook his blush for something else.

"Is it that bad? Do I look silly?" she asked, adjusting her jacket.

"No, you look the part. The hat covers your braids, which will have to come out eventually. The jacket is a good fit, very stylish." He smiled and folded his arms, wishing he had more to spend on her wardrobe. She looked like his servant might, and the thought made him feel wrong.

"It will make travel easier if Vortigras will take us

both," she pulled at the trousers. "T'ózha can follow behind, though by the time we enter Portshia next year, he may be strong enough to saddle and ride."

"I've been thinking about our accommodations once we reach Cordoshome," Jaron said, "The Freekirks have a villa there, overlooking the town. We might stay there and wait out the winter, perhaps even contact Sir Cord to let him in on your return."

Cindra did not need to ask if Sir Cord could be trusted, for she knew the bond between Jaron and the big knight was a strong one. "I hope the Freekirks and their staff can be discrete. I would hate for anything terrible to befall them for helping me."

"They can keep a secret; besides they need not know your true identity. Only Sir Cord has seen you in person, and he will likely spend the winter with his family when the school closes for the year. I think he will be pleasantly surprised." He gave Cindra a wry smile as she raised an eyebrow.

"I cannot imagine it will be pleasant, especially when we tell him of the plots against me and my family." Sir Cord had uncovered the intrigue with the enchanted roses that caused so much trouble before, but he would be floored by what she had learned during her absence.

"The worse the better; I can't wait to see the look on his face." He was grinning wickedly now and Cindra could not help but laugh at him.

"I hope he recovers soon after," she giggled, "we will need his help to enter the city and reach the castle."

"I was thinking about that," Jaron said reluctantly, "I don't think the castle would be safe. We don't know who is involved in this conspiracy, but if they can reach the king in his own castle, they can reach you in yours. If you are to return, it must be kept secret."

"But who could keep such a secret? Whom can we trust besides Sir Cord?"

Jaron thought for a long while before mumbling, "We can trust those who don't know better."

"What do you mean?" she asked.

"Well," Jaron motioned to her, "You are already dressed as a boy, so why not keep it that way? You can stay with Sir Cord at the school, or other provisions might be made; so long as you keep your disguise as you have done this last year, we might keep you safe while we search for these priests and their 'scion' or whatever they called it." He clapped his hands, "Ha, maybe you can pretend to be my squire," he laughed at the notion, thinking she would too.

Cindra just turned and looked at the ground for a long while. Jaron was worried he had upset her and was about to ask, when she said, "Why can't I be?"

Jaron thought she was making a joke of her own, but noticed she was not laughing. "My squire? Well, you're a girl, for one reason." He kept his smile in case she was having him on.

She was not. "I will not look like a girl. I will look like a young man among other young men. If I am your squire, you can train me at the school." Her face was so focused and sincere that it made his jaw drop.

"You can't be serious!" He proclaimed, "If you are found out it will be all over the city in hours!"

"It would be no different any other way. If I am discovered, everyone will know shortly."

"But you could be hurt! The Freekirk School trains knights for war, it is not like playing games with children." He was worried now and his brow furrowed.

She stood and spoke calmly, "I have risked my life for others before, I have even killed a Minozhian bull-man," she patted the *Kos* knife at her hip. "Can you say the same?"

Jaron was having none of it. "I have undergone the training and I have fought in battles, I have killed and seen many more killed. It is not the life for a woman, Cindra."

"I know what the life of a woman is like Jaron! I do what I am told, I go where I am bidden, and I must have men to protect me from other men. If I cannot fend for myself then I am nothing." Her pulse rose as she felt the inequities of life pressing around her like gripping fingers. "I will not be helpless, waiting for someone to save me from my enemies. I want to face them and beat them! I want to show people like those priests that they cannot tread on House Corrina." She took him by the arms and stared into his eyes, "You are my father's champion, or will be, when you return. I am his heir, and but for my sex, I would be defending my house by your side. If you can hide me at the school and train me as a knight..."

Jaron shook his head unwilling to hear her.

"You took me to see 'Princess Moon'," she told him and he raised his head at the memory. "She took up the warrior's sword when he could not. I never forgot that dance, the way she was so confident and skilled. I want that for myself. I don't want to beg others to fight my battles for me. I don't want to beg *you*."

He said solemnly, "I would gladly take up any battle for you, Cindra."

"Would you fight for my independence, my freedom to choose?" She squeezed his hands pleadingly, "If you will not, then I must. All I ask is that you stand with me."

Jaron closed his eyes and took several deep breaths. "We have six more months before I can enter Portshia again," he said, and his uncertainty gave her hope. "We will have much time to discuss it."

The next few days were spent preparing for their departure and Cindra used the time with her adopted family to talk over old times and think of the future. Teya promised that the caravan would visit Portshia in the next few years, though she could not promise a time and Cindra could not promise that she would be able to visit them properly. Haani and Luka made her a special meal with a variety of her favorite foods, and Navo played his flute afterward while they danced. On the morning of their parting, Haani promised she would make up a song about the Outlander girl that lived among them and became a sister to her, and it would be told forever after in her family's stories.

"And I will want to add to it, so you must see us again!" Haani told Cindra with a hug.

Teya presented her with parting gifts, which was a complete surprise to Cindra, who had not expected such a thing from her moody elder sister.

"I know you will not have to hunt in your castle, but I have made you a Shadowood bow so you may practice," she presented Cindra with a polished black bow carved in the curved, organic Galindri style, and painted on the face with dark crimson knotting patterns, like thorny vines. The handle was shaped to fit her hand, and the arrows were made of yew with vanes of black and gray snood hen feathers. There was also a hooded quiver of light leather that could be worn either on the back or at the hip.

Cindra was overwhelmed. She had seen the huntress making the new bow, but always assumed it was for her own use. "*Dep'ázhana k'ó-saya, b'á-ja!*" She took the bow and pulled it with effort, for it was weaker than that of the huntress but strong enough that she would have to grow into its power. "It's beautiful! I have always wanted one!" She grinned from ear to ear and hugged Teya in a bear grip.

The huntress smiled and said, "That is not all, I have another that is just as important," she took a strip of cloth from her blouse and held it out to the girl. It was dyed burgundy and embroidered with a dark line through the middle of its length. "This is the headband of a *Gatéth-sho'a* warrior. Wear it in battle and let your enemies fear it."

Cindra took it reverently and hugged her again saying, "Take care of yourself and our family, Teya." Haani and Luka hugged her goodbye as well, tearful but trying to make it a happy parting. Navo had no jokes for the occasion, but only embraced her and smiled.

Cindra came to Majii last saying, "Thank you for

taking me into your family, *ló-poh*. I would be lost without your kindness." She kissed his cheek, embracing him as he did the same.

He told her, "It was my joy to welcome another daughter into my family, even if she was not of my blood. We were meant to be together for a time, and now that time is done. Perhaps it will come again. Be well, Cindra, Menika, *mén-ko-she*. You will always be with us."

"And you will always be with me," she said through her tears.

Jaron helped her onto Vortigras and mounted behind her. With her bay pony in tow, they rode for the southern road, leaving Waynwell and Cindra's adopted family behind them. What lay ahead was an uncertain and dangerous future, but hope was in her heart and love held her in his arms.

The Author

Mark Rude, also known as Markalf the Going-Gray, is a wizard from Phoenix, Arizona, deep in the land of Mordor. He studied the Arts at Northern Arizona University, in the age when painting was done with paint, not pixels, and a photo shop was a place where you worked with something called 'film.'

It was in this age that he forged the story of Cindra Corrina, intending to make the story into a graphic novel, though it was not overly graphic, and not entirely novel. The comic book he called *Passage* kindled the spirit of the story. Three issues were forged in the land of Mordor, in the fires of Phoenix, before the effort was abandoned; yet the spirit of the story endured.

Cindra's tale was of epic proportions, untellable in quarterly comics that came out only once a year. Yet there was hope. Using fewer graphics, and with more emphasis on words, Cindra's story grew like the light of dawn over a darkened land. Markalf was able to spin his yarn as never before, making a nice sweater, some hand warmers, and a scarf.

Markalf the Going-Gray lives alone in a high tower, where he plots the doom of characters great and small.

www.markrude.net
www.facebook.com/markrude.net